HAWAIIAN SHADOWS

BOOK TWO: EMPATH

Edie Claire

To my own personal Zane —
who couldn't surf if his life depended on it,
but who can always make me laugh.

chapter one

Author's Note: This book is the second in a series. It would really, *really* be a whole lot more fun to read if you've already read the first one, *Wraith*. Reading out of order would be a serious spoiler. So please, check out the first one first. I promise you'll be glad you did!

Explaining everything to my parents was probably the weirdest, most awkward conversation I'd ever had, and for me that was really saying something.

"You see *what?*" my dad exclaimed. His jaw muscles tensed, his eyes widened, and the little blue vein over his left temple popped out and throbbed like it was ready to burst. The look had brought many a quivering airman to his knees over the course of Mitch Thompson's military career. But since I knew my father's relatively rare explosions to be all bluster, I didn't bat an eyelash.

"I see dead people," I repeated. "Not corpses walking around, like in horror movies. What I see are shadows — a playback of what the people looked like when they were alive. Scenes of people doing things in a particular place at a particular time. Maybe twenty years ago, maybe two hundred. The older ones are fainter, but they're kind of all mixed together."

My father, who had jumped to his feet at the first line of my confession, loomed over me stiff as a statue, his bottom jaw now hanging limply. My mother sat motionless on the motel bed across from me, her face pale and her eyes frightened.

Fabulous. It was happening all over again.

I was seventeen now, but the first time, when I was

five, I hadn't thought that telling my parents what I saw would be that big of a deal. I assumed that all the kindergartners at the base could see multiple sets of children milling around the classroom, some solid and normal, others wispy and vague. The vague ones never talked to me and didn't seem to know I was there, so basically I ignored them. But there were other shadow people, pretty much everywhere I looked, and some were harder to ignore than others. Some of them frightened me.

I can't remember a time when I *didn't* see the shadows, but I do remember my earliest attempts at trying to explain them. Like the time when I was three and my mother took me to see a movie, and I refused to sit in the seat she had chosen because a man was already sitting in it. She assured me the seat was empty. I couldn't understand what was wrong with her eyes.

Or the time when I was four and we lived in Biloxi, Mississippi, and my father took us to the Civil War battlefield at Vicksburg, and I spent the entire time screaming and trying to get back in the car. My father was so upset he threatened to spank me, but I couldn't care less about a smack on the butt, even if he had been serious. I'd never seen a place so horribly dangerous and frightening and gruesome and bloody — I couldn't believe they would take me there and tell me with a straight face that it was perfectly safe.

Were they nuts? Was *everyone* nuts?

Apparently, no. Only I was. Or so my parents came to believe after the third or fourth counselor / therapist / psychiatrist told them I was showing signs of severe psychosis.

That was what happened the last time I tried doing this.

Yet here we were again. And I couldn't back out now. I had promised Zane.

"You talked about seeing shadow people before," my mother said breathlessly. "Back when you were little. But then it stopped." Her voice was a plea.

I shook my head slowly. "No, Mom. I only *told* you that it stopped. I told you that because you guys were so scared and freaked out. I figured if I just stopped talking about it, that maybe everything would go back to normal in our lives. And it did."

My father dropped back down onto the bed with a plop. They bounced together in silence for a while, their faces as white as the sheets.

"I've always seen the shadows," I continued. Then I shrugged. "I just learned to live with them."

Another awkward silence.

It was my dad who finally cleared his throat and spoke. "But..." he said haltingly, "You seem perfectly fine!"

I allowed myself a smile. "I am perfectly fine, Dad. It's not a mental illness. I don't know what it is, but it's not that." I looked from one to the other. My heart pounded in my chest. "I need you to believe me."

"Of course we believe you, Kali," my mother said quickly. "We always believed you."

"But you thought it was all in my head," I reminded. "And it's not. I have proof of that now."

My dad was all over that one. "Proof?" he said, perking up. "What kind of proof?"

"This is about *him*, isn't it?" my mother asked before I could answer. "The boy who's in the hospital?"

I nodded.

"Wait a minute!" my dad exclaimed with frustration, "Back up and make some sense, would you? One minute we're all happy as clams picking out a house on Oahu, the next minute you say that a boy you know has been in a serious car accident and off you go on the next flight home to Wyoming... your mother and I end our vacation early to come chasing you all the way out here to the middle of Nebraska so you can see him before he dies, never mind that we've never even *heard* of this boy before... and I still don't get what any of that has to do with your seeing" — he nearly choked — *"dead people."*

"Everything," I said quietly.

"What proof do you have?" he repeated.

My mom laid a hand on his arm. "Mitch," she said knowingly, "just let her talk."

And so I did. I began with my first days of spring break in Hawaii, how I had enjoyed just lying on the beach on the North Shore and watching the waves. I saw shadows there, as usual. I ignored them, as usual. But then I ran into one who was unusual. One who could see and interact with *me*. His form was more solid than the rest of the shadows, although still transparent in places. He could change his appearance, move anywhere at any speed, walk through walls. But he was confused and lonely, because he had no idea who he was or even why he was there. And until he met me, not a single other soul had been able to see him. It was as if he were invisible.

"So he was dead," my dad interrupted. "Is he still dead?"

"Mitch!" my mom chastised.

"Sorry," he grumbled. "Keep talking, honey. I'm listening."

"He was in a coma," I explained, my voice shaking a little, just thinking about it. "The day I met him... on Oahu, I mean... he was very close to death. He lost a lot of blood in the car crash, and the doctors didn't think he would make it. He had what I guess you'd call an 'out of body' experience. Physically he was in a hospital in Nebraska, but his soul, or his spirit or his consciousness or whatever you want to call it, went on to finish the trip he had started. He wanted so desperately to get to Oahu... his life's passion was to surf on the North Shore, and that's where his spirit went."

My dad put a hand to his forehead. "Oh, my," he moaned. "This is way out of my league, Diane."

"Just chill, Mitch," my mom said shortly. "I've heard of such a thing before." Her words and tone were supportive, but her face was creased with worry. "I've never believed it," she continued, "but I've heard of it before."

"Mom," I pleaded. "I probably wouldn't believe it either. But I don't have a choice." I tried to catch my dad's eyes, but he avoided me. "Zane's physical body has never left the mainland," I continued. "He started driving in New Jersey, headed for California, and he got as far as Nebraska before the accident. He's been in a hospital bed here ever since. But I *saw* and talked to him on Oahu. For days. Right before he... faded away from me, he remembered some things about the accident — the accident we both thought, then, had killed him. When I realized he might *not* be dead, those details helped Tara find him for me. I knew things about the accident that no one else could have known... because he was still in a coma when I got here."

My dad's pained face turned toward me. "Has he come out of it yet?"

I felt a clenching in my chest. "Yes," I answered, my voice cracking again. "He woke up while I was with him." Those few, beautiful moments after he had first woken up, when I was alone with him, already seemed like years ago. Once I alerted the staff, his room had become Grand Central Station. There were examinations, tests, consults... I had been asked to leave. I'd moved to the lobby and waited for hours; finally I had fallen asleep. Between my last, sleepless night on Oahu, the flight across the ocean, and crushing jet lag, I had lost all sense of time. I still didn't know exactly how many hours I'd lain unconscious on that plastic couch before realizing I'd missed about a dozen calls… including the one from my parents saying that they had checked into a motel in Kearney, where my friend Tara had sent me, and where the hell was I?

"So he confirmed it then?" my dad pressed. "He said he had been on Oahu?"

Hot moisture welled up behind my eyes. They had no idea how hard this was for me. "Not exactly," I admitted, my voice weak. "He… he had a head injury and he was in a coma… his memory is foggy. He may remember it soon. But I don't know."

I was trying, really hard, not to totally freak out about Zane's loss of memory. We had shared so much in those magical days in Hawaii… even though I thought he was dead at the time. Finding him alive had been the most wonderful surprise of my life — and I was determined not to let his lack of memory bring me down. He was alive, he was going to get better, and he even said that I looked familiar to him… sort of. I had no reason to worry. We would have plenty of time to get reacquainted.

Which was a good thing, since I was hopelessly, madly in love with him.

So what if his first words to me when he woke up were, "Who are you?"

Everything would be fine. It had to be.

"There's a guy playing a guitar right there," I said mechanically, gesturing toward the pillows of the bed they were sitting on.

My parents' heads swiveled slowly to where I pointed,

then back again. "What do you mean?" my mother whispered.

I sighed. "A shadow. He's wearing a really ugly shirt with fringe on it, his hair is long and greasy, and he's picking away at a guitar. He seems really happy. I think he's writing a song." I looked around the modest room. "This motel's probably been here since what, the sixties? The beds must have been in the same place then. When buildings get remodeled, the shadows pop up in some strange places. They seem to be tied to their original locations in space, no matter what's happened since."

I couldn't bear to see their reaction to that info dump, so I kept my eyes on the guitar player. "It feels really awkward talking about this, after keeping it a secret for so long. But I got a little practice at honesty with Zane — he wanted to know all about the shadows, and I told him. He couldn't see them either, but he thought it was wrong for me to spend my whole life lying about them… particularly to you. Before he left me on Oahu, he made me promise to tell you the truth."

I took a breath and steeled myself to meet their gaze again. "So here we are!" I finished with fake cheer, giving myself a little bounce on the mattress.

My parents ogled me like hooked fish. Open mouths, bulging eyes. They had scooted to the foot of the bed, as far as possible from where I had pointed out the shadow. My father was nearly pushing my mother off the edge.

I had to grin. "There's nothing scary about that one," I assured. "They're just people. Or at least they *were* people. Sometimes I can sense their emotions, too. That guy's really happy at the moment. Despite his lame taste in clothes."

My mother swallowed painfully. "Fringed shirts were in style in the sixties," she croaked.

I chuckled. "Mom," I protested, looking at the shadow's skin-tight, striped polyester pants, which ended a good six inches above his bare ankles. "I promise, what this guy is wearing was *never* in style."

"I can't believe you two are talking about clothes!" my dad barked, standing up again and moving away from the bed. "We have to talk about this... this *thing*. We have to figure out what to do!"

"There's nothing *to* do, Mitch," my mother said reasonably. Her voice was still rough, but she did seem to be getting some of her color back. "Whatever this is, Kali has already figured out herself how to deal with it. She just needs our support."

My dad's face was pained. "Well, of course," he said miserably. "But surely there's something somebody can—"

"Dad," I interrupted quickly, being familiar with his compulsion for action. "I don't think anyone can *fix* me. I just didn't want to have to lie to you anymore. But there is a way you can help me." I threw a beseeching look at my mom. "Both of you."

They made no response. I took another deep breath. I had been thinking about the plan ever since I'd found Zane alive, and as crazy as it was going to sound, I had to make it happen.

"Zane has no family," I began. "None at all. His parents are both dead and they were never married, to each other or anybody else. He has no siblings, step or biological. No aunts or uncles. No grandparents. If he has distant cousins, he doesn't know about them. That's why the hospital had so much trouble looking for next of kin. He was seventeen when his mother died, and because he was alone, he got stuck in foster care until his eighteenth birthday. That's when he bought a car and headed west."

I paused a moment. They were listening quietly. My dad's breathing was a little labored, but at least the vein in his temple wasn't throbbing anymore. All good.

"Zane is going to take a while to recover," I continued. "I'm sure that his father's estate will take care of his medical bills wherever he is, but he doesn't know anyone here. He doesn't even have friends in New Jersey anymore; he told me he lost touch with them after his mother—" I broke off, not sure how much of the more unpleasant side of Zane's life he would want me to share. "The point is, he doesn't have anyone to help him through this. Except me."

My mother's eyes, always perceptive, studied me. "You want us to see if he can be transferred to a facility back home in Cheyenne? Is that it?"

"Exactly," I said with relief. Many times I cursed my mother's uncanny ability to read me. This was not one of them. "He'll probably need one of those physical rehab places. There's something like that in town, isn't there? Then we could all help him out, make sure he gets whatever he needs while he recovers… he wouldn't have to be alone."

"Didn't you say he doesn't remember you yet?" my dad asked.

The words cut me like a knife. "Not *yet,*" I admitted. But surely Zane would be happy to have the company, the offer of friendship, at least.

Wouldn't he?

My mom turned to my dad. "I don't see any reason why not, Mitch. The boy has to recover somewhere, and everyone who's hospitalized should have some advocate on the outside. Not to mention the boost to his spirits if Kali and her friends could visit him." She threw me a sympathetic smile.

My heart leapt. It could all work out. It *could*.

"Dad?" I asked hopefully.

The man looked thoroughly tortured. He still probably thought I was half crazy. Mitch Thompson lived in a black and white world of friends and enemies, good and evil, right and wrong. Having a daughter who saw shadows from another time didn't fit in his boxes. I could imagine the wheels turning furiously in his brain… what could he make of it? What could he do with me? How could he fix everything and get us all back to normal?

My personal guess: a punt.

He let out a long, dramatic sigh. "Whatever you think, Diane."

Bingo.

"I need a walk," he announced. He snatched his hat, wallet, and keys from the bureau, offered us both an artificially cheerful smile, and took off into the dark.

"He'll be all right with it eventually," my mother said gently. "He just needs some time."

"I know."

She started to say something else, then paused. I didn't think it was possible, but the mood turned even more awkward.

"Kali," she said tentatively, "that last night, at the beach house. You were standing out on the deck by yourself…"

I nodded, remembering against my will. It was all I could do not to tear up again. I had thought I was losing Zane forever.

"I thought you were talking to someone," she continued. "I was sure of it. The way you were looking at a certain spot… but there wasn't anyone else there."

My eyes did tear up. Zane had grown so faint, by then. He had tried to kiss me, but I couldn't feel it… he wasn't real. "He was there," I croaked.

My mother drew in a breath, sharply. "He was?"

I nodded.

"Could he…" her cheeks flared suddenly. She seemed almost embarrassed. "Could he see us, too? I mean, your father and me?"

I swiped a hand across my moist eyes and grinned. "Of course."

"Oh, dear," she said uncertainly.

I had to grin at her expression. Her only daughter had just been revealed as a potential nutjob, and she was worried about the impression she'd left on a teenaged ghost. "Don't worry," I added. "He liked you both a lot. And I made him promise to stay out of the bathroom."

Her face reddened.

I laughed out loud, and my eyes teared up all over again. "You're going to like him, too, Mom," I insisted. "I know you are."

She smiled back, but it was a smile tempered with concern. "I'm sure I will, if you do," she responded. "But you should be careful not to get your hopes too high… about how he'll respond to all this. You have to remember that you didn't exactly meet under normal circumstances. And now if he can't remember—" she broke off, clearly uncomfortable. "I just don't want you to get hurt any more than you already have been."

Another icy blade sliced through my chest. Why, oh why, did they have to keep saying such things out loud? Wasn't I afraid enough already? Weren't my feet itching, even now, to get back to him and put things right, before he could slip away from me again?

I rose. "I need to get back to the hospital."

My mother got up with me, her hand on my arm. "Oh, no you don't!" she ordered. "You are going to stay right here and get some sleep."

"But I just woke up!" I protested.

Her lips pursed. She pointed at the darkness outside the window. "It's the middle of the night here, Kali," she reminded. "Hardly visiting hours. They wouldn't even let you in."

I sank back down on the bed. "First thing tomorrow, then," I said miserably.

Then I would talk to him. Then I could invite him to come back with me to Cheyenne, and we could start all over again.

We could.

chapter 2

I was met at the front desk of the long-term care home by the tall, friendly nurse who had led me in to see Zane yesterday morning. "There she is!" the woman boomed in her drill-sergeant voice, even as she smiled broadly. "It's about damn time! Our boy's been asking about you."

Warmth flushed my cheeks. "He has?"

The nurse grinned knowingly. "Mm hmm."

My joy was mixed with regret. I had intended to arrive as soon as the doors opened, but after having been awake half the "night" staring at the motel ceiling, I had overslept, and neither of my parents — maddeningly — had chosen to wake me.

"Can I see him now?" I asked, sounding more impatient than I wanted to.

The nurse merely laughed. "Sure thing. Go on back. Room 264. Just be sure to knock first, this time. Our boy's got a thing about his privacy."

I'll bet. I took off down the hall, wondering how awful it must be for any formerly healthy teenager to wake up in a world full of funny odors, IV tubes, and bedpans. The Zane I knew would hate having to rely on other people to take care of him. He would fight to get better as fast as he possibly could, think and plan and scheme a way to finagle himself out of here...

His door was standing open about a foot. As I approached I could hear him talking, presumably on the phone. His voice was even more hoarse than it had been yesterday. I knocked on the door, waited about two seconds, and slipped into the opening.

His bed had been adjusted to where he could halfway sit up. A tray table stretched before him holding an ancient-looking landline telephone, a notepad, and several pens. The curtains on the windows were drawn back and sunlight flooded the room. He looked up, and my stomach flip-flopped as his beautiful sea-green eyes lit up in recognition. He smiled and gestured for me to come inside. "That's great!" he croaked into the phone. "It's happening even quicker than I'd hoped. Thanks. Bye."

He hung up. I wondered, with a dull sense of dread, exactly what was happening so quickly. But my brain was too preoccupied to obsess on the point. It was all I could do to drink in the sight of him.

He looked different from how he had appeared on Oahu, true. When I first saw him, he'd appeared to me as a sun-bronzed, curly blond hottie glowing with health and vitality, despite his not actually being alive. The living, breathing Zane had a complexion that was unnaturally pale, and it was obvious from his slumped posture and the slow, halting way he moved that he was still very weak. But there was no mistaking the glint of joy and humor in his eyes, nor the killer smile that spread across his face to create the sexiest dimples on the planet.

"Kali," he said breathlessly. "You came back."

I crossed the room in two strides. Did he remember me now?

Easy, girl.

"Of course I came back," I answered, trying hard to sound casual and friendly, as if I would not have — with the slightest encouragement — launched myself into his arms and held onto him so tight it would take the entire nursing staff to dislodge me.

"My parents showed up yesterday and took me to a motel last night to sleep," I explained, keeping a safely polite distance between us. "But I'm here now. How are you?"

"Better now," he answered, not taking his eyes off me. "I was starting to think that maybe I dreamed you."

I felt a tug of guilt at the worry in his voice. Waking up from a coma must be completely disorienting under the most normal of conditions, and his last twenty-four hours had been anything but normal. Of course my bizarre appearing-disappearing act would seem surreal.

"I'm sorry, but they made me leave the room while they were examining you," I explained. "Whenever I asked if I could come back in, they told me that either you were busy with tests or you were napping, and then it was after visiting hours."

His mouth twisted. "I asked about you, but they told me you were asleep in the lobby and they hated to wake you because you were jetlagged."

"Yes," I admitted ruefully. "That was true, too."

His expression turned serious, and a wave of coldness swept up my spine. The Zane I knew never got serious without good reason.

"I am so totally confused," he said. "I need you to explain some things to me."

My joy dampened. Is that the only reason he was glad to see me? "Of course," I answered. "If you don't remember what happened on Oahu then it figures nothing else would make sense to you."

He blinked at me. "I understand we're in Nebraska." His voice was steady enough, but I could sense the pain — and bewilderment — beneath it.

I fought back another desire to hug him. "That's true. We are."

"But you said we were on Oahu together. You were talking about it yesterday before I opened my eyes. When did all that happen? Why can't I remember it? They told me that I should expect some memory loss, particularly what happened right before the accident. But I *can* remember the accident. I remember the whole trip!"

A swell of panic rose. He still didn't remember me. And if he didn't, why should he believe anything I said? He had no reason to accept my story and every reason not to. I could just be some stalker chick who saw a picture of him somewhere and got obsessed (not as unlikely as it sounds, given his gorgeousness) or some fortune-hunting schemer who knew his dad had money and read about the son's accident online. I could be anybody. Why should he —

"Could you sit down?" he asked mildly.

Now I blinked at him. "What?"

He smiled at me. "It freaks me out looking up at a girl. I'm used to looking down at them. Messes with my manly ego, which is taking a pretty big hit already with the whole 'bedridden' thing. Can you grab that chair?"

I would have smiled back, but I was too petrified. How could I ever make him believe me? I grabbed the visitor's chair, dragged it to his bedside, and sat down. "I know I need to explain," I said uncertainly. "I'm just not sure where to start." I ran a hand nervously through my long, curly locks. They were clean, at least. I'd shampooed last night for the first time in about three days. When I'd finished, the bottom of the motel tub had been gritty with beach sand, and I'd almost cried. I could almost cry at nearly anything lately.

To my surprise, he reached out and touched my hair.

Yeah. Anything like that.

My eyes teared up. I swiped the moisture away savagely. How unbelievably embarrassing.

He pulled his hand back. For a moment, neither of us

said anything.

Then I pulled myself together and straightened. "I don't know how to tell you this except to just tell you. Then if you want to call me crazy and throw me out, you have every right."

I didn't look at him. I couldn't bear to see the inevitable doubt in his eyes.

"I've been on Oahu for the past week. You've been here in a hospital bed. At least, your physical self has been. But…"

This was incredibly, unbelievably hard. It sounded even crazier explaining it to him than it had to my parents.

"But all my life I've had this weird thing — I call it a curse, but you called it a gift — where I can see things other people can't see. And even though it makes no logical sense, I saw *you* on Oahu, surfing on the North Shore. We thought you were dead — that you were a ghost. Except you didn't remember your life and didn't know how you had died. We spent days together, doing all the things I talked about before. You started to remember, but you also started fading away from me, the same time the staff here noticed signs that you were coming back. Finally, you faded away from me completely. I was really upset, but then I saw another shadow, or ghost, just like you who *wasn't* dead, and I figured out that you must be alive somewhere too. And so I—"

"You told me about that yesterday," he interrupted. "I remember. Your friends helped you figure out where I was."

I looked up at him. He was studying me intently, his green eyes blazing. "You came all the way from Hawaii to Nebraska just to find me?"

So much for acting casual.

I nodded.

He had been holding himself off the bed a little, his arms shaking with the tension. In one motion, his eyes dropped from mine and he fell back onto the pillows.

Another pain slashed through my chest. He didn't believe me.

I sat motionless, waiting, for what seemed like half an hour. It was probably only five seconds, but it was all I needed to feel utter despair. If he didn't believe me, I would never see him again. He would recover and go on with his life alone, remembering me forever as the whack job who'd showed up at his bedside blubbering like a baby and making a complete ass out of herself. Later on, he and his girlfriend would laugh about it...

No. He had to believe me. He just had to!

I stood up again. "I'm not lying to you, Zane!" I pleaded. "I swear, I'm not." My mind began to race, searching for the kind of 'proof' that men like my dad needed to hear. "I knew that the accident was with an old woman driving the wrong way down the interstate, because you told me that. You told me she had the dome lights on and her headlights off, and that she looked scared. You were really hoping you didn't hit her — did they tell you that you missed her, that she's okay? How could I have known those things before you even woke up?"

He said nothing. I didn't know what he was thinking because I couldn't bear to look at him. I just kept pacing. And thinking. How could he be convinced?

Inspiration struck. "You told me a lot about your childhood, back when that's all you could remember. You told me about having your first surf lesson when you were nine, and how your dad's girlfriend bought you ice cream and took your picture. You said your mother was an actress, that she was a star on one of the soaps. She did commercials, too, and your favorite was one she did with a dressed-up dog."

"Kali," I heard him say hoarsely, but I went on. I was afraid to stop.

"You showed me a scar on your forehead, and you told me that a ramp broke and you went over the handlebars of your—"

"Kali!" he repeated, louder.

Reluctantly, I stopped my feet and turned. I cast a glance in his direction and his eyes caught and held mine.

"Will you stop?" he said good-naturedly, a smile playing on his lips. "Sheesh, you're making me dizzy! I can do without the rundown of every embarrassing thing that ever happened to me when I was a kid. I believe you, okay?"

My heart skipped a beat. "You do?" I squeaked.

"Of course I do. Why wouldn't I?"

The blood in my veins began to warm again. "Why *wouldn't* you?" I repeated. "Because it's the most ridiculous, messed up, unbelievable story ever! It makes no sense. Why *would* you believe it?"

To my amazement, he laughed out loud. "Don't ever go into sales, Kali. You'd totally suck at it."

"Thanks," I returned in an appropriate deadpan, pretending annoyance.

In reality, I was fighting another urge to go jump on him.

"Please," he begged. "Come sit down again. You really are making me dizzy."

"Sorry," I said, sitting. "You mean it? You really believe I'm telling the truth? About everything?"

"It is some pretty weird stuff," he said thoughtfully. Then his eyes began to twinkle. "But if it brought you here, hey — I'll take it."

I melted in my chair. If he kept looking at me like that, I'd be a puddle on the floor.

"Besides," he continued. "I am cheating, kind of. I may not remember anything about being on Oahu, but whatever happened did seem to... well, leave an impression on me."

My head snapped up. "How?"

He let out a long, slow breath. "The first thing I remember after the accident is hearing people talking. Nurses and doctors, I guess. They kept asking me to open my eyes, but I didn't want to. I was so tired — but it was more than that. I knew they were trying to help me, but I just didn't want to be here, with them. Plus they kept calling me Zachary — like the first day of school. It was annoying."

I grinned. "They told me they didn't know your nickname."

He stared at me. "But you did. You said my name and you sounded like you knew me, like we were... close."

My pulse pounded. "You could tell that?"

He nodded. "Now you're going to think *this* sounds weird, but I swear, it's true. When I heard your voice, before I ever opened my eyes, I had a picture of you in my head. I wanted to open my eyes and look at you, to prove to myself that I wasn't making that up. But for the longest time, I couldn't get my eyelids open. It was like trying to lift a pickup truck with one finger under the bumper... it just wasn't happening. But I kept on working at it, and gradually it got easier, until finally I did it. At first I couldn't see anything — the room was a blur. It took a while to clear up, and I was afraid you had left because you'd stopped talking. Then I realized you'd fallen asleep. I hated to wake you, but I wanted to see your face — I had to know if it matched the picture in my head. Once I got my hands moving, I couldn't resist checking out that incredible hair." He grinned mischievously. "So I woke you up. And you lifted your head and looked at me. And sure enough — it *was* you. I knew your face as well as I know my own. The only thing was — I had no clue why. I had no idea who you were; I didn't even know your name."

My cheeks flushed with warmth. I could only hope I looked rosy, rather than manic. "So you do remember," I said in a half-whisper. "At least, some part of you remembers some of what happened."

"I must," he agreed. "Although it's maddening to get such a tiny glimpse of the whole picture. To think that I've lost all memory of seeing you stroll along Sunset Beach in a bikini… that's just criminal."

His face was deadly serious, but his eyes were dancing, and the sight made me chuckle. "You can rest easy on that one," I assured him. "I promise, neither you nor anyone else has ever seen me in a bikini. I don't *do* swimsuits."

"Well, that's even more criminal," he protested with a frown. "You said yesterday that I promised to teach you to swim. I did mention that the Zane Svenson School of Aquatic Instruction has a dress code, didn't I?"

"You did," I teased, suddenly fighting tears again. "I've got my official head-to-toe wetsuit all ready to go."

He didn't miss a beat. "Fishnet?"

"Shut up!" I smacked him playfully on the shoulder. My hand tingled pleasantly from the touch of his now wonderfully solid body, but his visible flinch just as quickly filled me with horror.

"I'm sorry," I gushed. "I didn't think. You must be sore all over from the accident."

He attempted a smile. "A little, yeah."

Don't rush it, I ordered myself. *One step at a time.*

"Have you thought about where you'll go now?" I blurted. "I mean, to finish your recovery. You don't want to stay in Nebraska, do you?"

His eyes looked away from me. He seemed suddenly tired. "No, I don't," he answered. "I've been working that out just this morning. The lawyer who's handling my dad's estate is helping me get a medical transport to California. He's setting me up at a rehab hospital near his place in Malibu."

My stomach dropped into my shoes. "California?" I repeated.

"Right," he answered, making a lame attempt to sound cheerful. "It's where I was headed before the accident anyway, a little stopover on the way to Hawaii. I need to work out some things with him, like seeing exactly how much I have to live on until I'm twenty-one, and figuring out what to do about college. I haven't met him yet, but he seems like a nice enough guy. He was my dad's friend, too, not just his lawyer."

I sat perfectly still, staring at him stupidly. I felt like a fool. Zane might have no family, but that didn't mean he was helpless. He could go wherever he wanted to. He had other options. He didn't need me.

"That sounds good," I forced out. Then I just went for it. "I was going to say, if you didn't have any other offers, you could transfer to someplace in Cheyenne, where I live. My parents and I could make sure you have whatever you need."

Zane's eyebrows lifted. I could often read his thoughts, but this time I was confused. He seemed surprised... and maybe touched... but at the same time, pretty obviously horrified.

"That's really nice of you, Kali," he said awkwardly, looking down at his hands. "But I think I should stay near

Craig and his family. At least for now."

"Sure. Whatever," I said quickly. "I understand. No problem."

Can I crawl under the bed and die now?

"I thought you lived on Oahu," he said, his voice strangely flat.

I tried to paint a smile back on my face, but failed. I couldn't look at him. He wasn't coming home with me. He didn't want to. "No," I responded, fighting another eruption of accursed tears. I had never been so crazy emotional in my life — I had to get a grip on myself. "I was only there for spring break. We live in Cheyenne, Wyoming. My dad's—"

"But," Zane broke in, "Weren't you talking about plans for Oahu? About seeing me again there?"

My gaze lifted. His expression was troubled. He was trying to prop himself more upright, but his arms were trembling from the strain.

"Were you just trying to humor me?" he continued. "About doing it all again?"

"Of course not!" Hope flickered within me, even as my stomach churned to realize how physically weak the accident had left him. "I meant every word of it. We're moving to Oahu in June — I was just about to say that."

Zane fell back against his pillows. He looked weak and exhausted. How could I expect anything else? The guy had only just come out of a coma. Before that, he had nearly bled to death.

I waited a long moment, hoping that he would explain what had gotten him so upset, but he said nothing. He just lay still and closed his eyes.

"I'm sorry," I said quietly. "I've been here too long." *And I've expected too much.* "I guess I'd better go, and... let you rest for a while."

I started to move toward the door.

"Kali, wait," Zane said firmly, even as his voice seemed weaker. "Come back for a second."

My heart thudded. Was this the end? The last time I would see him?

I went to stand beside the bed. His complexion was frighteningly pale, but the flicker of humor I knew and loved so well still shone from behind his drooping lids. He seemed to want to stay awake and talk, but he was having to fight to make it happen.

"I want to see you again," he said finally, his eyes holding mine. "If I promised to teach you how to swim, then dammit, I'm going to do it. I don't know when, but it's going to happen. If you're on Oahu, I'll find you. Just as soon as I'm…. more myself. Okay?"

His eyes twinkled into mine, and I felt as if the clouds had parted and the sun had begun to shine. "I'm absolutely holding you to that," I said with a gulp. "But I'm telling you, the bikini thing isn't happening."

He smirked. "We'll see." His eyelids fluttered. It was obvious that he could barely keep them open.

"I should go," I said softly.

"Leave your number," he ordered, even as his eyes closed. "Write everything down for me. And don't let—" his words began to slur.

He gave his head a shake, his eyes fluttered open for another second. "No letting anyone else teach you how to swim before I get there. Promise?"

I grinned. "That's not too likely. Many have tried; all have failed. But yes, I promise. I'll write everything down for you."

His eyes closed again, and this time they stayed shut. After a few seconds, his head listed to the side. He was asleep.

I reached out a hand and ran it gently down the cheekbone of his beautiful face, entwining my fingers in a ringlet of his newly washed, golden brown hair. There was hope, still. He might not want to come to Cheyenne, but he *did* want to see me again.

Just a few months from now. On Oahu.

We were going swimming.

chapter 3

I took a sip of diet root beer. The glass had been sitting on Kylee's nightstand for about four hours, and it was lukewarm and flat. But I needed to soothe my throat. I'd been talking all night; I was so hoarse I could hardly understand myself.

"What happened the next time you saw him?" Kylee asked, her dark eyes sparkling. My perky, always energetic friend had already lost one night's sleep when she had met my plane from Honolulu in the middle of the night two days ago — now she was losing another one. But she showed no fatigue. Just her usual, all-consuming curiosity.

I hadn't been back in Cheyenne for an hour before she and Tara had arrived together on my doorstep sporting a shopping bag filled with microwave popcorn, a bag of chips, a giant tub of French onion dip, and a half gallon of black-cherry ice cream… my favorite.

"Mandatory sleepover," Tara had announced without humor. "Pack a bag and get in the car."

The hours since ran together in my mind. It was late now. So late, it was probably morning. But when I had called my best friends in a total panic, asking them to help me find a guy I couldn't possibly have ever met, they had not done the sensible thing and dismissed me as delusional — they had jumped into action. Tara the bloodhound had gone online and tracked down Zane's location with almost nothing to go on, and Kylee had made sure I got there in time. The least I owed them now was an explanation. And that's what I'd been giving them. All night long.

"That was the last time I saw him," I said in answer to

Kylee's question, the latest of about a hundred. "I was going to go back a couple hours later, after he had some time to rest. But before I could get there I got a call from Craig Woods, the lawyer from California. He'd flown out to Nebraska and was with Zane there in his room. He said that Zane asked him to call me and explain that his medical transport had been all arranged and that they would be leaving soon. Craig said that Zane would have called himself, but his throat was in bad shape and the doctor wouldn't let him talk for a while. Zane wanted to tell me that he would see me on Oahu."

My friends were silent for a moment. "So..." Tara began finally, then stopped. Her large blue eyes were bloodshot; her voice tense. She hadn't said much since I'd told them both about the shadows. I had kept my freakishness a secret from them the same as everyone else, but there was no way to explain about Zane now without telling them the whole truth. And besides, for some strange reason, I kind of wanted to. I had always shared everything else with them; if I was going to finally be honest with my parents, it seemed only right that they should know, too.

Kylee, predictably, took all the creepy stuff in stride and moved right on to wanting to know anything and everything about my relationship with Zane. But Tara's reaction — which was *no* reaction — concerned me. Kylee lived half her life in a fantasy world anyway, but Tara was the daughter of two no-nonsense cops. She liked her world to be logical, orderly, and free of weirdball crap like ghosts and shadows. "So, you didn't even try to see him again?" Kylee finished.

"How could I?" I answered, the disappointment of that moment still smarting. "He pretty much told me not to come back."

"That sucks," Kylee sympathized. "You sure the lawyer was telling the truth?"

I shrugged. "Why wouldn't he? Zane wanted to go with him; I know that. I just wish he hadn't been in such a hurry."

"You can't blame him for wanting out of a nursing home full of old people," Tara said reasonably, pulling the band off her long blond ponytail, then putting it back in again. "He took charge and found a quick solution — you've got to respect that."

"That's true," I agreed, studying her. Tara never, *ever* wore her hair down. Readjusting the band was a nervous habit. She'd been doing it every five minutes all night.

"Tar?" I asked tentatively. "You haven't said much about… you know. My seeing the shadows."

Her troubled eyes met mine only briefly. "What can I say? I mean, it is what it is, right?"

"She needs to know that you believe her," Kylee said, her dark eyes blazing.

I felt suddenly uncomfortable. I appreciated Kylee's unqualified support more than I could say, and her and Tara's bickering was a constant of the universe, but I hated it when they argued about me.

"Of course I believe her!" Tara defended hotly. Then she turned back to me. "Look, Kal — if you say you see dead people, I believe you see dead people. You're not the kind of person to make up something like that." She shot an accusatory glance at Kylee. "But I *am* allowed to freak out about it. You know I've never believed in ghosts."

"What she sees are not 'ghosts.'" Kylee corrected. "Ghosts are the souls of people who've died but haven't moved on yet, or ones who have moved on but then come back again for some special purpose. Zane was never a ghost because he never actually died. The other things she sees aren't ghosts either."

Tara raised an eyebrow at her. "And you would know this how?"

Kylee stiffened uncomfortably for a moment, then lifted her chin with a determined gesture. "I know things because my *ba noi* is an expert on this stuff. Seriously. She reads the books, she talks to people… she just knows. It's always been a thing with her. And I've—" she broke off. "I think it's pretty cool, too."

Neither Tara nor I needed to ask who Kylee's *ba noi* was; we knew she was referring to her Vietnamese grandmother. Kylee had always been close to her paternal grandparents, even though they had long since disowned her deadbeat father, who had abandoned Kylee's mother when she was pregnant.

"Well," I asked nervously. "What is it you think I *do* see?"

Kylee's forehead creased with thought. "I don't know," she admitted. "In Zane's case, I'd say his spirit was wandering from his body, but it didn't separate completely, because he was still alive. I think the term for that is a wraith — a spirit that's hovering, not knowing which way to go, because the body is very near death but the outcome still isn't sure. But these other things… these shadows of historical people… I've never heard of that before."

I had to laugh. "Fabulous. Even people who actually believe in this stuff think I'm weird!"

"Don't say that," Kylee soothed. "Just because I haven't heard of it doesn't mean nobody has. I bet my *ba noi* would know."

"Do you see shadows now?" Tara broke in gruffly. "I mean, like right here in Kylee's room?"

I looked around. Kylee's bedroom was small, barely

big enough for her twin bed and two sleeping bags on the floor. I didn't see anything except the two of them. "No," I answered, "at least, not now. I see them over and over in the same place, but they're not there all the time. It's like watching a video that loops, but with more downtime than playtime. Does that make any sense?"

"Sure," Kylee said with enthusiasm. "Have you seen any in my room other times?"

"I can't remember any," I answered.

She frowned with disappointment.

"If it makes you feel better," I added with a grin, "whenever we used to go water sliding on the slope in your backyard, I'd see a really old, faint shadow of a Native American boy jumping up on a horse."

Kylee's eyes widened. "Seriously?"

I nodded. My eyes turned toward Tara. She was staring blankly back at me. Should I, or shouldn't I?

What the heck? It did feel good to come clean after all these years. "One of my favorites is in your driveway," I told her. "Right by the basketball goal. It's a teenaged girl with one really long braid down her back. She's wearing a long skirt, but it's not fancy; all her clothes are pretty ragged looking, and she's barefoot. She's falling from somewhere or something up high — I've never been able to tell what. And this guy catches her, right before she hits the ground. He's wearing these shapeless trousers and a tattered shirt, and he has this bizarre floppy hat on. I've never even seen a picture of one like it — I swear I think he sewed it together himself! But anyway, every time he catches her, she looks up at him and she just beams… it's so obvious she's in love with him! And when he looks at her, he has the oddest expression on his face. Like he can't believe she's looking at him like that, but it's the best thing that's ever happened to him. But at the same time, I can feel his fear, too. Like he was afraid he wouldn't catch her!"

I stopped only because I had run out of breath. My cheeks were flushed. Talking about the shadows had always seemed so risky and personally exposing that doing it for the first time with Zane had felt like parading around school in my underwear. Yet here I was, babbling on… and I didn't ordinarily babble, about anything. What had gotten into me?

I looked anxiously at my friends. Kylee's eyes were wide, her mouth open slightly. Tara stared back at me with an expression that was unreadably blank. Almost like she was in shock.

"Sorry," I said weakly. "Too much information?"

They both stared at me another moment. "No way!" Kylee said finally, her face lighting up. "That is so totally freakin' cool I can't stand it!"

I smiled back at her, then turned to Tara. Her expression was still completely blank. She sat unmoving for a good five seconds. Then she gave her head a shake and looked around the room. "Is there any more dip?"

Kylee and I exchanged a glance. "No," Kylee answered. "We finished it off hours ago."

"Oh, right," Tara responded, not looking at either of us. She smoothed out her sleeping bag, plumped up her pillow, and laid down. "Sorry, guys, but I've got to crash. It's been a long day." She pulled a sheet over herself, then buried her head in her pillow facing away from us.

I opened my mouth to say something, but was stopped by Kylee's hand on my arm. She shook her head, her dark eyes sending me a silent message. *Not now. Give her time.*

I decided to take her advice. I'd only lived in Cheyenne a few years, but Kylee and Tara — despite their very different personalities — had been best friends since elementary school. I suppose that was why they fought so much. They felt like sisters.

"Yeah," I agreed, my voice sounding almost as hoarse as Zane's had. "I'm pretty tired, too." I stretched out on my own bag, and Kylee crawled into her bed. "Goodnight," I offered.

"Night," she returned.

"Samesies," Tara mumbled.

I grinned hopefully. "Samesies" was one of Kylee's favorite made-up words, the kind of cutesy nonsense that Tara ordinarily rolled her eyes at.

She would be all right with it. With *me*.

Eventually.

chapter 4

"I don't know what you're so nervous about," Kylee said brightly, practically shoving me up the steps toward the back door of her house. "You've met my *ba noi* like what — three times already? Chillax!"

"That was different," I insisted. "Then I was just some random friend of yours, not a freak of nature."

"Will you stop with that?" Kylee chastised. "I haven't told her anything about you yet — you can do that yourself. Besides which, what makes you think you're so special? My *ba noi's* dealt with some seriously weird people in her lifetime, believe me. It's like she attracts them. You and your shadows are *not* going to shock her."

I reached the door, but refused to open it.

"Kali," she said with a groan. "Just *what* are you afraid of? My *ba noi* is not some creepy third-world medicine woman who's going to exorcise you with a bloody rooster — she's from San Jose! She's lived there since the seventies, and aside from being into supernatural stuff, she's a perfectly normal person!"

I had a strong urge to crawl behind the nearby air-conditioning unit. "I know," I apologized lamely. "I'm sorry. I'm just nervous about anybody else knowing."

The flash of heat in Kylee's eyes cooled. She knew my freak-out had nothing to do with her grandmother's ethnicity. With me being one-quarter Hawaiian and Kylee being half Vietnamese, we'd always considered ourselves in the same multiracial boat. The only difference was that while her beautifully toned skin, hair, and eyes were unmistakably Asian, I didn't look Hawaiian. My hair was dark and curly and my skin was a tad darker than average, but my gray eyes and long "Roman" nose made me look more like the Greeks on my mother's side. "I guess what I'm really afraid of is…"

Kylee waited patiently.

"I'm afraid she really *will* know what's wrong with me," I admitted with a croak. "And I'm not sure I'm ready to hear it."

Kylee reached out and gave me a quick hug. "Sure you are," she said lightly. "And you can't put it off anymore. She's going back home tomorrow. Now get your wussy butt in there." She reached around me, opened the door, and shoved my wussy butt inside.

Twenty minutes later, I found myself sitting in a lawn chair on Kylee's deck, sipping a tall glass of salty limeade, her grandmother's specialty. "It's so much better when *you* make it," Kylee said with a sigh as she drained her drink. "When I try, it's just gross."

"You have to start with good limes," her grandmother responded, enjoying her own drink in the unusually warm spring sunshine. "Besides which, everything always tastes better when you're not the one doing the work." She threw a friendly grin at me, further wrinkling her wizened face.

I smiled back nervously. I had always liked Kylee's grandmother, but I was also a little intimidated by her. Joan Dong was a small woman in stature, but the twinkle in her dark eyes showed wicked intelligence and a spirit as tough as nails.

"Kylee says you have something to ask me," she suggested. "I'm assuming about something other than limeade. Well, don't be shy. Whatever it is, I've probably heard it before."

I hesitated. Why was this so terribly, bone-chillingly

difficult? Didn't I *want* to know the truth about myself? Wouldn't it help to understand? Or would everyone be better off if I just stopped talking about it and went to back to ignoring the shadows and pretending to live a normal life?

Pretending. That was the key. I could either deal with it, or I could pretend. Forever.

"I see dead people," I blurted, before I could lose my nerve. "Lots of them, all the time."

Kylee's grandmother didn't blink. She cocked her head slightly to the side. "How do you know they're dead?"

I swallowed. It was a reasonable, if unexpected, question. "Well, they're not solid; they're transparent. And they're wearing clothes from other times, and the older ones are fainter."

The creases in Joan's brow creased further. "When did you start seeing such things?"

"As long as I can remember."

"And did you ever have a near-death experience? As a child? A baby?"

I considered. "No. Not that I know of. I thought I was drowning one time when I was little — that's why I'm still so afraid of the water. But they tell me I was never in any real danger. Other than that, I've never even been that sick."

She gazed at me a long time, her eyes searching. "Tell me more about these people. Tell me everything you see, and everything they make you feel."

My stomach felt queasy. But I took a deep breath and started talking. I told her what it was like when I was a child, and how, more and more now, I was being affected by the shadows' emotions. I explained that during my brief time in Hawaii, the whole crazy business had seemed to flip into hyperdrive, causing me to feel the emotions of a live human being I didn't even know. I told it all like giving symptoms to a doctor, and I didn't say one word about Zane.

I couldn't bear to. It had been four days since he'd left Nebraska, and I hadn't heard a word from him.

When I finished, I grabbed at my glass of limeade and buried my face behind it. Now Kylee's grandmother would say something. She would tell me some horrible thing I didn't want to hear. Like how I had a moral responsibility to buck up and do something good with my "talents." Whatever it was, I knew I couldn't bear it, not if Zane was lost to me forever. My ability to see his spirit had helped him survive the accident, and I would always be grateful for that. But from this point forward, the "gift" of seeing souls in need was one I could do without.

It hurt too damn much.

"Have you ever heard of anything like that, *ba noi?*" Kylee asked eagerly. "I told her, I don't think what she's seeing are ghosts. Do you?"

Kylee's grandmother raised a hand to her mouth and drummed her fingers thoughtfully across her narrow chin. "She doesn't see as you see, no."

I set down my glass and looked at Kylee. Her eyes avoided mine. "What does she mean?" I demanded. "What do *you* see?"

Joan shook her head at her granddaughter reprovingly. "Still, you don't talk about it? Even to this friend?"

Kylee, the most hang-it-all-out-there, never-ashamed-of-anything girl I knew, had the gall to look sheepish. "I don't mind Kali knowing, *ba noi,*" she answered softly. "I would have told her before, if it weren't for what happened with Tara."

My pulse sped up. I looked from one to the other. "What happened with Tara?"

Kylee rolled her eyes and sighed. "It was a long time ago. Tara and I were, like, in the second grade. We'd been best friends for a while already, and we were used to sharing all sorts of embarrassing things. But then I shared one particular story I shouldn't have, and little Tara totally freaked out. And I mean: *Totally. Freaked. Out.*"

"She was raised differently," Joan said gently. "She wasn't prepared."

Kylee snorted. "She wasn't anything. First she looked like she was having a stroke, then she started screaming about what a liar I was, and then she started crying so hard they had to take her to the nurse's office. I had no idea what her problem was; I was terrified *I'd* done something wrong. When she finally calmed down, she wouldn't even look at me. For days, she pretended I didn't exist. Then finally, about a week later, she told me we could be friends again — *if* I admitted I'd made the whole story up."

A pang of sympathy roiled my stomach. "So you did."

"Yep!" Kylee acknowledged. She took a loud slurp with her straw. "And all was forgotten. And I do mean, *forgotten.* I honestly don't think Tara remembers it anymore. But I do."

"You have lied to her other times, about other things, yes?" Joan said slyly.

Kylee smirked. "Well…"

Her grandmother chuckled. "You've always been a storyteller, my dear. You dramatize. You 'embellish.' You can't blame her for not believing you. Or for forgetting what seemed like just another story."

"Believing *what?*" I said impatiently. "Tell me!"

Kylee gazed out into space, her dark eyes hooded. "It happened when I was five. My mother and I were visiting *ba noi* at her house in San Jose, and I was out in the backyard, playing with my Barbies under her apricot tree.

None of my cousins was around, and I remember feeling kind of lonely. But then a little Vietnamese girl popped up at the back door and asked if she could play with me. I'd never met her before, but *ba noi* always had lots of neighbors visiting, so it was no big deal to meet somebody new. We started playing — she was really funny, and I liked her. But then all of a sudden she got really upset, and she told me we had to go inside right away. I didn't want to go — I was having fun where we were. But she wouldn't stop, she said that Hoa wanted me — that I had to go in and see her right away. I'd never heard of anybody named Hoa and had no idea what she was talking about, but she was practically flipping out about it, so I finally laid down the dolls and followed her to the back door."

Kylee lowered her eyes. "What happened next was like a bad dream. I was standing on the steps with the door open, and suddenly it was like the whole backyard just blew up. There was this terrific crash, and then another, and when I looked back, everything had changed. The place where I'd been sitting was just... gone."

Joan smiled at her granddaughter. "You make it sound as though a bomb exploded."

"That's what it felt like!" Kylee insisted. "I was terrified."

"What did happen?" I asked.

"A man driving an SUV had some kind of seizure at the wheel," Kylee explained. "*Ba noi's* house is on a corner, but the streets are kind of staggered, and this car was going straight, came to a T in the road and just kept going. It crashed through her wood fence and shredded it to splinters, then plowed through the yard and smashed into the apricot tree."

"Oh, my God," I said weakly. "The one you were sitting under?"

Kylee nodded slowly, then raised her head. "My Barbie doll was still there. I could see her yellow hair sticking out from under one of the tires."

Joan reached out a skinny arm and hugged her granddaughter's shoulders. "It was a terrifying day for all of us," she told me. "The driver turned out to be all right, thanks to his air bags. But there was no question that if Kylee hadn't gotten up and moved when she did, she wouldn't have survived."

A moment of painful silence followed, during which I got the creeping idea that I could see where the rest of the story was going. "The girl who warned you," I asked. "She wasn't... alive?"

The two exchanged a glance, then shook their heads. *"Ba noi* never saw her," Kylee said. "She was keeping an eye on me from the window and never saw any other girl, even though I seemed to be talking to one. She thought I was just playing pretend. Once I came into the house, I couldn't see the girl anymore, either. She just disappeared."

"So you never knew why... I mean, who she was?"

Joan smiled. "Oh, we know. As soon as Kylee told me the story — I knew."

"She was dressed funny," Kylee explained. "Not that I cared at the time. I was bored enough that I would have played with her if she'd been wearing black leather with a snake for a belt. But I did notice that she looked odd. Her hair was very long and she was wearing this brown tunic thing. She said her name was Tien, but that didn't seem strange — it's a pretty common name."

"She wasn't transparent?" I asked.

Kylee shook her head. "Not at all. She looked just like you and me."

"So she was... what you'd call a ghost?"

Kylee nodded. "The ghost of a real person who died a long time ago."

Joan put out a tiny hand and touched mine. "She was my sister. My dearest *Tien*. My twin. She died of typhoid when we were seven years old, back in Vietnam."

I felt a sudden urge to pull my hand back. I wasn't ready for all this. I knew I should be, given my own macabre history. But I wasn't.

With a mighty effort, I left my hand where it was. "How do you know?"

"She called me Hoa," Kylee's grandmother said with a smile. "The name I was born with. Only when I moved here did I become Joan."

"I didn't know that Hoa was her name," Kylee insisted. "I'd never heard anyone call her that before. And then there was the picture."

"A picture of Tien?" I asked.

Joan shook her head. "No. No pictures of her were ever taken. But there was one of me, when I was a little older. I didn't show it to Kylee, then. But later, I left it out where she could see it."

"I didn't know it was *ba noi,*" Kylee recounted. "To me, it looked nothing like her. But I took one look and started telling everyone that the child in the picture was Tien, the girl who had saved my life. I still thought that she was a real girl."

I took a deep, shuddering breath. No wonder "little Tara" had run screaming. No doubt she could see, just as I could, that this time Kylee was telling the absolute truth. I just wished I could understand. "But why could you see her when your grandmother couldn't?"

"I'm sensitive to many things," Joan explained. "But I've never glimpsed death. All my life, I've been fortunate with good health. Our Kylee here was not so lucky. At six months, we almost lost her." She leaned over and twirled a lock of her granddaughter's sleek black hair around her fingers. "Meningitis, the doctors said. She survived, but they told us she would have brain damage."

"Explains everything, doesn't it?" Kylee said, throwing me a grin.

I smiled hesitantly back at her. I had heard this particular story before. Kylee's struggling mother had moved in with her in-laws before Kylee was born, and after her illness, they had stayed with the family for nearly two years. Kylee's complete recovery was considered miraculous. "Is that why you asked me if I'd ever had a near-death experience?" I asked Joan.

She nodded. "The souls of those no longer living are never completely separated from us. I feel the presence of Tien every day, *here.*" She touched a knotted fist to her heart. "But I can't see her. I've never seen her. To appear to the living, to manifest as something visible, a soul must expend great energy. To appear to someone without sensitivity is almost impossible. But those who have been close to death have already stood with one foot on the other side. They recognize the very *feel* of it — even without realizing. Children are especially perceptive, because they lack doubt. Tien could appear to my girl because with her, the bar was lower. The barriers to overcome, not so great."

"I haven't seen her since, though," Kylee added. "They can't appear for just any reason. Right, *ba noi?*"

Joan shook her head solemnly. "Once a soul crossed over, to show themselves even to a sensitive person requires great effort, great love, great devotion. Those who have newly crossed do not have the strength — but some may acquire it over time. For many decades no one saw so much as a glimpse of my Tien, yet she was able to appear to Kylee to save her from death, because she knew it was not her time. Our Kylee has a purpose to fulfill yet. We all have a purpose."

Don't look at me now, I thought, even as I cursed my cowardice. *Do NOT look at me!*

I searched my mind desperately for a change of topic. "But what if Kylee couldn't see ghosts?" I blurted. "Could Tien still have saved her?"

Joan's face turned thoughtful. "I don't know. But I believe she would have tried. I've heard of people without near-death experiences who have seen manifestations, but lack the means to understand them. Rather than the image of a person, they may see a mist, or a column of light, or nothing at all. They perceive that someone is with them… but they can't interpret what they perceive."

"So what is it that you think Kali sees?" Kylee asked with sudden urgency. "If they aren't ghosts, what are they?"

I wanted to run. Right now, before Joan could answer. Whatever it was I saw, I didn't *want* to know any more about it. I didn't want to be saddled with some cosmic destiny that would link me forever with the spooky and the creepy and the dark. All I wanted was to be normal. To be normal, and to hear from Zane. I wanted to be with his living self, on Oahu, walking along the beaches in the sun, smiling and laughing again…

"I'm not sure what Kali sees," Joan said heavily, snapping my mind back to the present. "I've never heard of anything quite like it before. Unless," she said dreamily, her dark eyes assuming a far-away look, "there was that one man…"

My heart all but stopped.

"There was a story the old people told," Joan continued after a moment, still looking off into the distance. "The story of a man long before my time. A ways upstream from where I lived as a child, there had once been another village that lay in a bend of the river. As the story goes, a newcomer came into that village one day looking for work, but after looking about, he refused to live there. He said it wasn't safe, that the river would flood. Of course the people only laughed at him, because the village had sat in the same spot for as long as anyone could remember, and it had never flooded, no matter how hard the rains came. Other places flooded, but not their village. No, the man insisted, your village *has* flooded before, and many people died. He was accused of trying to tell the future, but he insisted that no — he spoke only of the past. He claimed that he could *see* it. He pointed to places that were dry, and insisted that he could see the water roiling, and houses tumbling, and flailing limbs tossing helplessly in the current. He said that he could hear the people's screams."

A cold pit sat heavy in the depths of my stomach, even as a part of me wanted to cry aloud, *Yes! That's just like me!*

"He told them he often saw scenes from the past," Joan continued, "But the villagers didn't believe him. They grew angry with him, and he moved on. A few years later, the village did flood, killing many, many people — an unspeakable tragedy. It was a hundred years' rain, they said, the kind most people went a lifetime without seeing. Those who survived remembered what the strange man had said, and then they did believe him. But no one could ever find him again. It was said that he must have had a gift — a very rare and special gift. Yet no one could explain what it was."

Kylee's eyes sparkled; her mouth drew into a smile. "I'll tell you what it was. It was *Kali's* gift."

I could say nothing in return. My mouth was bone dry.

Kylee turned back to her grandmother. "What could it be, do you think? Some kind of energy in the environment that only rare people are sensitive to?"

Joan looked at me thoughtfully. "I'm only guessing, of course. But I wonder if what our Kali is perceiving isn't some kind of imprint. Not an action of those souls in the present, but a trail they have left behind. I've heard that when a person's soul is most awakened, by an event of great emotional importance such as falling in love, or suffering from grief, or horror, or fear — there is a burst of spiritual energy. Perhaps when this energy spikes, it leaves traces behind to which Kali is uniquely sensitive. She sees not the souls themselves, but a projection of them. A residue."

"That makes sense!" Kylee said with enthusiasm. She shot a brief, sideways glance at me, then turned back to her grandmother. "What about people who have separated from their bodies, but haven't died? You know, the out-of-body experiences where people claim they saw the top of the doctor's head who was resuscitating them, and stuff like that?"

My heart began to race again.

Joan's lips twisted with thought. "Some people think that those souls actually leave their bodies and come back, but I've never thought that myself. I've always believed the soul is captive in the body until it is truly and permanently released by death. But I do believe that some elements of a soul can travel — even when the body is alive and well. Like an octopus stretching out an arm, the tentacles at the tip can perceive what the head cannot."

She turned and studied me keenly. "A temporary vacation from the body... one might consider that a 'projection' of the soul as well. I wonder..."

My phone jingled suddenly, startling me. It was a text

tone I didn't recognize. "I'm sorry," I apologized, unable to resist pulling it out and looking at the number. I had different ringtones for pretty much everyone who ever texted me — to hear the generic one was strange.

I looked at the words on the screen. There were eight of them.

Got a phone! How's everything with you? – Zane

"Kali!" Kylee said sharply, grabbing my arm. "Are you okay? What is it?"

I could barely hear her, what with all the hot blood pounding in my ears. It was pounding pretty much everywhere. I said nothing, but turned the phone where she could see it.

Her face brightened instantly to a smile, followed by a very Kylee-like shriek. "He does still care, Kali!" she shouted. "I *told you* he did! I told you!"

I read the text again. And again.

And again.

Sheesh, I was pathetic!

"Well, that answers my next question," Joan said dryly, smiling to herself.

"What's that?" Kylee asked, still beaming at me.

"Kali said that her abilities grew more acute while she was on Oahu," Joan continued smoothly. "Those with gifts of extraordinary perception often find that when their own emotions are in turmoil, their sensitivity is heightened. With girls your age, that may be most of the time. But some emotions carry more firepower than others."

The older woman's eyes twinkled into mine. "I was going to ask if Kali had fallen in love."

chapter 5

"So is he still texting?" Tara asked, catching up with me as we headed out of advanced bio, our last class of the day and the only one we had together.

I turned to her with a smile. Ever since my revelations at the sleepover, Tara had been avoiding me... sort of. Technically we were still together as much as ever. She still cracked jokes and shared her genetics notes and complained about the cafeteria food and her beastly little brothers. But whenever any subject even remotely resembling my abilities came up, she either became suddenly preoccupied or disappeared completely. The chance for a private conversation never did seem to come up. Her seeking me out today to ask about Zane was a first.

"Yes," I answered, beaming. "Not too often, but as much as any guy texts, I guess." I had no intention of telling Tara, or anyone else, how much time I'd spent reading and re-reading the few texts Zane had sent — analyzing every syllable, reading ridiculous amounts of totally insane infatuated-girl crap into every line, obsessing over what was there, what wasn't there, what he *really* meant...

It was embarrassing. My pre-Zane self would have absolutely no respect for me now.

But I did it anyway. I couldn't help it.

"What's he saying?" Tara asked, swinging her backpack off her shoulder as we reached our lockers.

I didn't tell her that I could recite every text by heart, in order, with footnotes. "Just that he likes the rehab place, and he's got a laptop now, and he's getting ready to take the GED so he can graduate high school and apply to college."

She blinked at me. I didn't realize, until I summarized it, how dry and impersonal such news sounded.

Great. Something else to obsess over.

"He seems his usual, optimistic self," I defended, finishing at my own locker and slamming it shut. "It's just a little awkward, I guess. With him not really remembering me."

Tara's expressive blue eyes held mine. "He doesn't have to text you at all," she pointed out. "If he's trying to keep any kind of conversation going, that says a lot."

I sighed with relief. "You're right, as always." We walked out toward the bus lines, where our paths usually split.

"Tara, do you think we could—"

"Don't get in line," she interrupted, then gestured toward the student parking lot. "Kylee's giving us a ride. You don't have anything going on this afternoon, do you?"

I looked at her suspiciously. She knew that although I had dance three afternoons a week, I was free today. It was her schedule, not mine, that was almost always booked, since she had to be at home to watch her little brothers. Tara was the second oldest of six, and her parents' hours in law enforcement were irregular. No one expected her older brother Damon to babysit, partly because he was just as likely as the younger ones to burn the house down, and partly because he was always at practice for some sport or other. But Tara was no willing victim of gender discrimination. At the age of thirteen she had sat her parents down and explained that she could, like her brothers, play soccer and basketball and run cross country, *or* they could fire the current after-school babysitter and hire her at a reasonable discount. The rest had been history. Over the years she had amassed a sizeable bank account, chortling all the while that she had never wanted to play organized sports anyway.

"My dad's off today," she explained. "And I thought of something interesting we can do."

My eyebrows rose. Tara was definitely up to something. And when Tara got an "interesting" idea in her head, you could be pretty sure it was either going to be fantastically fun or positively horrifying. Her brain in action was like a registered weapon.

"Like what?" I asked timidly.

Tara made no response; we had reached Kylee's car.

Kylee stood waiting by the side of it, watching us curiously. "So what's this all about?"

Tara moved toward her and stretched out a hand. "Can I drive?"

Kylee made a skeptical face, but allowed the keys to dangle from her fingers.

Tara swooped them up and popped into the driver's seat. "Come on!" she encouraged.

Kylee and I exchanged a confused glance. Tara drove both our cars occasionally, since she had no wheels of her own, liked to drive, and could get anywhere in the county on sheer instinct. Her wanting to drive today was not surprising. What was weird was the cool determination that lurked beneath her obviously fake cheer. The girl was on a mission.

Kylee turned and opened the passenger door, and I slipped into the back seat.

"Where are we going?" Kylee asked.

Tara switched on the ignition. She didn't look at either of us, but kept her eyes trained straight ahead. "Ghost hunting," she answered.

—⟋⟍⟍—

I squirmed anxiously in the back seat as Tara turned
the car onto a gravel road and drove away from the city.
The skies had been blue this morning; now the horizon in
every direction was studded with ominous gray clouds.
The scene fit my mood perfectly.

"Kali," Tara said, her voice understanding. "You don't
even have to get out of the car if you don't want to. I just
thought it would be, well... interesting. Kylee's wanted to
go on one of those ghost tours ever since we were kids,
but I never would — the thought of tromping around at
night through graveyards and dingy basements always
creeped me out, even if they weren't really haunted."

"I did go on the Cheyenne ghost tour!" Kylee
exclaimed. "I've been ghost hunting other times, too." She
smirked knowingly. "Makes for a great date."

"But why do you want to do this now?" I asked Tara.
She couldn't seriously expect me to believe this had
nothing to do with my confession.

Tara paused a moment. "Believe it or not, Kali," she
answered softly, "I'm trying to be open minded."

"Woohoo!" Kylee cheered sarcastically.

"Shut up!" Tara responded. "I'm not saying I believe in
the supernatural." She threw a worried glance over her
shoulder. "It's not that I don't believe *you*, Kali, because I
do. I swear I do. I'm just not convinced that what you're
seeing isn't being generated internally, by brain chemicals
or something, you know what I mean?"

Kylee sighed dramatically. "Open-minded... *right.*"

I didn't say anything, but I did get Tara's meaning. I'd

thought about it myself, but I knew it wasn't possible. I could give her any number of examples where the shadows I'd seen revealed information I couldn't possibly have known otherwise. But what would be the point? My knowing about Zane's accident was as convincing as any of them, and Tara had clearly blocked that out. She wasn't ready to accept that what I experienced was supernatural, and she might never be. But she still accepted *me*. For now, I was cool with that.

"Look guys, I'm just trying baptism by fire, here," Tara tried to explain. "I want to meet this stuff head on. I don't believe in ghosts. But if we happen to run into any today, then hey — they're welcome to prove me wrong."

Kylee frowned at her. "Don't be saying crap like that! If you want to antagonize the spirits, you can do it when I'm not around, thank you very much!"

Tara rolled her eyes.

Kylee winked at me over her shoulder.

I let out a nervous chuckle. If no ghosts happened to present themselves wherever the heck we were going, I was pretty sure Kylee would manufacture some. The fact that doing so would undermine her case for the supernatural wasn't likely to sway her — messing with Tara's mind was too much fun.

"So where are we going?" I asked, trying to sound more upbeat than I felt. I had less than no interest in fake ghost stories. The real ones were disturbing enough.

Tara shot a playful glance at Kylee. "Guess."

"Hmm…" Kylee took the bait. "Well, it can't be the Plains Hotel. We passed that. And they wouldn't let us roam around it just for fun, anyway — although Josh and I did sneak down the fire stairs one time, and I swear I saw a woman in a long blue gown—"

"Heard it already," Tara interrupted. "Everybody's

heard the 'murdering ghost bride' stories. Not buying it. Next?"

Kylee's lips pursed. "Fine. But I *did* see her." She thought a moment. "We've already passed the Atlas Theater and the Knights of Pythias building... Terry Bison Ranch?"

Tara shook her head. "None of the above. We're going to Striker Schoolhouse."

Kylee squealed with delight. "Oh, that place is *so* cool at night! I went there with a bunch of guys one time. Dustin was there, and Ryan... who else? Maybe I've been twice. I forget where it is, exactly... Oh, my gosh, Dustin was so funny. He hid behind a tombstone, trying to scare me, but then Ryan came up behind him and he got so scared he screamed like a woman — it was hysterical!"

She went on, but my mind wandered. I gazed out the car window at the endless Wyoming plains, once waving with prairie grass and teeming with buffalo, now chopped up into rectangular fields dotted with the occasional farmhouse and barn. Off in the distance, an oil tank farm loomed. The landscape looked pretty much the same in any direction, for miles around. Some might call it bleak, but thanks to Kylee and Tara, I'd been happy here.

Since I was now officially being honest with them, you might think I'd mention that even as Kylee spoke of imaginary spooks, we had in fact driven past the shadows of a half-dozen long-dead miners and railroad workers, any number of farmers, and at least a dozen Native Americans. But you would be wrong. Not even Kylee could grasp the sheer volume of "spiritual energy" I was forced to view, even in such a sparsely populated area as this. Facing the full scope of my reality would be overload for them.

It certainly was for me.

"You've heard about Striker Schoolhouse, haven't you, Kali?" Tara asked.

"I don't think so."

"What?" Kylee exclaimed. "Nobody gets through elementary school in Cheyenne without hearing that story!"

"Kali didn't go to elementary school in Cheyenne," Tara pointed out.

"Oh, right," Kylee admitted. "Well then, you're in for a treat!"

"Wait a minute," Tara said. "It's just up ahead. I'll pull off and then you can tell her."

We reached the intersection of two gravel roads, and Tara turned to the left. There, sitting in the midst of countless acres of perfectly flat fields, lay a small, square plot of land covered with mature trees. As we turned off the road and onto bare dirt, clusters of ancient looking white tombstones appeared scattered among the trunks ahead of us. There was no building on the property. Nor was there any kind of sign.

"I see no schoolhouse," I remarked.

"Oh, it's long gone now," Kylee explained. "But you can see the foundation where it was."

Tara rolled down the car windows and killed the engine. "Tell her the story," she urged, turning around in her seat.

Kylee's eyes sparkled as she, too, turned sideways in her seat to face me. "Well, way back in the olden days, when this place was first being settled—"

"It was in the 1880s," Tara noted.

Kylee's eyes rolled. "Whenever. It was a long time ago. Wild West and all that. There were little settlements scattered around all over, what with the railroad camps and mines and everything, and Striker was one of them.

There were families here, and they built a one-room schoolhouse for the kids that doubled as a church. They planted trees on the lot and started a cemetery behind it. I don't know how long the school had been around before this happened, but at some point they hired a teacher who was *majorly* messed up — twisted and sadistic. She was abusive to the students, beating them for all sorts of imagined crimes, and threatening them not to tell anyone. Some of the children tried to complain about her, but the settlers didn't believe them. Teachers were allowed to whip students back then, so this witch's authority went unquestioned. Horrible, horrible things went on in that little schoolhouse, but none of the adults would intervene. Around *them*, this woman was calm and reasonable — she was like a split personality. One day, as the story goes, the teacher started to beat on one particularly sweet little girl for doing nothing at all, and the students had had enough. The bigger kids overpowered the old woman and tied her to a chair. Then they all got out, lit the schoolhouse on fire, and burned it to the ground."

I flinched. "They *burned her alive?*"

"So the legend goes," Tara answered skeptically. "At least, that variation of it. You hear it different ways."

"I also heard it where the kids beat her to death with schoolbooks and lunch pails," Kylee admitted. "But they always end with the building burning down."

"Let's check it out," Tara suggested, opening her door and popping out of the car. Kylee followed.

I sat still another moment, letting out an unenthusiastic sigh. I knew that many perfectly normal people had a fascination with horror stories — even enjoyed letting themselves be scared by them. I wasn't one of those perfectly normal people. I *hated* the grim and the gruesome. Dwelling on any sort of pain and agony, real or imagined, made me feel way too much like I was experiencing it myself.

And I did not care to be burned to death this afternoon.

I gritted my teeth and opened the car door anyway. With luck, the legend wouldn't be true — or at least there would be no shadows to remind me of it. I tried not to blame Tara for my predicament — she had no idea how deeply scenes of tragedy affected me. Kylee knew, but even she didn't really seem to understand. For her, tromping around the ruins of a schoolhouse and a spooky old cemetery was harmless fun. And she could actually see ghosts!

Could it be that she, too, secretly thought these local legends were crocks?

Feeling a bit more confident, I stepped out of the car. We were near the edge of the cemetery, and Kylee approached a group of tombstones and waved us over. "These are the oldest ones," she said knowledgably. "Most of the writing is worn off, but they look about the same age. I heard that a bunch of people were buried all at the same time because of a cholera epidemic."

I looked at the aged stones, now leaning randomly this way and that, many of them tumbled and broken. The wind gave a sudden gust, buffeting their ragged surfaces with overgrown prairie grass. I felt a chill, but not because of the wind. It was always windy in Wyoming. I just didn't like cemeteries.

"Kali?" Kylee asked tentatively. I looked up to find both of them watching me. "Do you see anything here?"

I had to force myself to look around. I knew that a lot of people thought of graveyards as places where evil lurked — ghosts and ghouls and restless spirits — but I had yet to sense any evil in a cemetery. It was the emotions of the dead people's loved ones that made me miserable.

"I see mourners," I explained tonelessly. "And I can feel their sadness." I walked away into the clearing, and the stifling sense of grief gradually lifted. I breathed deeply. The rainclouds in the sky had only continued to thicken; for a weekday afternoon in broad daylight, it was eerily dark.

"Geez, I'm sorry," Kylee apologized as she and Tara moved to my side. "I didn't think about that. We'll stay away from the graveyard."

"It's okay," I said honestly, feeling better. I really didn't want my issues to be a drag on the day. I was happy enough that the three of us were hanging out together again. "Where did the schoolhouse used to be?"

Kylee smiled at me encouragingly. "Over here." She led us to a spot in the clearing where a rectangular depression was visible, its borders loosely lined with large, half-buried stones. I bent down and took a closer look at one. Its exposed edge was scorched with black. Others bore similar scars.

"Wow," I said, a little surprised. "Whatever building was here really did burn down."

Tara nodded. Her eyes watched me intently, her face uncharacteristically pinched and nervous. "Do you see anything?"

Reluctantly, I looked up. Maybe I would get lucky. Fortunately for me, *every* episode of pain and death that had ever happened in a place wasn't represented by a shadow. Why some were and others weren't, I had no idea. I only knew that I had been in sites of documented tragedy where I neither saw nor felt a thing. I hoped this would be one of them.

My eyes scanned the area where the schoolhouse had

stood. For a long time, I saw nothing. Tara and Kylee stood motionless, watching me.

The shadow took shape before me with a swirling motion, as if it were created by a gust of wind. Higher than I stood, no doubt where the original floor had been. It was a girl, with long skirts, a high-necked blouse, and hair swept up in a massive bun. She looked my age, not much older. Her eyes were wide with terror.

Guilt. It hit me like a slap in the face. The girl might look like a frightened fawn, but she was no innocent.

Hatred. I whirled around as someone else's eyes seemed to bore into the back of my head. Another woman. This one dressed similarly, but shabbier, and a good deal older. Her hair was also in a bun, but an unkempt one, with wisps hanging limply around her face. Her eyes, fixed squarely on the younger woman, burned fiery with rage.

"Holy crap," I murmured, sensing, but not focusing on, the presence of Kylee and Tara right behind me. The shadows' dueling emotions pummeled me from either side, and my instincts screamed for me to back away.

But I didn't. Not this time. My friends were here, standing right behind me. And I had nothing to hide from them anymore. I began to wonder… What would happen if, instead of running away, I actually *tried* to interfere?

Feeling bold, I stepped between the two shadows. I extended my arms as if to ward them off — both from me, and each other.

I should have known better. My actions made no difference whatsoever. The scene the shadows were enacting had happened over a century ago; no one could do anything to stop it. It was going to happen all over again.

"Please," the teenaged girl pleaded, her heart beating so loud that I swore I could hear it, even over the wind.

"I'm sorry. Truly I am. He told me—"

Her last words were lost, smothered into a choking gurgle by hands that reached out and wrapped around her throat. She resisted, but only feebly, as the older woman launched herself forward through my own, pointless self and delivered a body blow that knocked both women to the ground.

The shadows disappeared.

I stood still for a moment, staring at my shoes, which a second ago had been obscured by a dust-caked prairie skirt. The guilt, the fear, the mindboggling fury... it was all gone again.

Just like that.

"Are you okay?" Kylee said softly, approaching my side.

"I'm fine," I answered mechanically.

"From the look on your face," she said sympathetically, "that must have been pretty dramatic."

I felt a strange surge of joy. I looked up again. A man three feet away lifted a crown of lacey fabric up and over a woman's head. Her freckled young face smiled shyly. He kissed her. His blood thundered in his veins with anticipation.

A wedding.

They were gone.

"Kali?"

I could only shake my head in answer. A church and a school, built in the middle of nowhere and never rebuilt after the fire. So many emotional moments and events crammed into a relatively small area of earth over a relatively short period of time... yet for the entire rest of history, it had been just another patch of ground on the plains.

It was practically like a time capsule.

I focused on where I thought desks might have been, searching the air for shadows of students. It felt strange. I wasn't used to looking *for* shadows.

I saw nothing else.

No students. No abusive teacher. No tying to chairs or beating with lunch pails. No fire. Just one inexplicable catfight and a man who was anxious for his honeymoon.

"I think that's it," I announced. "At least for now."

I whirled around with a satisfied smile. Kylee blinked back at me, her dark eyes brimming with curiosity. Tara looked mildly ill.

"Tell us!" Kylee urged with a squeal. "Tell us everything!"

And so I did.

When I finished, Kylee was speechless with awe. Which was a little weird, since Kylee was rarely speechless about anything. But what bothered me more was the fact that Tara looked like something dug up from the cemetery. She always had a fair complexion, but at the moment, she appeared to have no blood.

"Tara!" I cried, moving over and shaking her arm. "What is wrong with you? Are you okay?"

Her blue eyes turned slowly my direction. Her lips trembled. "No," she answered feebly. "No, I am not okay."

Kylee came to her other side. "Do you feel sick?"

Tara took a step backward, stumbled slightly, then dropped down to sit on one of the foundation stones. "It can't be. It just *can't.*"

"*What* can't be?" I demanded. "I told you I saw weird crap!"

Tara swallowed. "Yeah, you did. But it could have—" her voice broke off. She stared at the former center of the schoolhouse with a glazed look in her eyes. "Only it couldn't be. You couldn't—" She stopped herself again. Then after another moment, she uttered a very un-Taralike word.

"Tara!" Kylee chastised. "What *is* your problem?"

"This didn't turn out like I thought," she answered. "Kali was supposed to see... you know... what the legend says."

"I don't always see everything that happens in a place," I explained. "In fact, I usually don't. Just because I don't see the shadow of something in particular doesn't mean it didn't happen!"

Tara swung her head around to face me. Her voice steadied. "But it *didn't* happen, Kali. That's just it. The whole story about the kids mutinying against a teacher — it's not true."

"And you know this how?" Kylee challenged.

Tara frowned. "It's perfectly well documented, if you make the effort. Striker's Schoolhouse has been written about more than once in the last hundred years — just not lately. There are archives: local newspapers and magazines. It was even mentioned in one guy's thesis I dug up from the 70s, as an example of how local legends get started and then assume a life of their own, no matter what the facts."

My knees felt wobbly. I dropped down on a stone next to Tara. "So..." I prompted. "If the legend was wrong, what *did* happen? What caused the fire?"

"The legend was wrong on several counts," Tara explained. "The church/school building burned down in 1887, that much is true. It's also true that a woman's body was found inside, and that that woman had been the schoolteacher. But that's about it. There's nothing in the earliest articles about the fire to show that the school children had anything to do with it. One source mentioned that the kids made wreaths for her tombstone and sang songs at her funeral."

"So why was she in the schoolhouse when it burned?" Kylee asked. "Was she locked inside accidentally or something?"

"That question is what started the mystery about her death," Tara continued. "They couldn't find any evidence that the door was locked. Besides, her body wasn't found by the door, like she was trying to escape. It was found on the other side of the room, where her desk had been."

My eyes followed Tara's to the spot in the foundation where I had just been standing. I felt another chill.

"You mean," Kylee suggested, "that she might have been dead before the fire?"

"That was the theory," Tara answered. "Because even though the kids seemed to like the teacher just fine, she had issues with the rest of the community. *Home-wrecking* issues. Rumor had it that she was having an affair with a married man. They didn't come right out and say that in the papers, of course. But the language about "suspected moral turpitude" made it pretty clear. The guy writing the thesis found evidence that some men in the community had gotten together a few weeks after the fire and debated whether a particular woman should be turned over to the authorities. It wasn't specific about who or why, but it was clearly related to the teacher's death. They ended up not doing anything. And that was the end of it. Of the *real* story, anyway."

Tara's pained blue eyes looked into mine. "You saw it, Kali," she said quietly. "You didn't know any of that, but everything you saw fits those facts exactly. A vicious attack by a jealous wife. Maybe she strangled the teacher to death. Maybe the teacher hit her head on the way down and was knocked unconscious or something. But the desk would have been right there." She pointed to the spot where I had watched the scene unfold. "And that's where her body was found. Her murderer almost certainly torched the place afterward, to cover it up."

The expression on Tara's face was sheer misery.

I didn't know what to say to her. "I might have been seeing something else," I suggested lamely. "The girl who got attacked looked too young to be a teacher. She was our age!"

Tara turned to face me. "Sarah Plimpton, the teacher in question, is buried in this cemetery, right over there." She pointed. "She was seventeen years old."

This time, it was Kylee who said the bad word.

"Tell me about it," Tara agreed.

"No!" Kylee insisted, dropping down to sit beside us. "I mean, this is like, so amazing! It proves everything! Kali, you're a miracle. You're like a human window to the past. How totally cool is that?"

I couldn't speak. I was too worried about Tara having a heart attack.

"I thought it was..." Tara mumbled, looking at the ground again. "But it couldn't be. If the images were coming from inside your head, you would have responded to Kylee's suggestions. You would have seen something from the story. But you didn't. Despite what your conscious brain *thought* to be true, you saw stuff that didn't agree. You saw..." her voice cracked. "You saw what really happened."

She spoke the words as if pronouncing a death sentence.

"Passed your little test with flying colors, didn't she?" Kylee said lightly. "That's what all this was about, wasn't it? A test?"

Tara nodded stiffly. She turned to me. "I'm sorry, Kali. Please don't be mad at me. I was just so sure... and I thought maybe it would make you feel better if we could find a scientific explanation."

"You mean it would make *you* feel better," Kylee accused. "Kali is cool with the supernatural. It's always been a part of her life. How could she not be?"

Cool with the supernatural, I thought to myself. Was I? Just a month ago, I would have said No with a capital N. But now?

As much as I shrank from the idea of having some assigned cosmic role that I didn't want to play, it was equally disheartening to think that everything I had gone through — and still went through — had no purpose at all. Could this sensitivity of mine have some practical use? Clearly, I could not change history. But could my ability to see the shadows affect the present? What if the people in that village in Vietnam *had* believed the man like me?

Before Zane faded away from me on Oahu he had begged me to look at my abilities as a gift, to be honest with my family and friends. He wouldn't even remember saying those things now, but he had been right. Despite the rough reactions from both Tara and my dad, I did feel better now. Less like a freak. Less alone.

More cool with the supernatural?

Maybe.

"It's okay," I said, getting up. The shadows might repeat any time now, and despite the new and intriguing thoughts swirling inside my head, I really wasn't up to that. "Look, guys, this has been fun and all. But could we just, like, go get some ice cream or something?"

Kylee leapt up with a grin. "We'll do better than that. We'll get a quart of vanilla and a bunch of toppings and make suicide shakes in my blender." She reached down and grabbed Tara's arm. "Come on, you hopeless skeptic," she said good-naturedly. "You've had a shock, but you'll survive."

Tara rose without complaint and followed us to the car, walking like a zombie.

"I think *I'll* drive this time," Kylee announced, taking the keys and getting in the driver's door. Tara shuffled to the back, got in, buckled, and sat staring blankly forward. I slid into the passenger seat next to Kylee.

"Tara?" I said worriedly. The girl still had no blood in her face. "You going to be all right?"

"Peachy," she mumbled.

"Don't worry," Kylee told me. "We'll throw an energy drink in her shake." She started the car and pulled back out onto the road. "It is kind of a sad story," she said sympathetically. "I mean, a teenaged girl takes her first teaching job, and her reward is to get whacked by some crazy paranoid farmer's wife?"

"The wife was crazy," I agreed. "But she wasn't paranoid."

Kylee's eyes widened. "You mean, the teacher *was* messing around with the other woman's husband?"

"Oh, yeah."

"But how do you *know* that?"

I remembered again the girl's feeling of terror, and how absurdly mixed it was with anticipation and a certain macabre excitement. She felt guilty, but not that guilty. She felt... smug. As if she knew she'd done wrong, but expected to get away with it. Even *deserved* to get away with it.

Miss Sarah Plimpton had been a serious piece of work.

"I can't really explain how I know," I answered, marveling at my own certainty. "Some things, you just have to feel."

chapter 6

My mother watched me with an amused smile twitching at the corner of her lips. "You could always just call him, you know."

I slipped my phone self-consciously back into my pocket. Yes, I checked it occasionally, just in case I had gotten a text but didn't hear the ringtone. Maybe I checked it often. And just maybe I had gotten into the habit of staring at it mournfully every other second of every waking moment of the day. What of it?

"Mom," I reminded her with frustration. "Nobody *calls* anybody anymore." To give her credit, my mother was reasonably well up to date on the real world, despite the fact that she and my dad were older than the parents of most kids my age. She was a technical writer, so she was computer savvy, and she did text and send pics. But some things, she would never get. Like the fact that it was perfectly okay to go around with your bra straps showing, but that it was *not* okay — under any circumstances — to wear jeans with an elastic waistband.

"Of course not," she teased. "Why would you call, when you can take six times as long sending short little typed messages back and forth with no nuance or context?"

"I cannot just call him," I explained. "It would be too awkward. I don't have anything to say."

My mother gave a shrug. "Maybe he feels like he doesn't have anything to text. After all, he's probably not doing much besides physical therapy. I imagine it will take quite a while for him to recover his strength. Oh, look at this one. How pretty!"

She held up a cream-colored formal with delicate spaghetti straps and an unusual layered skirt that looked like it would float when you moved. It actually was really pretty. And I had been thrilled when my dad — of all people — insisted I buy myself a new dress for the upcoming junior/senior prom. It would be my first real formal dance. So why couldn't I get excited about it? About *any* of the dresses we'd looked at?

My mother hung the gown back up on the rack with a sigh. "Kali," she said heavily. "For heaven's sake, I know you miss this guy and you can't stop wishing he was the one taking you to prom, but you can't just put your whole life on hold! You should be enjoying these last few months in Cheyenne with your friends."

I hated it when my mom read my mind.

I hated it even more when she was right.

"So has Dad mentioned anything about... you know?" I asked, changing the subject.

My mother frowned. "No, I'm afraid he's still not ready to talk about it. He's worried about you, and he wants to help, but he doesn't know how. He can't wrap his mind around what you told him, and his way of coping with things that he can't act on is not to think about them."

"I know," I said with a sigh. "Maybe it's better that way. Scientific minds seem to need their happy little cut-and-dried boundaries."

"Any improvement with Tara?" she asked, reading me again.

I shook my head. "She's the same. Acts like everything's fine, but doesn't want to talk about it."

"I'm sorry about that," she said sympathetically. "Maybe she'll still come around. Does she have a date to prom yet?"

I shook my head again. It was a sore subject among the three of us. Kylee would be going with her current boyfriend, Eric, and she desperately wanted Tara to go with his best friend, Steve. But Tara was less than excited about it, and — perhaps because he could tell that — Steve hadn't asked her yet anyway. I hadn't been asked either, but two guy friends of mine had been hinting at it. They seemed to be waiting for some kind of encouragement, but I wasn't capable of giving any. I didn't want a "friend date." Not this time. I would rather go alone. At least then I wouldn't have to pretend I was enjoying myself.

I took out my phone and stared at it again. Then I realized I had taken out my phone and stared at it again. I stuffed it angrily back into a hip pocket.

Sheesh, this was bad. Zane *did* text, just not nearly as often as I wished he did. I missed him terribly and was always anxious to hear from him, but I had to get a grip on the anxiety of it all. If Kali Thompson did not go postal in seventeen years of seeing dead people, she was *not* going to lose it over some guy!

Any guy.

"I like this one!" I said with enthusiasm, pulling out the first dress I saw. Too bad it was bright orange with full ruffled sleeves, a high neck, and a gargantuan yellow daisy at the waist.

"Really?" my mom asked, her face pained.

I laughed out loud. "No. I hate it. But maybe this one over here—"

My phone made a sound. It was the sound I heard in my dreams all night long.

Zane's ringtone. And it was *ringing*.

I pulled the phone out so fast my butt cheek got

friction burn. "Hello?"

"Hey, Kali! What's up?"

My heart started beating like a jackhammer. The voice on the other end of the line was not the hoarse, thin croak I had heard back in Nebraska. It was the beautiful, smooth baritone that had warmed my days on Oahu like sunshine, and hearing it now took me back like a whirlwind to sandy beaches, blue water, swaying palms, and a brisk ocean wind.

"H-hey," I stammered back. "I'm just out, looking at... stuff. What's up with you?" My mom stood four feet away, pretending to be focused on the clothing racks. I grabbed up two random gowns and headed for the dressing rooms.

"Oh, same old, same old," he answered cheerfully. "All physical therapy, all the time. I know you've been thinking about running your car head-on into a concrete overpass too, but I really wouldn't recommend it. It's not nearly as much fun as it sounds."

I grinned. "But you know how I idolize you."

"Yeah," he returned. "I know. But maybe you can imitate some of my surf moves instead."

"I should probably learn how *not* to drown, first."

"Chicken."

I laughed as I swung into a dressing room, closed the door, hung the gowns on a hook, and settled onto the wooden bench in the corner.

"Seriously, are you feeling better?" I asked.

"I am," he answered. "Just bored out of my mind."

"Aren't you studying for the GED?"

"Oh, I passed that already."

My eyes rolled. He *would* pass the test after studying about two seconds. For all his efforts to act chill, he was obviously wicked smart.

Call me crazy, but I liked that in a guy.

"I'm applying to the University of Hawaii for fall term," he added.

I smiled. I would be spending my senior year of high school in Honolulu. *Perfect.*

"Look, Kali," he began, his tone suddenly becoming more serious. "We may get interrupted in a minute, but there's something I wanted to... ask you about."

I tensed. "What's that?"

He was silent for a moment. I pictured him running a strong, tanned hand through his mane of curls. I knew he wouldn't be tanned, but I couldn't help myself.

"Well, you said you see weird stuff," he said finally. "You saw me when I wasn't really there, right?"

"A part of you was really there," I corrected, feeling a fierce desire to defend... something. I wanted to make clear that I knew the *real* him. Whether he remembered it or not. "But yeah, I see weird stuff. Stuff most other people can't see. Why?"

A cold surge of dread crept along my veins. He'd had no trouble accepting my supernatural side when we first met... but of course, he'd been a wraith himself then. After he woke up in the hospital, he still seemed to accept my nutball story. But what if, after further reflection, he decided that everything about me was just a little too weird?

I couldn't stand it.

"I was hoping maybe you could explain—" he broke off awkwardly.

My blood was giving me frostbite. "Just say it," I encouraged.

Another pause.

"I think I saw a ghost," he blurted finally.

My limbs flooded with warmth again. "Holy crap," I

murmured to myself more than to him, nearly weak with relief. "Is that all?"

"Is that *all?*" he repeated, sounding insulted. "It was kind of a big thing for me."

I laughed out loud. "Zane," I teased, "you being freaked out about seeing a ghost is just too rich."

After a moment, he chuckled too. "Yeah, I see your point. But it *was* pretty intense."

My mind went back to my conversation with Kylee and her grandmother. "You've never seen anything like this before?"

"Um... *no,*" he said firmly. "I'm pretty sure I would remember that."

"According to my sources," I said, trying to sound scholarly, "having a near-death experience sensitizes a person to picking up on the presence of souls who are no longer living. You've had one foot on the other side of the curtain — so now what's over there makes more sense to your brain."

"Oo-kay," he said uncertainly. "So you mean, it's going to keep happening?"

"Probably." I couldn't resist a smirk. "You should consider it a gift!"

He was silent for a beat. "Are you quoting me?"

I laughed again. "Yep."

He grumbled.

Still chuckling, I slid off the bench onto the floor and made myself more comfortable. There was a woman in the stall next door who probably thought I was insane; but for once, I didn't care.

"What happened exactly?" I asked. "Tell me about it."

"Well," he began, "it started with, a couple times, me seeing this guy wandering around the halls. I noticed him because he was wearing a hospital gown, and nobody in this place wears those things — the whole point is *not* to feel like you're stuck in a regular hospital. But he's wandering around barefoot, looking confused... I asked a couple staff about him, but none of them knew who I was talking about, which was really weird. How could they not notice? Then one morning I woke up and there he was, standing right inside my door, staring at me."

"Did you scream?" I teased.

"You could say I was 'startled.' Particularly when I noticed that the guy wasn't right. He looked solid and everything, just like a real person. But his hand was sticking right *through* the door handle. And when he walked toward my bed his movements were bizarre — like not the right speed or something. Too fluid, too effortless. He got up right in my face and said, 'You can see me, can't you?'"

"Hmm," I grinned. "Seems like I've heard that line before."

"I guess it's a pretty obvious question, coming from a ghost. Anyway, as freaked out as I was about the whole non-living thing, the guy himself wasn't threatening. He just seemed upset, really sad. He looked like he was twenty-something, too skinny, bad complexion — he had that hollowed-out druggie look to him, if you know what I mean."

"Check."

"So I said, yeah, I could see him, and what was he doing in my room? And he said he'd been wandering around the place for years, ever since it was a regular hospital. He told me that he'd died in the ICU after a car accident. He and his cousin had been drinking at a bar, and he tried to drive them home. They hadn't gone two blocks when he ran a light, swerved to miss another car, and crashed into a brick wall. His cousin never made it out of the ER. He knew because he found his body down in the morgue."

"That's awful," I sympathized.

"He was really torn up about it," Zane continued. "I mean, it had been years ago, but I think he sought me out because he wanted to talk. It was still torturing him. He said he saw a light — that he still sees a light — but he doesn't want to go into it."

I sat up straighter. "You mean there really is a light and everything? I've heard of it, but you said you never saw one."

"I didn't actually die," he reminded me.

Thank God. "No, right. But why didn't he want to go into the light? Isn't it supposed to be peaceful and welcoming and all that?"

"Oh, he said it was. Like, the best thing ever. But he couldn't go. He couldn't face his cousin after feeling like he'd killed him — I guess the cousin wasn't as drunk, and had asked if he could drive. And he didn't want to face his aunt, either. She had practically raised him and then died young of cancer, and on her deathbed she'd asked him to look after his cousin. He felt horribly, horribly guilty. The bizarre thing was, he wasn't afraid of hell or punishment or anything like that. He just couldn't bring himself to face his family!"

"That's pretty rough," I commiserated. "What did you say to him?"

Zane exhaled uncomfortably. "What could I say? I mean, since when do I know anything about this stuff?"

I chuckled again. The irony was way too amusing. "I bet you winged it just fine."

"I'm not so sure about that."

"Well, what *did* you say?"

"I, uh… suggested he might feel better if he did something useful with himself — something good. Besides just wandering the halls looking miserable. He said he wanted to keep other people from making the same stupid mistake he made, so I suggested he go hang out at the bar down the street and scare the crap out of drunks heading for their cars."

I cracked up laughing so hard I nearly did roll on the floor. "Are you *kidding?*"

He sounded embarrassed. "No."

"Zane, that's awesome!" I praised between peals of laughter. "How perfect!"

"You really think so?"

"Absolutely. Most of them probably won't be able to see him, but if even one does, or even just sees a mist or gets a creepy feeling, it might actually work!"

"Yeah," he agreed, sounding more confident. "I figured if he felt better about himself, maybe he'd go into the light the next time."

"See," I praised again, "you're a natural. And you told me—" I broke off when I heard the sound of a knock on his end of the line, followed by a door opening.

"Guess what I've got?" a Hispanic-accented female voice said silkily. "Your favorite!"

Zane's voice sounded farther away. "Chile rellenos? It is! Coleta, you are an angel."

"Anything for you, handsome," she purred back. "Let me know if you need anything else, hmm?"

My teeth gritted. There were some muffled noises, then the sound of a door closing.

"Sorry about that, Kali," Zane apologized, his voice back to full volume. "My dinner is served. A better than usual one, thank goodness."

"So I guess you like Mexican food?" I asked, my voice cracking.

Crap! Did I sound as ridiculously, lamely jealous as I

felt? I *knew* he liked Mexican food!

"Love it," he answered. "I love most food. And right now, I'm starving. Set a new record today for laps in the pool."

I got a mental image. My blood felt warm again. I crawled back up onto the wooden seat. "You're back to swimming already? That's awesome!"

He chuckled. "Yeah, well, I'm not going to tell you how *many* laps made a record. I am getting better. Just not quick enough." A dish clinked. "Wow, this smells good. Coleta outdid herself. Got the chef to add some extra cheese!"

I bet she did.

I made an effort to unclench my jaws. Handsome, indeed. Who was I kidding? Zane was beyond handsome. He was freakin' *gorgeous*. The only reason I'd had him to myself in Hawaii was because nobody else could see him!

Duh.

I was done for.

"I've got to go, Kali," he said, rattling some silverware in the background. "But I'm glad I called. You made me feel a lot better about... you know."

"No problem. It was good to hear from you."

Cripes. Now I sounded like I was talking to a distant uncle!

"Did you get your uniform yet?" he asked.

I did a double take. "My what?"

"Your uniform. For the Zane Svenson School of Aquatic Instruction. The new policy manual allows for a one-piece, but absolutely no swim shorts, and none of those god-awful cover-up things either. Too dangerous. The extra fabric attracts sharks."

My cheeks flared with heat.

"I really am going now because I'm starving, but keep

in touch, okay?" he continued.

"Okay," I said lamely, my stupid eyes starting to tear up again. I wanted to be with him again, on Oahu. I wanted to be with him again *now*. Before he fell madly in love with some Mexican beauty and decided to surf the Bajas instead.

"Oh, and Kali," he said slyly.

"Yes?"

"Coleta's like, forty-something. Bye."

I sucked in a much-needed breath.

"Bye."

chapter 7

"Pretty, easy to move in, and understated," my mother praised, hanging up my newly ironed prom gown on the door of my closet. "I think you made the perfect choice. I'm glad Kylee and Tara were able to talk you into it!"

I smiled back weakly. The dress had not been my first choice. My first choice had been a stunning, elegant black number studded with tiny sparkling jewels and dipping into a low-cut V neck. Tara and Kylee had said I looked amazing in it. But what was the point in wearing such a thing if Zane wouldn't be there to see it? I couldn't care less what any of the Cheyenne guys thought.

"Our dresses all kind of coordinate," I explained. "This shade of violet goes perfectly with Kylee's fuchsia and Tara's teal." It also had wide shoulder straps and a flowy skirt, which made it more comfortable to dance in. So what if it was so modest it was almost prudish?

"You three are going to have a wonderful time," my mother prophesied.

"We always do," I agreed.

Since "going stag" to the prom wasn't a particularly big deal at my high school, Kylee and Eric's rather spectacular breakup just ten days ago wound up being a positive for all of us. For Kylee, because "he was getting boring anyway"; for Tara, because she really did not want to go with the force-fed Steve; and for me, because I had never wanted a date in the first place.

I had been looking forward to the big event, if for no other reason than I loved to dance. But all day now, I had been feeling unsettled. After weeks of fairly regular texting, the last word I'd had from Zane was a cryptic note saying that he was being discharged from the rehab facility and would get back in touch when he "got where he was going." When I asked what that meant, he hadn't answered. It had been four days now, and just this morning I had given in and texted to ask what was up.

He hadn't answered that message either.

I was trying really, really hard not to worry about that.

I had other worries, too. The shift in my attitude toward my "gift," however slight, was having dramatic consequences. Now that I wasn't actively fighting it, the emotional end of the spectrum had cranked up another notch. I wasn't just feeling the shadows anymore; I was starting to feel *everybody*. The lunch lady who rang up my salad: depressed. The guy in line behind me at the grocery store: worried. The computer geek in my civics class who never said anything to anybody: crazed with lust (and not over any one girl in particular, either). The ballet instructor for my Thursday night class: ditto (except that he was very specifically interested in the guy who was remodeling the studio).

It could be amusing, at times. But it could also be deafening — and exhausting. I tried to prevent overload by avoiding crowds; but at school, that was impossible. The funny thing was that the signals I picked up most strongly came from strangers, or from people I barely knew. With people I was close to, my impressions seemed garbled. Maybe because my brain, which was already used to reading all sorts of personal cues from them, got in the way? However it worked, I knew I couldn't keep on like this. I needed help. And thanks to Kylee's willingness to consult her grandmother, who was apparently linked into half the supernatural knowledge base of the West Coast, I felt like I might actually get some.

It felt amazingly good not to have to deal with everything alone anymore. I just wished that everyone else I loved could be as matter-of-fact about it as Kylee was.

The doorbell rang, interrupting my mother in mid-sentence. She had been saying something about my dress, but I had no idea what. "I'll get it," she offered, moving toward the front door. "It must be Tara or Kylee. You snip off those loose threads before we lose track of them."

Loose threads. Right. I grabbed some scissors from my desk drawer and snipped off several violet-colored strands that were escaping from the bottom hemline. The dress had been cheap. I would rather save money for the black one. And senior prom…

Footsteps sounded in the hall, and I looked up to see Tara coming through my doorway with a full-length plastic wardrobe bag and a duffel. I stood still for a moment, stunned.

"Tara!" I exclaimed, gawking at her. "You got contacts!"

She waved a hand in dismissal and dumped her stuff on my bed. "Yeah, I figured it was time to give it a try. Mom's new insurance covered it, so I figured whatever."

I tried not to stare, but I couldn't help it. Kylee had been trying to talk Tara into getting contacts ever since the fifth grade, and lately so had I. I didn't wear glasses or contacts and felt a little guilty telling her what to do, but Tara's eyes were so gorgeous and her taste in frames was… well… pretty appalling. With contacts, she looked like a totally different person. Dark, cobalt blue orbs sparkled out from behind long, thick lashes and a set of never-before-seen perfectly shaped eyebrows. Even with her hair still skinned off her forehead and held prisoner in the inevitable ponytail, her appearance was mesmerizing.

"You look fabulous!" I said inadequately.

Edie Claire

She waved a hand in dismissal again. Only the slightest tilt to the corner of her mouth let me know she appreciated the compliment. "Never mind my stupid eyes," she said impatiently. "I came a little early so we can talk. I hope you don't mind."

She sat down on my bed, and I joined her. "Of course not. What's up?"

"I think I found a scientific explanation for you."

My eyebrows rose. "For me?"

She smiled a little sheepishly. "Okay, for *me*. You know I've been having a hard time with this stuff."

"Yeah, I noticed."

She turned toward me, her newly visible eyes radiating regret. "I'm so sorry, Kal. I wish I could have been there for you all along, like Kylee has been, but I've been so freaked out—"

"I know," I said. "I get it. This stuff affects people differently. My dad still acts like I never said anything."

She looked at me with surprise. "Really? The Colonel?"

I nodded. "He can't deal with it either. So he doesn't."

"I guess I can see that," she said thoughtfully. "He and I both want everything in our lives to be rational and understandable."

I made no response.

She turned toward me again, this time with a smile. "But here's the thing. I've finally come to realize that what you're seeing *isn't* supernatural at all!"

I blinked back at her. This should be interesting. "It isn't?"

She shook her head. "Look, Kali. Two hundred years ago, if you'd tried to explain to people about wireless networking and bandwidth and how moving pictures and sound and data can travel through the air in the form of invisible waves, they would have thought you were nuts.

Three hundred years ago, they would have burned you for a witch! We can look back now and say they were stupid and closed-minded to think of electromagnetic waves as supernatural, but what else could they think, when they lacked the scientific tools to measure and describe them? And how do we know we're not still doing the exact same thing to other perfectly natural phenomena that we see glimpses of today, but don't have the technology to understand yet?"

My heart leapt. "I guess we don't."

"Exactly," Tara beamed. "I told you I don't believe in the supernatural, and I still don't. But everything that's real *is* natural."

"So you think what I'm seeing is real?" I asked anxiously.

"Absolutely," she answered with a smile. "I think it's some kind of residual as-yet-undescribed type of energy, left over in the atmosphere."

I chuckled, resisting the urge to tell Tara how much she sounded like Kylee's grandmother.

"I don't know how or why you're able to translate that energy into 3D moving images when no one else can," Tara continued. "But the fact is, you do it, so there must be a way. Probably a recessive trait carried in your DNA. As for seeing Zane on Oahu — I think I've found an explanation for that, too."

I grinned at her. "Go for it."

"Well," she began in her best lecture voice. "I've been reading up on near-death and after-death experiences. A lot more people are having them now, because resuscitation methods have gotten better and more people are surviving after their heart has actually stopped. If you look at what those patients are saying in a scientific way — as opposed to assuming that it's either a religious thing or that they're making it up — it's pretty clear there's something real there. What they report back is way too uniform to be pure coincidence. And we know it can't all be generated by a dying brain, because the brain isn't even functioning when a lot of this stuff happens, and if your brain cells aren't working, you can't hallucinate. Some part of our consciousness *has* to exist separate from the brain, simple as that. And I think that some part of Zane, some form of energy associated with his body, did travel to Oahu. And you, being you, were able to interpret that energy where you saw a 3D living person."

My cheeks flushed with warmth. "You have no idea how good it is to hear you say all this," I gushed. "Particularly when you make it sound like it's coming from a college professor!"

"It will, someday," she answered. "Don't you see? It all makes a weird kind of sense when you look at it scientifically, instead of just running scared, like I was doing. Of course Zane can't remember what happened on Oahu — his brain wasn't there, and it's the brain that lays down long-term memories of events. But he did carry back into his body whatever that energy is capable of carrying. Feelings, almost certainly. Images, perhaps. I'll bet you anything that when he gets back to Oahu, the things that he sees and hears and smells are going to bring back all sorts of feelings, even without his brain remembering the events that actually happened there."

I couldn't restrain myself anymore. I lunged at her with a hug, bowling her over onto the mattress and knocking her stuff off onto the floor. We both bounced back laughing. "Tara, I love you! Do you have any idea how much I've wanted to hear something, *anything* like what you just said?"

"Yeah, I'm getting that."

I could not stop smiling. "If Zane remembers feelings, then that's all that matters!" *Because he'll remember how he felt about me!*

Tara smiled back. She started to say something else, but was interrupted by a knock on my door, which came at the same time that Kylee opened it and stepped inside. She took us both in with a glance, but her gaze stopped dead on Tara. A very slow, delighted-in-an-evil-sort-of-way smile spread across her face, twisting her features like the cartoon version of the Grinch. She dropped everything she was carrying at her feet, then crouched down, unzipped her backpack, and extracted a shiny new curling iron.

"Tara, my dear," she said ominously. "Tonight, the hair is coming *down.*"

—✺—

"I am so excited I can't stand it!" Kylee squealed as we approached the "red carpet" that led from the parking lot to the side door of our rather excellently decorated gymnasium, which the junior class had helped transform into a showplace for the seniors' "Night in Hollywood."

I grinned back at her, feeling the same.

We were walking three across, with me in the middle and with Kylee looking past me every couple seconds to make sure that Tara hadn't bailed on us. The gown that Kylee had picked out for herself was appropriately dramatic — a hot neon pink that hugged her curves with no apology and showed off her dark hair and eyes to perfection. Ordinarily, Kylee could be counted on to spend at least an hour preparing herself for even a casual dance. But this evening she had shrugged into the dress, fluffed her hair, and thrown on her own makeup in about

five minutes — spending every other available moment
working on Tara.

"I have been waiting for this moment since we were
thirteen years old," Kylee proclaimed, her voice nearly
catching as we reached the door. She turned and stood a
moment, looking at the results of her labor with
moistening eyes. "Tara, babe," she said with pride. "You
look like a freakin' Disney princess."

"Oh, crap!" Tara exclaimed.

Kylee and I both laughed out loud. But it was true.
Tara did look like a princess. Her dress, which was the
exact same shade of blue as her eyes, was elegance itself,
sweeping down her lean frame to reveal a feminine form
never before seen beneath her usual baggy tee shirts,
sweats, and I-swear-those-came-from-her-brother's-closet
jeans. Her dark blond hair flowed halfway down her back,
ending in soft, gentle curls. A few shorter blond tendrils
curled around to frame her china-doll face, from which
her newly uncovered blue eyes shone like sapphires.

"Tara," Kylee chastised, scooting around me to take
hold of her opposite arm. "You are *not* going to wimp out
on us now. Remember what you used to keep telling
yourself, whenever the mean girls made fun of your glasses
and your clothes and you felt like crying? *Brave like a
warrior.*"

Tara's eyes rolled. "That was in the third grade!"

"Still applies," Kylee ordered. "Haven't you been
wearing whatever you darn well please ever since? And
tonight, you are *choosing* to look amaza-freakin-throw-down
gorgeous!"

"Thanks," Tara replied. "But... you know I hate
attracting attention. A lot of people are bound to notice
I'm not wearing glasses."

Kylee shot me a wry, sideways glance. Tara really had

no clue how beautiful she was.

"Come on, Tara," I said, putting my arm through her free one and propelling us all forwards. "We're doing this thing together. We promised. Now, let's go!"

The red carpet led past an outdoor security checkpoint with the chaperones and then passed through the double doors to a cleverly designed "grand entryway." Here, everyone got to walk down a short flight of steps and have their picture taken while Hollywood spotlights spun around illuminating the newcomers in full view of the crowd.

All Kylee and I could say, in defense of the decorating committee, was that it had seemed like a good idea at the time. Somehow, the word "intimidating" had never come up. But as the three of us neared the entrance, Kylee and I exchanged worried glances. When Tara saw the gauntlet she had to walk through, would she bolt?

Definitely. No sooner did we step through the doors than Tara saw the lights ahead and the crowd gathered below and halted like a mule. "Oh, I am *so* not doing this!" she exclaimed, shrugging off our arms and whirling around.

But Kylee and I were prepared. We darted behind her and stood shoulder to shoulder at the door, blocking her retreat. *"Brave like a warrior!"* we chanted.

Tara stared at us for a long moment, her blue eyes blazing. Then, much to our surprise, she laughed. "Oh, *fine!* Let's just get this damned spotlight thing over with so we can dance!"

Smiling with relief, we turned Tara around again, took deep breaths, and made our grand entrance.

We couldn't see who waited below, because the lights were in our eyes. But I could sense the crowd's reaction. Both guys and girls were... speechless. And not over

Kylee or me.

We posed for a quick picture, then stepped down onto the dance floor. It took a second for our eyes to adjust, during which I felt a manly elbow jabbing me in the ribs. "Hey, Kali," Tara's older brother Damon said offhandedly, giving Kylee and Tara on my other side only the briefest of glances. "Where's Tar? I thought she was coming with you."

I fixed him with an appropriately withering look. "She did," I answered, refraining from adding, *you moron!*

"Well, where'd she get to? I gotta ask her—" His eyes widened suddenly to saucers. His stubbled jaw dropped nearly to his chest.

The next word out of his mouth was *that* word. He said it clearly. He said it really, really loud. And he said it, quite unfortunately, just as the last chords of the song died out, making his astonished voice reverberate to every corner of the room. "No!" he continued shouting, oblivious. "Get out! Tara? Is that really you?"

The entire assembled crowd stared right at us. Kylee and I exchanged a tension-filled glance. Damon wasn't a bad guy, really. He was friendly enough, and like his sister he was actually quite good looking — tall and athletic with sandy brown hair and blue eyes. Unlike his sister, however, he was neither particularly interesting nor particularly bright. Tara always said that her brothers had the collective intelligence of a bran muffin.

A few people tittered. A nearby chaperone threw Damon a disapproving glare. The next song began, but despite its familiar upbeat sound, no one moved.

Kylee and I watched anxiously for Tara's reaction. Would she bolt again?

But Tara merely groaned. "Of course it's me, you idiot!" she snapped. "Who did you think it was? Now shut up and make yourself useful. I like this song." She grabbed him roughly by the hand, spun him around, and led him, unresisting, to the dance floor.

Kylee and I relaxed. "She's going to be okay," Kylee assured.

We watched together as Damon clumsily began to dance with his sister, only to be replaced within seconds by one of his smarter — and smoother — senior friends. "Something tells me we won't be seeing her for a while," I said happily.

"Nope," Kylee agreed, her dark eyes sparkling. "My job here is done." She then turned and looked at me with equal fervor. "Now, back to you. I had a long talk with *ba noi* this afternoon. She says you're an empath."

My eyes widened. "I'm what?"

"An empath," she repeated. "It means that you have the ability to pick up on other people's emotions. Anybody can try to read emotions by picking up on obvious cues, like tone of voice, facial expression, body language. Some of us are better at that than others — and women tend to be better at it than men. But a true empath is different —they actually *perceive* other people's emotions and *feel* them like they're their own. That's what you've been doing. It's a separate gift from seeing the shadows, but it's a lot more common. *Ba noi* knows a bunch of empaths in San Jose, and she's going to ask them for advice on how to control it. You know, learning how to shut out the background noise so it doesn't get overwhelming. How cool is that?"

"That's…" I said breathlessly, "pretty darn cool."

I felt a surge of giddy excitement. Part of it, no doubt, I was picking up from the people around me, most of whom were mindlessly enjoying a good party. But it wasn't all them. I felt like a sick person must feel when — after a string of doctors tells them their symptoms are all in their head — one doctor finally takes them seriously, diagnoses their trouble, and prescribes a cure. I was *not* crazy, and I never had been. I had some rare and unusual gifts, true. But aside from that, I was a perfectly normal person.

Sweet.

"Hey, Kali!" came a voice to my left. I looked over to see one of my guy friends, Lucas, smiling at me from behind a cup of punch. "You look awesome!"

I smiled back. Lucas was a bit of a nerd, but he was a nice guy. I noticed he had trimmed his ordinarily shoulder-length hair for the event, and might have actually looked decent if he hadn't chosen to wear an eggplant-purple tux with a bright red vest and bowtie. But what did I care? At least he could move to music, which made him the closest thing to a good dance partner my high school had to offer.

"Thanks," I responded. "You don't look so bad yourself." *Relatively speaking,* I added silently. "Want to dance?"

He threw back the remainder of his punch with one gulp, then shrugged. "Not much else to do, is there?"

I turned back to Kylee, but the spot where she'd been standing was empty. She was already out on the dance floor, demonstrating some moves to a circle of adoring guys who couldn't imitate them if their lives depended on it.

Oh well. So what if the guys at my high school weren't into dancing as much as the ones I'd met at the Spring Fling on Oahu? I had a lot of friends here, and I would miss them when I moved. Even if the guys did continue to swoon over Kylee and the flirty girls while thinking of me as just another "gal pal." The music was good and my best friends had my back.

I would not think about Zane. I would not try to

imagine his reaction to seeing me in this dress, certainly not in the one I *didn't* buy. I would not remember how he could always make me feel attractive, no matter what I was wearing or what I was doing, just because I was me.

I was going to dance with a bunch of guys who saw me as just another one of the guys, and I was going to enjoy myself anyway.

I turned back to Lucas. Awkward, too-skinny, apparently colorblind Lucas. We'd known each other since before my braces came off. He saw me just like the others did: a down-to-earth, undemanding tomboy of a friend.

He held out an elbow and smiled at me. "Shall we dance?" he said jokingly.

Lust.

My breath caught in my throat.

Holy crap!

I tried to clear the system; reset the channels. The face he turned to me looked as it always did: self-conscious but good-spirited, slightly sarcastic, always ready for a laugh. But what was he actually feeling?

Lust.

Oh my. Was it the dress? The occasion? Or had he been giving off the vibe all along, but I wasn't sensitive enough to feel it? Surely not!

"Something wrong?" he asked, lowering his arm again.

Concern.

I managed to return a weak smile. He really was worried about me. How sweet was that?

"No, I'm fine," I lied, taking his arm with a flourish. "Let's show these losers how it's done, shall we?"

He grinned back at me broadly. "After you."

Lust.

Ackk!

I averted my eyes and led him briskly out onto the

dance floor.

chapter 8

Lucas was not the only one. The only thing keeping me from feeling totally creeped out by the rapid-fire onslaught of desire I felt from every guy — yes, *every* guy — I danced with was the even more powerful vibe of excitement and fun that radiated from nearly everyone in the room. It was a great dance. The DJ was tons better than last year's (so I understood from the seniors), all the songs were familiar, and the sour-cream guacamole dip on the back right table was to die for.

For whatever reason, at least a third of the crowd had come without dates, so there was plenty of mingling and flirting going on, which meant Kylee was in seventh heaven. And as for Tara... well, Tara was having the time of her life. She insisted, on the few occasions when she could shake off enough admirers to have a word with me, that it was all about her lack of glasses. I could have told her that her face was in fact *not* the focus of Jack Mason's attention during their frequent dances together, but I decided she was better off not knowing that.

And I would be better off not knowing that Caitlin Martin was ridiculously jealous of Erin Pruitt, even though Caitlin had been the one to break it off with Nick over a month ago. Or that my precalculus teacher was *way* too fond of my American history teacher, considering that they were both married with kids. And I could definitely stand to live another day without realizing that Amy Alexander felt horribly guilty every time she looked at her super-sweet boyfriend, which probably meant that she'd been cheating on him with her thoroughly despicable ex.

Again.

"Hey, girl!" Kylee chirped, joining me at the guacamole table. "Is this a fun one, or what? Do you *see* Tara?"

I nodded as I finished swallowing a mouthful of chips. "Listen, Kylee, when did your grandmother say she would call again? I've *got* to shut this empath thing off!"

She threw me a puzzled look. "Really? Like, totally off? But why?"

Because, despite her saying about a thousand times that she forgives you for stealing her boyfriend freshman year, I know now that Maddie Silverman still hates your guts. And I really wish I didn't.

"Because it's driving me nuts," I answered. "There are some emotions that people are better off keeping to themselves, you know?"

Her eyes gleamed. "Like *what?*"

I shook my head. "Just let me know as soon as you hear anything, okay?"

"Will do," she answered cheerfully. "Oh, look! Bryan is calling me over again!"

She sailed off into the crowd, and I dipped another chip into the guacamole. *Calling you, indeed,* I thought ruefully, remembering how Bryan's "emotions" regarding the new Tara had nearly burned a hole in my back every time I had accidentally stepped between them. Too bad the guy was not only an operator, but an all-around, first-class jerk — something it didn't take empathic abilities to pick up on.

I made a mental note to chaperone Tara home tonight.

A group of hungry-looking people approached the food table, and I reluctantly gave up my spot by the chips and dip. As I stepped away, I was struck by a sudden feeling of melancholy. I looked around, wondering if I was sensing someone else nearby. But I didn't see any likely suspects — living or dead. This time, the feeling was my own.

I sighed. Everyone else's good spirits had kept mine up so far, but left to myself, I was short on cheer. I might as well face it: I missed Zane. Despite knowing better and constantly warning myself to cut it out, I couldn't help daydreaming all spring about how much fun we could have together at prom. He was such a fabulous dancer — untrained, but with natural talent. We could rock out like no one else.

But it was more than that. Even if he came in a wheelchair with his leg in a cast, I would have fun just being with him. Laughing with him, enjoying his killer smile...

Missing him was seriously painful.

Kylee and Tara had urged me to go for it and just invite him. "What could it hurt?" they had asked. What they didn't know was how many times I had already hinted to Zane in texts — and not at all subtly — that I would be happy to road-trip out to visit him in California. It would have required no effort on his part. I had money saved up. But every time I had mentioned the possibility, he had deftly made a joke of it, or twisted my meaning, or changed the subject. He didn't *want* me to come.

I wasn't sure why, when everything else he texted was so reassuring. He never left any doubt that he wanted to see me again, but in his mind that clearly didn't mean *now* — it only meant at some unspecified point in the future, and on Oahu. I still had no idea exactly what his injuries were, or how quickly he was recovering from them, because his few texts on that topic were intentionally vague. So how could I ask him to travel to Wyoming, when he obviously wasn't well, just to indulge me with a stupid high school dance?

I couldn't. So I hadn't. End of story.

I wound my way back around to the table where we'd left our bags and pulled out my phone. There was no point in pretending I wasn't checking for a message from Zane, since pretty much everyone else I knew was either in the room with me or knew it was prom and was leaving me alone. There wouldn't be any messages. But I had to check...

I had missed a call.

A call from Zane!

My hands fumbled so badly I dropped the phone on the tabletop with a clatter. Luckily the music was so loud and the room so busy that no one noticed.

Chill, girl!

I picked up the phone again. He had called ten minutes ago. It was only the second time he had actually called me, ever. He hadn't left a voice mail message. There was no text. Should I call him back?

The phone vibrated in my hand.

I dropped it again.

Breathe!

In one motion I swooped up the phone, hit answer, and sailed away from the noise of the music toward the relative quiet of the alcove by the locker rooms that was designated as a "cell phone area." That had been Kylee's idea. The girl was brilliant.

"Hello?"

"Hey, Kali!" The sound of his voice sent a shudder through me. He sounded so full of energy, so alive... so excited. "I've got something I want you to hear. You ready?"

I hustled toward the farthest corner and covered my other ear. "Sure."

I strained to listen over the drumming bass beat. At

first, I heard nothing. Then it came through loud and clear. *A rooster crowing.*

A pleasant warmth flushed my face. I knew that sound. He was on Oahu!

"Did you hear it?" he asked brightly. "There are, like, three hens and a rooster right outside my window! Guess where I am."

I laughed. "Where else would you go to find wild chickens but Hawaii?"

"Ding ding ding!" he said, imitating a bell. "Where in Hawaii?"

"Haleiwa?" I guessed, naming the small town on the North Shore where I'd nearly tripped over a chicken myself.

"Almost," he conceded. "I'm in a little apartment just off Kaunala Beach, near Backyards. You know where that is?"

My smile broadened. I did know. Backyards was a surf break. He had taken me there. "Just north of Sunset Beach!"

"Awesome!" he praised, obviously pleased.

"You have an apartment?"

He laughed. "Well, that's probably not quite the right word for it. It's more of a room. Tacked onto the side of somebody's garage, with a bathroom about four feet square. But it's livable. And the location is amazing. I can *walk* to Backyards. And once I get a bike, I can be at the Pipe in, like, three minutes!"

He sounded like his old self again — talking about surf breaks like a kid talks about Christmas. And he was sharing his excitement with *me.* "Zane, that's fabulous!" I gushed.

He went silent for a couple beats. "Hey, what's all that noise?" he asked. "You at a party?"

I tensed. "Kind of. It's the junior/senior prom."

He was silent another moment. "Oh, wow," he said, sounding a little deflated. "Sorry. I didn't know I was interrupting the big event."

"You're not!" I said quickly. "I needed something to get me away from the guacamole dip, anyway."

More silence. I didn't know what he was thinking, but I couldn't bear for him to misunderstand.

Honesty, Kali.

"The truth is," I blurted. "I really wanted to invite you to come, but I was afraid you would say no. I didn't know if you felt up to traveling so far... and besides, you said you'd see me in Hawaii."

"Oh."

Oh? Was that it? Oh?

"But I really wish you were here," I finished bravely. "I mean, not that you wouldn't rather be in Hawaii, of course!"

"I wish I was there, too," he said quietly. "I missed all my own dances in high school; I was always working. I guess I probably told you that already." After another beat, he cleared his throat and his voice became cheerful again. "So did I brag to you before about what an awesome dancer I am?"

I smirked. "Actually, you did. And I didn't believe you. Until I saw you in action."

"You saw me dance?" he said skeptically. "When?"

Awkward. When I thought he was still unconscious, I'd given him a pretty good rundown of all the fun we'd had together on the North Shore. But of course I'd left a few things out. Like the fact that I'd gone to Frederick High School's "Spring Fling" with another date. "It was a dance at the school in Honolulu that I'll be going to next year," I explained. "And yes, you are an amazing dancer." A sudden mental image made me smile. "Think you can still do an arabesque on a moving shortboard?"

"Um..." he answered uncertainly, "that's not exactly the kind of dancing I was talking about. What's an arabesque, again?"

"Never mind," I laughed. "How about I show you when I get there?"

"Can't wait," he said immediately. "Listen, Kali..."

"Yeah?"

"I shouldn't bother you when you're on a date. I'll call you later, okay?"

"I'm not on a date. I came with Kylee and Tara. And I promise you, neither one of them is missing me in the slightest."

I couldn't hear anything. But I imagined him smiling.

"Send me a pic!" he insisted, his voice jovial again. "You talk about those two so much, it'll be nice to have some faces to put with the names."

"Hang on a minute." I flipped through the series of pictures my mother had taken on my camera before we left the house. I picked the one where my hair looked the least like I'd stuck my finger in a light socket, and hit send.

"Okay, done." Did I dare? The fact that I didn't have a single picture of him had caused me no small amount of grief in the endless months since I'd last seen him. I never thought to take a picture of a semi-transparent wraith (would he even show up?) and it seemed beyond crass to whip out my phone and capture a shot of him while he lay in a hospital bed. All I had to look at was one low-res pic from his ninth grade swim team that I'd pulled off the internet (in which, despite his age, he looked totally hot). "Now it's your turn," I dared.

"Fine," he answered. I heard a series of muffled noises, then a ringtone on his end. He whistled. "Wow," he said in a deadpan. "Remind me, when I'm running the world, not to hire any guy who went to high school in Cheyenne, Wyoming."

"And why not?"

"Because they must all be complete morons. How could they let the three of you get to prom without dates? The incompetence! Boggles the mind."

"Um... thanks for that," I said with a chuckle. "Kylee had a date, but — well, it's kind of a long story." My phone beeped. I pulled it away from my ear and saw that I had received a picture. I opened it eagerly. Then I groaned out loud.

"Zane!" I fumed. "This is a freakin' *chicken!*"

He cracked up laughing. "Isn't that what you wanted?"

"No!"

"So come to Oahu," he said smoothly. "When are you moving?"

I gave him the latest date range; we wouldn't know the exact day for a couple weeks yet.

"That ought to be enough time," he responded.

"Enough time for what?"

A beat. "Nothing. Kylee's the brunette, right?"

"Yep. How'd you guess?"

"She looks like a Kylee. And Tara's the blonde."

"That's right." I suddenly wished I hadn't sent the picture. How good could I possibly look standing next to the two of them?

"I'm sorry I'm not there, Kali," he said with sudden seriousness. The regret in his voice made my heart melt. "I didn't even think about your having a prom this spring. But of course you would."

"It's okay," I managed, my eyes threatening to tear. "It's not a big deal. Really."

He chuckled sadly. "You really do suck at lying, you

know that?"

I laughed. "Yeah. So I hear."

"So if you're really not busy at the moment," he asked. "Tell me, what's a prom like, anyway? Are Kylee and Tara having fun with the blind idiot guys? Is there a DJ or a band? I've always wondered what I missed. You're a good storyteller. Take me there."

I imagined him in the perfect tux, his blond curls contrasting sharply with a tailored black jacket and crisp white shirt, his green eyes sparkling as he danced...

Frederick High School, Honolulu, Hawaii. Senior prom. One year from now.

I *would* make it happen.

"Well," I began with enthusiasm, settling myself into a folding chair in the corner. "Proms always have a theme, for one thing. This one's is 'Night in Hollywood...'"

I took him through the whole evening, starting with Tara's makeover and the effect of our grand entrance. I remembered how easy he'd always been to talk to. On Oahu, I figured it was because he was already dead and I felt like I had nothing to lose... but now I wasn't so sure. Maybe it was because he was a good listener, and he seemed genuinely interested in what I had to say. Whatever the reason, I found myself sharing way more than strictly necessary. Like, for instance, the whole guy-lust-empath thing.

"Wait a minute," he interrupted. "Let me get this straight. You're getting this vibe from every guy you dance with... and you're surprised by this, why?"

I bit my lip. How exactly had I stumbled into this minefield? Just because I was as comfortable talking to him as I was to Tara or Kylee didn't mean I could forget he was a guy!

"You don't understand," I argued uncertainly. "These

aren't guys who actually *like* me — it's not like we're dating or anything. We're just friends."

"Yeah. And?"

He was confusing me. "And?"

He chuckled. "Well, what emotions would you expect them to feel when they're watching a girl as gorgeous as you move around in a dress like that? Puzzled? Sleepy? Morose?"

"No!" It sounded stupid, now. "But just... I don't know! Exhilarated by the music, maybe?"

He laughed out loud. "They're *guys*, Kali. They can't help themselves; it doesn't matter who you are or what your relationship is. It's a reaction. You can't blame them for having basic instincts. Now how they *act* — that's a different story. Do girls really not know this stuff?"

I couldn't help but think it was better if we didn't. Lucas's primal fantasies could stay in his own head, thank you very much.

I had to turn this empath thing *off*, ASAP!

"Maybe it's just as well," Zane proclaimed. "The guys in Cheyenne clearly don't deserve your understanding. In fact, I take back my previous defense. They're sexist barbarians, all of them."

I grinned.

"And by the way," he added. "Can you tell what I'm feeling right now?"

I concentrated. I imagined him sitting in his tiny apartment. It would be cramped and probably a little dingy, but brightly painted. It would be early evening there now, right around sunset. The breeze would be blowing in through opened shutters, carrying the sound of waves crashing on the sand. I could guess what he might be feeling. But the "emotion vibe" was a different animal. It was a unique sensation that I either picked up or I didn't.

Right now, I was getting zip.

"No," I answered, disappointed.

"Excellent. In that case, I'm exhilarated by the music."

I cracked up laughing. "I don't think you have to worry about me spying inside your head; I can't feel Kylee or Tara, either." I explained about the paradoxical "stronger with strangers" thing. "So your evil secrets are safe, at least for now."

"There you are!" I looked up to see a jarring display of purple and red. Lucas was beaming at me from the entrance to the alcove. "Everyone's looking for you! You coming back to dance some more?"

"That must be one of the barbarians," Zane said dryly.

"I'll be back in a couple minutes," I answered Lucas.

He raised a cup of punch in the air, as if toasting me. "Cool," he stated. Then he did some kind of marching band move — a stiff about-face which caused half his punch to splash out onto his pant leg — and left again.

Lust.

Sheesh!

"I should let you go, Kali," Zane insisted. "You only get one junior prom. Go enjoy it."

"All right," I said reluctantly, sliding off the chair. "So..." I dared, "What are you going to do with all your free time, now that you've made it to the North Shore?"

It was kind of a joke, but not really. Of course he would be dying to surf, but was he physically able to?

"I'm trying to remember things," he answered.

It was hardly the response I expected. "Remember things?"

"I meant to tell you earlier," he began, his tone serious. "Seeing the ghost wasn't the only weird thing that's happened to me since the accident. Ever since I've gotten to Oahu, I've been having these sensations... like deja vu, I guess. I'll see a place, and I'll *know* I've been there before. But no matter how hard I try, I can't remember a thing about it. It's crazy making!"

My pulse quickened. *Yes.* It was happening just as Tara predicted!

In a rush, I explained her theory. "So when I get there, you can tell me what seems familiar, and I can help you fill in the blanks."

"That'll be great," he said, sounding relieved. "Now enough about me. Go back to your friends and dance!"

I smiled. "Will do."

We said goodbye and I hung up, my face glowing.

When I get there.

I *would* get there.

The "do-over" was coming soon!

I moved through the doorway and back out toward the crowd, realizing only then that, once again, Zane had cleverly avoided my question about what kind of shape he was in. He'd also avoided sending me a picture of himself. A wave of fear struck through me. What if he *was* hiding the extent of his injuries? What if he was afraid to tell me that he could never surf again?

Lust.

I wheeled around to see Lucas approaching. "Ready now?" he asked politely.

I nodded absently and followed him to the dance floor.

Zane wasn't hiding anything. I would know it if he was.

Lucas flashed me a smile of pure innocence.

Wouldn't I?

Chapter 9

The last day of school. The last period. The last minute. Sad as I was to be leaving my friends so soon, every second of the day had felt like an eternity. *One week*. Seven days from now, I would be on Oahu.

This time with a living, breathing Zane. And this time, I would be staying there.

I was so excited, I couldn't allow myself to think about it... or I might explode.

Kylee and Tara didn't want to think about it, either.

"This," Kylee announced, flipping the switch on her blender to pulverize our celebratory smoothies, "will be the best we've ever made."

We smiled at each other silently while the motor whirred. None of us wanted to talk about my leaving. In the beginning, we'd made plans that maybe they could visit me at Christmas break. But airfare was expensive. Tara had money saved up, but I knew she needed it for more substantial things, like college. And Kylee could work all summer and not make enough to cover both airfare and spending money for senior year. Maybe, I had suggested meekly, they could check out the University of Hawaii and consider it a college visit? I knew that Kylee, who loved the ocean, wanted to go to school somewhere on the coast. Tara didn't care where her future college was located, as long as it had the engineering program she wanted and would give her a good enough scholarship. But while Kylee's parents could help her out with the costs of a legitimate college trip, Tara's parents could not.

My coming back to Cheyenne for a visit was the

backup plan, of course. But none of us could get quite as excited about that.

The blender ground to a halt, and Kylee poured the smoothies. "To summer," she toasted, raising her glass.

"To summer," Tara and I echoed, clinking the tumblers and taking a sip.

The drinks were heavenly. Strawberries, kiwi, pineapple, and lime. Kylee had thrown in some mystery ingredients, too. She was good at that.

"You're right," Tara agreed. "They are the best ever."

"You do have a way with combining flavors," I praised.

Kylee smirked. "Must be my fab multi-continental gene pool. My profile had the greatest 'ancestral diversity' of anybody's I saw. What did you guys get?"

Tara and I exchanged a startled glance. "We forgot all about it!" Tara answered for both of us. She moved out of the kitchen to where our backpacks lay on Kylee's family room floor. She handed mine over to me, then began to rummage through her own. "Mr. Stedman didn't hand them out until after the bell rang," she explained. "And then everybody was partying in the halls..."

Mr. Stedman, our advanced biology teacher, had asked for volunteers months ago to enroll in an ancestral genetics study. It was the same type of DNA test other people were paying big bucks for on the commercial market, but we had gotten it done for free in exchange for swabbing a cheek and filling out a survey about our known family tree. We were supposed to analyze the results in class, but they took too long to come back and he had taught the unit without them.

"I came out 49% East Asian, which is a no-brainer," Kylee explained, pulling a crinkled piece of paper out of her back pocket. "But my mom had no clue where her ancestors came from. She thought one of her grandmothers was Irish, but she wasn't sure." She hopped up on a kitchen stool, shook out her paper, and took another sip of her smoothie. "So it turns out — everybody ready? — not only am I half Vietnamese, I'm 22% Scandinavian, 16% British Isles, 6% Central European, and 6% European Jewish. How totally cool is that?"

"That is totally cool," I agreed, impressed.

Tara whistled. "I think you've got both sides of most major wars covered there. Good thing your ancestors got along!"

I rummaged anxiously through my own backpack, but the envelope remained stubbornly hidden. Where had I stuffed the thing? I couldn't wait to see my own results. I knew that my grandmother Kalia, whom I was named after, was Hawaiian, but I couldn't wait to see that fact verified in writing. She had died when my father was young and he'd been raised by his father and stepmother in Minnesota, so he had pretty much zero cultural association with the islands. Still, blood was blood, and I was proud of mine.

"Mine is going to be totally boring; I know it," Tara prophesied, finding her envelope and ripping it open with haste. "My mother says she has Native American ancestors, but out here everybody says that. I bet it's not true. That company probably laughs its head off at how many people's family trees are completely wrong."

She unfolded the paper, and her eyes grew wide. "Get out!" she shouted with glee. "I *am* part Native North American! 4%!"

"I always did think you looked a bit Cherokee," Kylee joked.

I laughed with her. All Tara's siblings looked like they'd fallen off a Viking ship. "I bet you're mostly

Scandinavian though, right?" I asked, still looking for my own envelope.

Tara nodded, her face beaming. "Yeah, 63%. But I'm also 32% Central European. That makes sense too, since my one grandfather was definitely German. This is too cool!"

"What did you get, Kali?" Kylee asked, just as the stubborn envelope at last made an appearance (inside my English folder). I pulled it out. It was labeled only with my identification number; the testing had been anonymous. I ripped it open.

"Yours should be really interesting," Tara predicted. "The Hawaiian islands have so many different populations mingling. You're sure your grandmother was native Hawaiian, right?"

"That's what my dad says," I answered, unfolding the papers. *Please, please, please be true!*

My hands were practically trembling. My eyes roved over the gibberish, searching for the words I longed to see. What category did native Hawaiian fall under?

"Pacific Islander!" I shrieked with joy. "It's here! It's really here!"

My friends cheered. "Awesome!" Kylee praised. "You'll fit right in!"

"What else do you have?" Tara asked. "Your mom's like, totally Greek, isn't she?"

I nodded. "Both her parents were born in Greece, and she never heard anybody in the family ever claim to be from anywhere else." My face was still buried in the paper. Something didn't seem quite right. "What category is Greece?"

Tara looked at the map on her papers. "It would be Eastern European. You have it?"

I nodded again. "I'm 49% that, so that makes sense."

But did the rest of it?

"What's wrong?" Tara asked. "You look confused."

"I..." my heart started to pound. "I am confused. It says I'm 31% Pacific Islander. But I couldn't get more than 25% from Kalia. Right?"

Tara's forehead creased.

"That must mean you have other relatives who were Hawaiian, too!" Kylee suggested brightly.

I shot a glance at Tara. "But my dad's father's people were all from Minnesota. The name Thompson is British, but all the other family names were things like Abramsen and Gulbrandsen. My dad was showing them to me when we filled out the forms..." My voice trailed off. I stared at the paper another moment, then looked back at Tara.

"But I don't have any Scandinavian here. *Zero.*"

Tara's eyes held mine with understanding. "What do you have?"

I took a breath. "It says 49% Eastern European, 31% Pacific Islander, 12% Southern European..." I hesitated. "And 6% East Asian."

"East Asian!" Kylee squealed, hopping off her stool. "Seriously? Where did *that* come from?"

"2% uncertain," I finished. "And I don't know."

"Well, aren't there lots of Asians in Hawaii?" Kylee suggested. "Kalia could have been a mixture."

I shook my head. The effort made me a little dizzy. "But I'm already more than 25% Pacific Islander!"

"Can I see the paper?" Tara asked softly.

I handed it over to her. Her eyes scanned the numbers, and I could picture the calculations she was running in her head. The same ones I had been running. The ones that didn't add up.

After a long moment, her eyes met mine. "Your dad went through all his father's ancestry with you, and he knew it was for a DNA project?"

I nodded.

She exhaled. "It could be a mistake," she offered.

"What mistake?" Kylee demanded.

"All of the Pacific Islander and Asian background in Kali's profile couldn't have come just from Kalia," Tara explained. "And her mother's parents are already accounted for with the 49% Eastern European. That leaves her father's father. Even if Kalia herself wasn't all Polynesian, but had some Asian or even some European thrown in, the fourth grandparent couldn't possibly have been Scandinavian. According to this, he was Southern European... possibly with Asian blood. He must have had some Pacific Islander blood, too."

Kylee's dark eyes shone with grim understanding. The room went quiet a moment.

"Like I said," Tara offered again, gently. "It could be a mistake."

"Of course it could," Kylee agreed. "Did you see that disclaimer form? It was a mile long! It's a new technology — it could be way off. Plus, it was all done by the numbers, so you know a few are going to get switched around."

I shook my head stubbornly. "If it was *all* off, maybe I could believe that. But it's dead on with my Greek grandparents. And how many Americans outside of Hawaii have Pacific Islander blood at all? For it to be right about all that, but totally, completely wrong about one grandparent out of four..."

Nausea rose in my middle. I remembered how eager my father had been to help me with the project. How proud he had been to show me his Swedish grandmother's family bible, with its generations and generations of carefully penned birth and death dates. Of Kalia's parents, he had known almost nothing.

I had to wonder how much he knew about Kalia herself.

"I don't think it is a mistake," I said weakly. I didn't want to say it. I didn't even want to think it. But my lips formed the words anyway. "What I think is that Albin Thompson was *not* my biological grandfather."

The nausea got worse.

"And my dad has no idea."

chapter 10

"Here," Kylee ordered, setting a peanut butter cup on the table in front of me. "You need chocolate. Eat."

We were sitting in the food court at the mall, eating frozen yogurt. At least, Kylee and Tara were eating theirs. I had only been staring at mine.

"Kal," Tara cajoled. "The official Cheyenne last-day-of-school junk food binge crawl isn't nearly as much fun if you don't actually eat the junk food."

I tried to smile. "Yeah, I know. Sorry." I picked up the candy and nibbled on a corner. It did taste good. Tara was only kidding about the junk food crawl, but we did have microwave popcorn along with the smoothies before coming to the mall for yogurt. They were trying to get my mind off my mystery grandfather, and I was trying to let them.

"How's the blocking coming?" Kylee asked, looking around at the crowd. The mall was busier than usual for a weekday afternoon, swelled with high-energy kids ready to celebrate the summer.

"Getting better," I answered. "Slowly."

Just a month ago, I would have avoided the mall like the plague. But thanks to some pretty weird advice coming from Kylee's grandmother's network of similarly cursed/gifted people in San Jose, I was beginning to get a handle on the empath thing. Sort of.

I sat up in my chair, "opened" my mind, and looked around. I had always seen surprisingly few shadows in the mall, and today was no exception. There were two men standing in the hallway near the cinemas arguing, but from their clothing and their position in space, they appeared to have been there before the building was built. The city of Cheyenne had more shadows than did the countryside around it, but neither had as many as Oahu. I realized now that being a military brat had worked to my advantage, because so many of the bases where my father had been stationed were in the middle of nowhere. Wyoming in particular had never been a thickly populated place, which was a big part of why I liked it. As much as I longed to see the world, I dreaded the thought of setting foot in a city like London or Rome, which had been populated for so long by so many that the shadows must overlap each other in gnarly masses. What such a place would *feel* like to me now, I couldn't bear to imagine.

Unless I could learn better control.

"What's the situation?" Kylee asked, as was her habit now. She had been helping me with the exercises. Much to my delight, Tara had been too.

"Only two shadows," I replied. "Too far away to feel. But I'm getting all kinds of other stuff."

A mother, frustrated and angry with her misbehaving toddler. A toddler, hungry and miserable. A mob of middle school girls: nervous, excited, mortified, anxious, jealous, sad, restless.... *Yikes! Go away. Been there, done that!* A man with his girlfriend: bored. The girlfriend: bored. *Trouble there!*

I shook my head at the overload.

"Okay," Kylee coached. "Bring down the blind. Picture it. Reach up and grab the handle..."

I had a hard time believing that such a simple trick could work, but it did. I set all my powers of concentration to imagine a giant circular blind that surrounded and cut me off from the people outside my chosen circle. I started rolling it from the top, slowly, smoothly, and slid it down my field of vision like an invisible protective film. Even before it was halfway down, I could feel a lessening of the emotional noise. By the time it touched the floor, I felt nothing but blissful, peaceful quiet.

I exhaled with a smile.

"Got it?" Tara asked.

"Got it," I answered. I knew the block would not last forever. It only worked when I concentrated on it, or when I was wholly consumed with other thoughts. When I let my mind wander, I was vulnerable again. But as time went on, I seemed able to call it back more easily. And just knowing I had *some* control made me feel amazingly better.

"*Ba noi* says your progress is astounding," Kylee praised. "Her friends are all dying to meet you, you know."

"I'll bet," Tara said. "No doubt the real thing is a bit rarer than most of that crowd is willing to admit."

Kylee scowled. "How do *you* know how common the sensitivities are? Where's the research on that?"

I scarfed down the rest of my peanut butter cup. Kylee was right about one thing: I did need chocolate. "Here, finish this," I said quickly, spooning half my uneaten yogurt into Tara's cup and the other half into Kylee's, hoping to prevent another battle. Even with Tara onboard with the supernatural-that-really-isn't, the two's approaches to dealing with it couldn't be more different.

"Kali knows there are a whole lot of whackos out there who think they're gifted when they're really just delusional," Tara insisted. "She doesn't need to get derailed by all that hocus pocus. She needs to focus on what's going on with her, and what can be verified."

Kylee rolled her eyes with a groan.

"It's caramel supreme," I tried again, pointing to their cups.

"That 'hocus pocus' just taught Kali how to get her life

back!" Kylee protested.

Mercifully, my phone chose that moment to ring. It was my dad's tone — a trumpet fanfare. I shushed Tara's imminent comeback and picked up. My dad never texted and only rarely called, and when he did it was never just to chit chat.

"Hello? Dad?"

"Hey, darlin'," he said cheerfully.

I relaxed a little. "Hi. What's up?"

"I want you to come out to the base."

I paused. This was weird. "The base? For what?"

"There's something I want to show you. Won't take too long. You coming or not?"

I swallowed. The Colonel was used to quick responses, and those in the affirmative. My mother and I were allowed a certain leeway, of course, but there was something in his tone now that brooked no dissent. Still, I hesitated. I wasn't ready to see him. I had yet to wrap my own mind around the DNA results. What — if anything — should I do about them? What if he remembered the project and asked to see my profile, like, today? And what if he didn't ask about it? Ever?

"Kali!" he barked. "This is important. Where are you now?"

"I'm at the mall," I answered, rising. "Just give me long enough to drop off Kylee and Tara and I'll be there, okay? Where?"

"Park out by the BX," he instructed, his voice jovial again. "I'll keep an eye out for you."

We hung up. Tara and Kylee collected their cups and stood, studying me with concern. "What's up at the base?" Tara asked finally.

"No idea." I pulled my keys out of my pocket. The toddler was howling now, and his angst was eating at my stomach lining. Keeping the blinds down constantly wasn't easy. "But ready or not," I said weakly, "I guess I'm about to find out."

—ᴍ—

I didn't get to the base much, other than to drop off or pick up my dad, who considered driving himself to work every day to be "wasteful" and who delighted in bumming rides off anyone he could coerce. This habit had the unfortunate effect of leaving him stranded in bizarre places at bizarre times, to the point where my mother no longer blinked an eye at being called to fetch him at the hardware store, or on a street corner, or at a taxidermist's shop in the next county, and return him to wherever he was actually supposed to be. It was a quirk she found amusing, which I could only attribute to true love. But I wasn't complaining either, since the car I was driving right now would otherwise be sitting at the base.

I got clearance to pass through the gates and then wound my way around to the exchange. My dad was nowhere to be seen, so I pulled into a spot and parked. I was out of the car and walking toward the door when I saw them: my dad, another middle-aged man wearing business casual, and a guy in a yellow tee shirt and cargo shorts who looked like a football player.

All three of them turned to me and smiled.

"Matt!" I exclaimed happily, hustling toward him.

His eyes twinkled as he stepped away from our fathers and met me halfway, enveloping me in a brief, but hearty, bear hug. "Surprise!" he said, laughing. "Bet you didn't expect to see me here, did you?"

"Um... no!" I said, laughing with him. Matt's father worked at Hickam Air Force base on Oahu, and during

EMPATH   117

my family's house hunting trip, the two officers had coerced Matt into giving me a tour of the island. Despite high potential for disaster, it had worked out great. I genuinely liked Matt, who despite being a hopeless jock was kind, sincere, and generally fun to be around. He had even invited me to the Spring Fling at his high school and introduced me to all his friends. "What are you *doing* here?" I asked, still stunned.

"College visit," he answered cheerfully. "I knew we were going to do it sometime this spring, but I didn't realize you lived so close. Then this morning Dad said he wanted to drive up to Cheyenne and see some people at Warren before we flew back, and I said, 'Well, all right!'"

I smiled. I didn't need to ask *which* college. He meant the Air Force Academy, which was a couple hours away near Colorado Springs. I stole a glance at my dad. As expected, he was grinning like the cat who ate the canary. Matt, being the son of an Air Force officer who also wanted to be an Air Force officer, was the stuff my father's dreams were made of... his dreams for me, that is. Five minutes after meeting Matt, Mitch Thompson had been mentally walking his only daughter down the aisle and handing her over to a lifetime of preordained bliss.

It wasn't going to happen, of course. But that didn't mean I wasn't happy to see the guy.

"I'm so glad you made the detour!" I said honestly.

"You want to grab a bite?" he asked. "We can't stay much longer, but I'm starving. What have you got at the BX?"

"Subway and Burger King," I answered. "Take your pick."

"You two go on," my father said with a wink. "We'll catch up with you later."

The undisguised glee on his face disturbed me, given

that he knew full well how I felt about Zane. It seemed like, in blocking out all knowledge of my abilities, he had blocked out Zane's existence as well.

"I'm thinking Subway," Matt said, steering me away from our fathers and towards the entrance. "But I'm hungry enough I may do both."

"Go ahead," I laughed. "Knock yourself out. I just had a fruit smoothie, some microwave popcorn, part of a frozen yogurt, and a peanut butter cup."

He groaned. "No more talk of food until I get some, okay?"

I laughed again. In a few minutes we were settled into a booth and Matt sighed with contentment as he downed his first bite of burger. "Oh, yeah. That's the stuff."

I studied him as he ate. We had texted back and forth a few times since I left Oahu, but nothing too heavy. I knew that his water polo team had won the regionals; he knew that my parents had already preregistered me for Frederick High. I'd also been texting with a friend of his named Lacey, a girl I'd met at the dance whom I'd felt an instant connection with. Starting into a new school for senior year could have been a horror, especially since I was having to leave Tara and Kylee. But thanks to Matt, I was actually looking forward to it.

"So," he said after putting away most of a burger and a couple bites of sub. "Whatever happened with the guy who was in the car accident? He doing okay?"

I tensed. Of course he would want to know. I did recruit him, in a panic, to drive me to the Honolulu airport when I realized that Zane was alive and in a hospital on the mainland. It had all been a huge mess, because early on, before I realized that Zane (a) had feelings for me, too, and (b) was not deceased, Matt and I had started to date. I had been trying to reverse that course, but never really got the chance. Not that I left Matt in limbo — I was such a wreck when I left, the fact that I had deep feelings for the injured mystery guy would have been obvious to a deaf tomato. But he had every right to ask what the status was now.

"He's much better, thanks," I said evenly.

"You guys dating?"

I didn't hesitate. I just nodded. It might not be technically true, but to say anything else would be even more dishonest. I had no intention of playing mind games with Matt. I wanted my feelings to be clear. He deserved that.

"I see," he said lightly, reaching for another handful of fries. "So what happens when you move?"

"Well, actually," I admitted, "he's already moved to Oahu. He's there now."

Matt's face fell. He swore out loud.

Despite the implication, I couldn't help but smile. He was being intentionally comic about it.

"Seriously?" he railed. *"Seriously?"*

I nodded again.

"Well, fine," he said, raising his palms in defeat. "I give up. For now. But if you ever decide to ditch this guy, you let me be the first to know, okay?" His voice was so casual, his expression so friendly and guileless, it was difficult to tell if he was serious or not. But I rather thought he was.

"You got it," I agreed.

"So," he began, moving swiftly to another subject. "You all ready to move? Boxes packed?"

"Haven't done a thing," I admitted. "But I have a week still."

He nodded. "We military brats have it down. I was ready in 24 hours last time."

"Impressive!"

He smirked. "Not really. I got all my sports equipment packed, but I accidentally dumped half my clothes in the Goodwill box, and I left my bass guitar and my amp over at my friend Nate's house."

"You play the bass?" I asked, surprised.

"Not anymore," he said ruefully. "But Nate does."

I laughed. "So, what are you planning to do over the summer? You have a job yet?"

He smiled broadly. "I do. Got a great one. I'm going to wait tables at a Mexican restaurant with my buddy Alan. His uncle owns the place. Money's pretty good, with tips, and I'll get to hang on the North Shore."

I brightened. "You mean *La Ola*? In Haleiwa?"

"That's the one! You been there?"

"Not yet," I answered, remembering the colorful sit-down restaurant along the tourist town's main strip. It had looked inviting, but I hadn't sampled much in Haleiwa except fast food. "I'll make a point of it, now."

"Just make sure you bring enough cash for a decent tip," he teased. "What are you going to do this summer?"

The question stopped me cold. What *was* I going to do this summer? I had been so fixated on being with Zane, I'd forgotten all about my financial picture. When we were together before, I'd been on vacation, but I couldn't very well hang out on the beach doing nothing the entire summer. Not if I was ever going to save up enough to help Tara and Kylee visit.

"I don't know," I answered finally. "But I need a job. Any suggestions?"

His mouth twisted. "Gee, that may be tough, Kali. Pretty much everybody's already got their applications in, you know? Even fast food fills up over the summer." He thought a moment. "Maybe Lacey could get you a

lifeguard spot. She works at one of the county pools, and
she says they have trouble finding people."

I sighed. "I can't even swim." Hadn't I told him that
already?

He looked shocked. "Seriously? You'd make a pretty
sucky lifeguard then."

"You think?"

"I'll ask around," he offered with a shrug. "Maybe
somebody knows of something."

"Thanks. How's Lacey doing, by the way?"

A flicker of something crossed his baby blue eyes. I
couldn't feel his emotions in the slightest, which surprised
me, given how little I'd been around him compared to
random guys at school like Lucas. But where the empath
thing failed, my natural perception was often the keenest.
His fleeting expression of angst and the tense set of his
shoulders sent their message loud and clear. Something
was wrong with Lacey. He was worried about her.

"She's good," he lied. "Same old Lace, you know?"

I caught his eyes. "Not buying it, Matt. What's wrong?
Really?"

He blinked back at me with surprise. Then he sighed
and sat back in his chair. "Aw, man. I don't know. It's just
such a mess. With Ty and everything. I don't know what
to do."

I leaned forward and snatched one of his fries. "Go
on," I urged, sensing a need to talk. Guys resisted it,
usually, but I had learned that a sympathetic ear could
coax even the stubbornest of them to share, as long as
there was no judgment involved. I didn't get called the
"gal pal" of Cheyenne for nothing. "Maybe I can help," I
offered.

He sighed again and ran both hands roughly over his
head of short-cropped brown hair. "I don't know. I guess

a girl's point of view wouldn't hurt." He paused another moment, then groaned. "It's Ty. He and Lacey have been dating, like, forever."

"Since middle school, she told me," I supplied.

"Yeah," he agreed. "She's always been crazy about him. And he says he loves her, too." He went quiet again.

"But?" I prompted.

Matt let out a growling sound. "But he's cheating on her."

"No!" I cried out, upset. I had only met Lacey briefly, but her dedication to the unseen Ty had been obvious. She was a funny, genuinely sweet person... she didn't deserve that. I wanted to ask Matt "are you sure?" but that would be a stupid question. Of course he was sure. It was obviously eating at him.

"Yeah," he responded gruffly. "It's a girl Ty's been working with. He works crazy hours, but they're not as crazy as Lacey thinks they are."

I growled along with him. "Well, that totally sucks."

Matt drummed his knuckles on the table restlessly. "I don't know what to do, Kali. Ty's my best friend and all... But I really just want to wring the guy's neck, you know?"

"Want me to do it?"

He smiled sadly. "I wish to God Lacey would just break up with him. He's given her enough reason to about four times over, even without the cheating. But she's just built so loyal... she's like a damned puppy dog."

Matt was right. Lacey did seem like the kind of girl who would give a guy every benefit of the doubt.

"I wish I didn't even know about it," he lamented. "But the thing is, Ty admitted it to me himself. He was having some 'crisis of conscience,' if you can believe that."

"Nope," I said cynically.

"Well, you shouldn't," he agreed. "He told me about it

and I told him to cut it the hell out and he said he would. He claimed he really did love Lacey and didn't want to break up with her."

I knew what was coming. "But then he kept cheating anyway?"

"Yep."

I sat back in my seat and exhaled loudly. "Then you have to tell her, Matt."

His eyes held mine a moment, their depths plagued with misery. He let his forehead bang on the tabletop. "I can't," he groaned, his voice muffled.

"She has to know," I reasoned. "If she forgives him anyway, that's her business. But she has to know."

"Why?" he garbled, his head still down. "You know it'll kill her."

"She'll be devastated," I agreed. "But wouldn't *you* want to know, if you were in her shoes?"

He lifted his head and scowled. "If I were in her shoes, I'd have flattened the inconsiderate lying bastard years ago."

"He's *your* friend!" I said, surprised by his venom.

Matt looked suddenly thoughtful. For a long moment, he didn't speak. "You know what? I was wrong, what I said before. Ty isn't my best friend." He straightened. "Lacey is."

My heart warmed. "You said it," I noted with a smile. "I didn't."

He slapped both hands on the table, making the empty ketchup cup jump. "Damned right! To hell with Ty and whatever he wants. Lacey deserves better."

He smiled at me. "You're good at this stuff, you know?"

I laughed out loud. "I didn't do anything!"

"Yeah, you did," he insisted. "You helped me put

things in perspective. Thanks." His more easygoing grin returned. Then he rose. "So, no burger and sub combination is complete without a vanilla shake to top it off. Can I get you one, too?"

Now it was my turn to bang my forehead on the tabletop. How much more junk food could I possibly eat in one afternoon?

"Come on," Matt cajoled. "It's a special occasion. Your dad said it was your last day of school, right? And in just a week, you'll be back on Oahu!"

I turned my head sideways and grinned at him. "Make it chocolate."

chapter 11

"If you want any of that winter stuff, just take it," I urged, pointing to the growing mound of clothes I had thrown in a heap under my window. "The rest is going to charity."

Tara paused in her job of putting together cardboard boxes and sighed. "I guess you won't be needing the mittens and the snow boots so much, huh? After a couple months, you'll think fifty-five degrees is freezing."

"Ooh!" Kylee squealed, pulling something from the pile. "You really don't want your white ski jacket? I'll take it!"

I shrugged. "I'm keeping enough warm stuff for travel, but the new house doesn't have much closet space."

Tara handed me a finished box. "That's all of them. You want me to start putting stuff in?"

I fought back another wave of sadness. When I was alone, I was so excited about moving to a tropical paradise *and* seeing Zane again that I could hardly stand it. But whenever I looked at my friends, the thought of saying goodbye made my insides feel heavy as lead. And I knew that it was even worse for them. *They* weren't going anywhere. Still, they were obviously trying their best to be happy for me.

"Sure, thanks," I answered Tara. "Maybe that pile of books on my desk?"

My phone made my favorite noise in the world. Zane's new ringtone: a rooster crow.

I whipped it out of my pocket.

"Text?" Kylee said excitedly. "Do tell!"

"He sent me a picture," I explained, studying the

screen. "It's the military bunker on the beach near Turtle Bay."

"Why would he send that?" Tara asked.

I read the text, and my heart skipped a beat. "He says, 'So why does looking at this thing depress the hell out of me?'"

My friends blinked back at me, confused. "Say what?" Kylee asked. "I didn't know anything bad happened to you on the beach."

I sank down on the edge of my cluttered bed. "Nothing bad did happen *there,*" I explained. "But it's where we were sitting the day he told me about his mother. The whole story of her coming down from the high of being a famous soap actress to the low of being an unemployed addict, and his having to work all the time just to eat, and getting stuck in foster care the beginning of his senior year, and then her ODing and dying on him. It was horrible enough for him to tell it and for me to hear it. I can't imagine living through it."

"It makes sense then, how he feels," Tara said thoughtfully. "It's just like we thought, Kali. He sees that bunker now and has no idea what happened there, but he has a strong emotional association with it. A negative one."

I looked back at her. "You must be right." I texted him back quickly and explained that nothing bad had actually happened at the bunker — at least nothing he didn't already know about. Even as I did that, and even as sad as I felt myself to be reminded of his past, a part of me was newly excited. If he remembered how he *felt* at the bunker, I could take him to other places —

"Hey, girls! How's it going?" My father's boisterous greeting made us all jump.

Kylee and Tara greeted him with their usual nervous

respectfulness. The Colonel's attempts at playing "casual civilian dad" with my female friends always did fall woefully short — but he tried.

"Um... kind of slow," I admitted. "I can't believe how much stuff I've collected just since we moved to Cheyenne!"

"Same with your mother," he said ruefully, not being one to collect much of anything himself, except military memorabilia. "But here," he said, holding out a yellowed banker's box. "I found your grandmother's things. This was all the way at the back of the attic — I figured it'd take another move to unearth it!"

I rose slowly and took the box from him. *Kalia's things.* I hadn't looked through the box since I was a child. He had looked for it, halfheartedly, when we filled out the ancestry forms, but he hadn't wanted to unload the entire attic at the time.

"Speaking of which, did you ever get those test results back?" he asked.

I could sense Tara and Kylee stiffening; the room grew suddenly warmer. "There was a delay at the lab," I said truthfully. "But Mr. Stedman said he would get the results to us, even if he had to mail them over the summer."

My father shrugged. "Oh, well. They should get forwarded with everything else, then." He cast a glance around my room, which looked like a cyclone had hit it. "Better get a move on," he chastised. "The truck will be here early tomorrow. Thanks for your help, girls!"

"You're welcome, Sir," Tara and Kylee answered.

With a smile and a wave, he left.

I sank back down on the bed.

Kylee slipped over and shut the bedroom door behind him. She whistled. "Girl, you were *smooth!*"

"I don't want to have to lie about it," I said miserably.

"But I can't show him the results! Not yet anyway. Maybe never. I feel like... oh, I don't know. That it's not my place, you know? He's perfectly happy with the way things are. He loved his father, and his grandparents. You should have heard how proud he was reading through the names in that Swedish bible!"

"I see what you mean, Kali," Tara agreed. "It's obvious he has no idea. If he had the slightest suspicion, he wouldn't have put you in the position you're in. He would either have told you, or refused to consent to the testing, or something!"

"What about your mother?" Kylee asked. "Have you told her?"

I shook my head. "I've thought about it. But once I did, she'd be in the same awful spot I'm in. And I feel like she wouldn't be able to keep it from him, because they tell each other everything. If it's best he never knows, then she can't know either."

They said nothing for a minute. Then Kylee moved closer. "Maybe there's something in the box that could help? "

We all looked down at it. "I don't think so," I answered. "My dad's been through it all himself you know, more than once. It's mostly stuff about his parents' wedding, and birth announcements and stuff. There was a bronze baby shoe..."

"It can't hurt to check, Kali," Tara said gently. "Your dad might not have been looking for what you're looking for."

I stared at her. "What *am* I looking for?"

"A good reason to tell your dad the truth," Kylee answered. "Or *not* to. Either way, more information can't hurt, right? What little you know now isn't helping anybody."

I removed the lid. "I guess you're right."

Kylee and Tara gave the stuff on my bed a shove and made room to sit on either side of me.

"Her wedding dress was on top," I said. "I remember that." I set the lid aside and pulled out the carefully folded heap of aged fabric. It wasn't a typical wedding dress; it was too plain. Cream-colored cotton, tea-length, with a modest neckline and no lace or frills.

"Oh my, she was tiny!" Kylee commented.

"And to think I wanted to get married in it myself someday," I lamented. "I couldn't get *half* of me in it now, and even if I could, it would be a miniskirt!"

I refolded the dress carefully and laid it aside. "Here's my dad's bronzed baby shoe," I explained, pulling out the brittle, once-frilly little shoe and setting it aside with the dress. "I remember she had a scrapbook, and then a bunch of loose pictures and cards and stuff..."

My memory seemed to be accurate. I handed the scrapbook to Tara and a thin paper high school yearbook to Kylee. Beneath them was an envelope stuffed full of cards and letters. I moved that aside, reaching instead for the few loose photographs that lay at the bottom of the box.

"The picture I know Kalia best from is her wedding picture," I explained. "It's always been framed and kept out along with my parents' wedding picture and the one of my mom's parents. But I liked looking at these pictures of her too, when I could." I held up a tattered black-and-white snapshot. "This is Kalia with her parents, and her brothers. There were five kids in the family."

Kylee and Tara leaned in with interest. "Poor thing," Tara quipped. "Surrounded by all that testosterone. I can *so* relate!"

The picture was grainy, but the architecture of the old

wood-frame house and the tropical plants and trees surrounding made the whole scene scream Hawaii. I pointed to a girl of thirteen or fourteen, standing next to her mother beside a dilapidated car. Her four brothers looked both motley and mischievous, shirtless with ragged shorts, flyaway hair, and impish grins, but my grandmother — despite the plainness of her clothes — looked like a fashion model. She was a natural beauty, pure and simple. Her long dark hair hung to her waist, framing a striking face with high cheekbones, large expressive eyes, and a bright, happy smile. "She was the middle child," I remembered. "Her dad died of lung cancer a couple years after this picture was taken, and the family had a really hard time. Kalia worked a civilian job at the Air Force base, in the cafeteria, while she was going to high school. That's how she met my grandfather." I paused a moment, then corrected myself. "I mean Albin Thompson. He was stationed in Honolulu, at Hickam, during the Korean War."

I fingered through a few more photos: a picture of Kalia's parents when they were young, and several pictures of a young Kalia with female friends. "My dad never did know who any of these girls were," I said with a sigh. "She didn't label anything. I guess she figured she would always remember."

"Oh, look at that!" Kylee exclaimed as I flipped to the last picture. "Is that your dad?"

I nodded. It was a picture of Kalia as a young woman, her hair now short and fixed into the stiff, unnatural curls that were stylish in the fifties. She wore a dress that looked like Sunday best, and on her hip she held a toddler with a thick head of dark, unruly hair. I had seen the picture before. But this time I noticed something else.

"My dad said this was the last picture ever taken of

her," I explained. "He didn't frame it because it made him sad. Now I can see why."

The telltale curve of Kalia's abdomen, meaningless to me before, now spoke volumes. "She must have been pregnant with her second child when she died," I thought out loud. "I didn't know that."

"What did she die of?" Tara asked.

"A brain aneurysm," I replied. "Dad said that his dad told him it happened very quickly and unexpectedly. Albin was devastated. Not to mention completely clueless about how to take care of a toddler. Somehow Albin managed to get transferred closer to home in Minnesota, and my grandparents took care of my dad until my step-grandmother Lotta came into the picture a few years later."

Tara and Kylee asked no more questions, and for a long time they each looked through the books on their laps while I dove into the packet of correspondence. It was as uninteresting as I remembered. Mostly cards and brief notes of congratulations on her marriage and on my father's birth. Christmas cards signed simply with names and well-wishes. A few letters from girlhood friends, who wrote mainly about themselves. Two high school English papers, both about the war. Much of the paper was brittle and crumbling, and the packet bottom was littered with broken-off corners of notepaper and discarded bits of torn-open envelopes. I found no correspondence from anyone in Kalia's family. I might have been surprised by that, if my father hadn't told me that her mother had died not long after he was born, and that her brothers, all teenagers or young twenties by that point, had scattered. When no one from Kalia's family had showed up at her funeral, Albin got really upset, and he had never tried to contact them again.

"Here are the dates, Kali," Tara said finally, after she finished studying the scrapbook. I remembered that it was fairly short, having only been started at Kalia's wedding. It contained the usual: news clippings, ticket stubs, cut-outs from church bulletins, event programs. "Kalia and Albin were married on August 8th, 1953," Tara announced. "He was twenty-five; she was only eighteen. Your father was born on February 23, 1954."

I blew out a breath. "A shotgun wedding, obviously. Still, that doesn't really tell us much. My father would have been conceived in" — I counted backwards — "late May, probably. He's always told me that his parents met at a Christmas party at the base, and that for Albin, it was love at first sight. So they must have been dating eight months or so before they got married."

The ache in my stomach, which began when the results of my DNA testing first sunk in, was getting worse. All my life I had idolized Kalia... my hauntingly beautiful Hawaiian grandmother, who had died so young, so tragically. I had looked at her pictures and imagined that I knew her. Her bright smile and dazzling eyes had always seemed so full of warmth, and humor, and adventure...

But my father was not her husband's child.

"This is so funny, Kali," Kylee said suddenly, breaking my melancholy. "Kalia's classmates wrote in her yearbook, just like we do, and the funny thing is... they wrote all the same things! Seriously, you could swap out some of the names, and I would think this yearbook was mine. Never mind that it was all written like sixty years ago. Sounds like your gram was the life of the party!"

I looked at the handwriting scrawled over the blank pages at the end of the yearbook. Many of the entries were jazzed up with hearts and flowers and indecipherable cartoon drawings.

"The book itself is bare bones," Kylee continued. "Which isn't surprising since there was a war going on. They didn't get individual pictures, and the sports and clubs were pretty thin. But these guys still knew how to party! Look at these crazy dance pictures! And did you know your grandmother was voted 'Most Popular?'"

"I did," I said, able to grin a little again. No grade-school girl would ever miss *that*. Particularly one who'd never been "popular" with any school crowd except the faculty, which from a social standpoint was absolute death.

"I read every entry," Kylee continued, sounding disappointed. "But I didn't see anything about her dating anybody — either a dashing young officer from the base or anyone else. Not that anyone necessarily *would* mention that, but you never know."

"Let me have a look," Tara said, extending a hand.

Kylee passed the book over. "They're all talking about graduating in a matter of days, so I'm guessing it came out in May or June. It says 1953."

Tara flipped the pages at the end back and forth, staring hard at the binding.

"What is it?" I asked.

She turned her blue eyes up to mine. The glasses were back again — had been back ever since the prom. She claimed the contacts bothered her eyes and she wasn't ready to wear them full-time yet, but Kylee and I both suspected that what she really wasn't ready for was six foot two and went by the name of Jack. "Kali," she said intently. "A page has been torn out, here."

My pulse picked up a notch. I looked at the binding where she pointed. A thin, irregular ridge of paper poked out from its center.

"It was in here when everyone signed the book," Tara added. "You can tell from what this guy Kimo wrote down here in the corner. Part of it is obviously missing."

"I noticed that one was weird," Kylee said vaguely. "But I didn't think..."

"Torn out," I echoed, the sick feeling getting worse again.

What exactly had Kalia been trying to hide?

I took the yearbook from Tara's hands and replaced it in the box along with the rest of my grandmother's possessions.

The life of the party.

"Let's get back to packing," I said dully, standing up. "I've got to decide how much of this crap I'm taking with me."

My stomach ached abominably.

"And how much I need to let go of."

chapter 12

My dad was like a kid opening birthday presents. Nothing excited the man more than moving to a new location and a new base, which was one reason why he was one of the oldest colonels in the Air Force. The joke was that the military couldn't get rid of him. The reality was that he couldn't imagine a life outside of it. It was a miracle that my mother had convinced him to let us live off base in Cheyenne; it was a double miracle that she'd done the same on Oahu, considering the insane cost of housing anywhere around Honolulu.

But here we were.

"Now, Kali, darlin'," he said for the eightieth time as he drove into our new neighborhood in our new (used) car. "You could fit this whole house in your mom's living room and dining room in Cheyenne. And it needs a little TLC, for sure. The neighborhood's a bit congested and it's got a totally different feel from the wide open spaces out West... but I'm sure we'll all get used to it in time."

"I know, Dad," I said mechanically, my heart pounding. My face was so close to the glass of the car windows I might as well have squished my nose flat like a little kid. From my first view of the coastline as the plane landed — the raw beauty of breaking whitecaps on a sea of blue, surrounding a paradise of green — I had been mesmerized. Stepping outside at the airport, the warm wind and lofting scent of flowers were like a caress. The typical bustle and ugliness of city traffic didn't faze me; I saw only the palm trees, the tropical bushes, the sharp green volcanic peaks towering into the clear blue sky.

O.M.G.

After all these months, it was finally happening. I had my beloved Hawaii back.

Now all I needed was Zane.

"Here it is!" my father crowed, turning off the winding street directly into a carport framed with painted wooden latticework. "Home sweet home!"

From inside the carport, I could see nothing. I hopped out of the backseat and moved to the patch of grass outside the front door that could only be loosely termed a front lawn. I looked up. I had seen pictures of the house before, but the structure in front of me now appeared only half the remembered size. The paint on the trim was peeling and the concrete stepping stone under my feet was cracked and wobbly.

I didn't care. The breeze picked up my hair and tossed it across my shoulders while rumpling the fronds of the tall coconut palm beside the carport. A huge bush by the front window was covered with giant orange blossoms. Over the roof loomed the sharply angled side of a mountain peak that was lush and green as a jungle.

"Hello," I whispered.

I was inside the door the second my father opened it. The living/family room was a featureless rectangle. To my right was a small kitchen with frighteningly aged metal cabinets and scratched white appliances. Just beyond it was a square nook barely bigger than the average kitchen table. Other doors appeared to lead to the master bedroom and the bathroom. The whole place seemed close and smelled slightly musty.

I didn't care. All across both the front and back walls were large windows streaming with sunlight, with screen wire on the outside and movable glass louvers on the inside to let in the balmy breezes. And outside of those windows was my Oahu.

"There's a deck leading off the kitchen," my mother said to me. "I'm hoping we can eat a lot of our meals out there. The view is lovely. At least if you're looking up!" She turned to my father, and her voice lowered. "You'd think they could have cleaned the kitchen a little better," she grumbled.

"Now, Diane," my father soothed. But I was no longer paying attention. I had found the stairway and was on my way up. The house had only two bedrooms; mine was a sort of loft that occupied the whole of the small half second story.

The wooden stairs creaked under my feet. The twist in the stairway had a ceiling so low that even I had to duck my head. There was no upstairs bathroom; the one full bath below would have to be shared with my parents.

I didn't care.

I turned into my new room. The carpeting appeared to have been patched together from a stack of cast-off store samples. The ceiling was open to the gently slanted roof. At either end was a closet, each consisting of a recess in the wall with one shelf, a hanging bar, and no door. There were two windows, one on each side of the house, and just enough full-height floor space for a twin bed, a dresser, a chest of drawers, and maybe a trashcan.

None of that mattered. My hand went immediately to the glass-louvered door at the bedroom's back end. I unlocked it, turned the knob, and stepped out.

Perfect. My own private lanai was no more than a leveled spot on a patch of the first-floor roof. But it was almost as big as the bedroom. And the view... *oh my.*

A sweeping panoramic view of the Honolulu skyline and harbor, it was not. We couldn't have afforded that if it had come in a house half this size and twice as old. But to me, at this moment, it was the most beautiful view *ever*. The house was perched high among the sharp green peaks, and while a look down showed a mishmash of other houses and yards and privacy fences and barbecue grills and kids' bikes and lawn tools and just plain junk, a look up showed a glimmering, shining world of fresh, blazing green and azure blue. At present, not a cloud was in the sky, but I knew that before long, giant purplish masses would appear from nowhere, rolling in and around the dramatic peaks, promising brisk winds and a cooling splash of rain. Here I could sit, year round, looking out, breathing deep, drinking in the unending natural beauty and forgetting everything else in the world. Even the shadow of the little boy climbing on the rooftop beside me.

"Well, Kali?" my father asked. He and my mother had come up the stairwell behind me. "What do you think?" he begged hopefully. "Do you like it?"

I turned and smiled at them both.

"I *love* it."

I stared at my phone with gritted teeth. Its silence was killing me.

I had texted Zane as soon as the plane landed, and I still hadn't heard a thing. He didn't know exactly when we were arriving, true. I had been deliberately vague about that because I wanted the chance to surprise him. But the closer the big day became, the colder my feet had gotten. Could I even find where he was living? Did I plan to just stalk the beach until he appeared? And most frightening of all — would he really appreciate a drop-in visitor, when he'd so obviously discouraged me from visiting him in

California?

"It was in a box labeled 'Kitchen,'" my mother said, her voice harassed. "You'd think that would be plain enough. Unless they lost it altogether..." A lock of her hair, curly and unruly as mine, though much shorter, had escaped from her hairband and was hanging in front of her eyes. "It must be around here somewhere. If not, we'll have to shop tonight. I can't manage without the utensils and the cookware!"

I rose quickly from the kitchen floor, where I had been helping to unpack the dishes. "Shop tonight" was not a phrase I wanted to hear. We had only the one car still, and I *had* to get to the North Shore. Losing my wheels was not acceptable. "I'm sure it's here somewhere," I said with conviction, heading for the stack of boxes in the family room. "I'll find it."

My dad, who had been carefully placing his favorite books on his favorite bookshelf, also stopped what he was doing and joined in the search. He surveyed my efforts with a grin. "Got other plans for the evening, I take it?"

I grinned back, though I was pretty sure that the plans he was imagining involved different personnel than my own. My dad rarely acknowledged my situation with Zane, which was annoying; but I knew it was no reflection on Zane as a person. Even if the perfect son-in-law (a.k.a., Matt) were not in the picture, the unseen surfer boy's existence fell into the same can't-deal-with-it nether zone as my seeing the shadows. Out of sight, out of mind.

But that was about to change.

"I'm hoping to take the car and drive to the North Shore to see Zane," I admitted. I looked back at my phone. "But I'm not sure when, yet."

My father's face fell. He harrumphed. "Well, it can't be too late. You'll be jetlagged, you know. Midnight here will feel like three in the morning."

"I know, Dad," I said automatically, then realized that wasn't true. I hadn't even considered the time change. What did it matter? I was seeing Zane *today*, and nothing was stopping me.

I stared at my silent phone again, then shifted another box to read its label. Where *was* the stupid kitchen one my mom wanted?

"Have you heard from him since we landed?" my mother asked, poking her head out from the kitchen.

I felt a sinking feeling in my gut. So, she thought his silence was odd, too. "No," I admitted. "I'm not sure where he is."

"Did he know we were flying in today?" she pressed.

"Not exactly," I said with a sigh. "I kind of led him to believe it would be tomorrow."

"Why'd you do that?" my dad asked, sounding surprised. He knew I didn't play mind games with guys — something he appreciated in my mother as well, and had encouraged in me the second I hit puberty.

"I wanted to surprise him," I explained. "But now, I'm not so sure it's a good idea."

My mother came fully into the family room. "Maybe not, Kali," she said gently. "You still don't know exactly what his situation is... it might not be fair."

My dad looked from my mother to me with a frown. "What the hell are you talking about, his 'situation?' Does the boy want to see you or not?"

I swallowed. I couldn't believe we were seriously having this group conversation, when my dad hadn't so much as mentioned Zane's name in months. But I was glad that he remembered. And that he seemed to care. The truth was, no matter how regularly Zane sent his light and witty texts, I couldn't rid myself of the cold, hard knot of fear in my stomach. The fear that keeping up a texting relationship from a distance, and his wanting to be with me as much as I wanted to be with him, were *not* the same thing.

"Zane's always said he wanted to see me when we both got back to Oahu," I tried to explain to my dad. "He still says that. It's just that... Well, when the chance to get together came up for real, when I offered to go see him in California, it was pretty clear he didn't really want me to come."

My dad's eyes widened. Both eyebrows lifted. "Well, why the hell would he?" he asked sharply.

"Mitch!" my mother scolded, looking as horrified as I felt.

My dad flinched, then looked wounded, like a little boy who has no idea what he did wrong. He looked from one to the other of us for a long moment before a light seemed to switch on. Then he smiled. "Oh, for heaven's sake, honey," he said apologetically, touching my arm. "I didn't mean he wouldn't want to see *you*. What I meant is, he wouldn't want *you* to see *him*."

"And why not?" I demanded, still upset. He was making no sense at all.

My dad looked back at me with equal confusion. "Well... hellfire, girl! The boy nearly died, didn't he? He was in a car crash, had a coma. Most likely he was laid up in a bed, tubes coming out his arms, stuck using a damned bedpan. You think he wants a girl seeing him like that? You think he wants the likes of you within a hundred miles when he's struggling to get out of bed, ambling around with an old man's walker, letting a bunch of strange women poke needles in his butt?"

My heart skipped a beat. He seemed so certain. "But you let me invite him to come to Cheyenne for rehab," I protested weakly.

"Oh, I knew he'd never go for that," my dad said dismissively. "I'm sure he appreciated the offer. But trust me, the Florence Nightingale thing is a woman's fantasy. To a man, it's a damn nightmare."

I blinked, then looked at my mother. She shrugged. "He's probably right, Kali. The male ego knows no bounds."

"But why wouldn't Zane say so?" I asked. "If that was the only reason he didn't want to see me?"

My dad threw me a heavy look. "Did you ask him outright why he didn't want you to visit?"

I didn't answer for a moment. "No," I admitted. I had been too afraid of Zane's answer.

I put my head back down and examined the last few boxes. None were labeled 'kitchen.' "I'm going to look for that box upstairs, Mom," I declared, hoping to end the conversation. But before I could reach the staircase, a rooster crowed in my pocket.

"Speak of the devil," my father said with a grin.

I whipped out the phone. It was a text.

**Sorry – was out on the water! Where are you?
Want me to drive to Honolulu?**

I stood still at the bottom of the staircase, my blood all seeming to pool in my feet. "He wants to see me," I announced, my voice ragged. "Like... now."

"There's a shocker," my dad teased. He threw a triumphant look at my mother. "Tell me I don't know about these things!"

"You're brilliant, Mitch," she deadpanned back. Then she looked at me. "Do you want to take the car?"

I envisioned the reunion I had been looking forward to

for so long happening out front with my parents surreptitiously peeking out the window. They would want Zane to come in so they could meet him...

No way. Zane could face the Colonel's interrogation another day. But today we would meet where it all began — at the beach. "Could I?" I asked hopefully. The missing box had still not been found.

"Go ahead," my father said cheerfully, surprising me. "Your mother and I can always take the bus if we need to get to the store. One nice thing about city living!"

My mother's face showed less enthusiasm. But I knew she wouldn't stop me now. "It's fine by me," she said tiredly. "But don't stay out late or you'll get too drowsy to drive. And don't forget you've got more unpacking to do before your bed will be fit to sleep in."

"I won't," I promised, running up the stairs to change out of the grungy clothes I'd been unpacking in for the last two hours.

Stay where you are, I texted to Zane as I moved. *I'm coming to the North Shore!*

chapter 13

I was so nervous I couldn't stand it. It was a miracle I got the car out of the city traffic in one piece. But I *did* do it, and here I was. The Kamehameha highway. Ehukai Beach Park was just ahead.

My fingers had been gripping the steering wheel so tightly that my knuckles felt stiff. If my dad's motivational analysis was right, Zane could be as anxious to see me as I was to see him. But I couldn't help worrying that he might still be weak or struggling with injuries he wouldn't talk about. He said he'd been "out on the water," true, but he didn't say he'd been surfing; and if he had, he'd almost certainly be bragging about it. Maybe he wasn't strong enough to swim in such dangerous currents yet. Maybe he was just getting used to the ocean again, paddling around...

Sunset Beach Elementary School loomed up on my right. The playground stood empty; it was summer now for everyone. I turned left into the small beach parking lot. There were plenty of open spaces — a dead giveaway for lousy surf conditions.

I parked the car and took my keys from the ignition. I was beyond excited now. I was nearly sick to my stomach. I briefly considered sitting still a moment and trying to collect myself. But instead I jumped out, locked the car, stuffed the keys in my shorts pocket, and pointed my feet toward the beach. *It'll be okay,* I told myself. *No matter what kind of shape he's in, no matter how awkward it might seem, no matter how big a fool you make of yourself... it will be okay.*

I lifted my chin and looked up. I couldn't see the ocean; the beach sloped up from the parking lot to a rise where the bathhouse and lifeguard tower were. From that ridge, I knew, one could look down across a sweeping view of Ehukai beach and its world-famous Banzai Pipeline. But I wasn't interested in seeing that. I was interested in the lone figure who looked back at me from his perch on top of one of the concrete picnic tables near the ridge.

He smiled.

It was Zane.

Time seemed to stop as my eyes took in what my mind was still too muddled to believe. This wasn't the pale, frighteningly weak Zane who had left me behind in Nebraska. Nor was it the wispy, nebulous wraith I had seen here once before. This Zane was standing tall, barefoot, wearing a sun-faded tee shirt and board shorts still damp with seawater. His arms and legs were toned with healthy muscle and dotted with sand. His blond curls hung loosely about his face, fluttering with the breeze.

He was even freakin' *tanned*.

I watched, speechless, as he jumped off the table into the air and then down to the ground, his arc of movement so high and smooth I was sure it was deliberately theatrical.

He did stuff like that.

"Kali!" he called, still smiling.

I had been moving toward him; now I was ten feet away. He wasn't permanently injured. He was perfectly fine. He was better than fine. He was the most incredibly gorgeous thing I'd ever laid eyes on.

And he was smiling at *me*.

My feet stopped moving. It was too much. At any moment, surely, he would disappear. I was afraid to breathe.

But then he moved toward me. It was only a step, but

that was all it took to break my paralysis. Because with that step came a motion my heart couldn't resist even if I'd been totally and completely brain dead. He lifted his arms.

I ran into them.

What happened next was indescribable. I threw my arms around his neck; his own wrapped around the small of my back and lifted me off the ground. Beyond that I knew nothing, could think of nothing. All I could do was feel. Warmth. Ecstasy. Peace. Joy. His touch was sunshine, it was rain, it was hot cocoa and a crackling fire on a cold winter's day. I was enveloped, I was cared for, I was safe, I was *home*. I held him tighter and tighter still, savoring the warm, solid, human feel of him, marveling at his holding me back in equal measure, wondering how I could have ever lived one moment in the absence of such complete and utter bliss. The force that pulled me toward him was so strong, so alive, so insistent... This was good. It was right. It was real. It was forev —

OMG, how long have I been holding him?!

I broke away like a strong magnet lets go of metal — reluctantly and not without a kickback. I couldn't do it any other way. I took a step back and tried to collect myself. Had he let me go? Had he been trying to detach me before that? I had no idea. My brain hadn't been working.

And still, I could feel that incredible pull...

I took another half step back. Gathering all my strength, I looked up at him.

He blinked back at me. I couldn't feel his emotions, which didn't surprise me. But his green eyes weren't particularly difficult to read. Joy. Excitement. Puzzlement. Perhaps a stunned sense of shock.

Or maybe that's just what I was feeling.

At least he didn't seem embarrassed. That was all me.

We looked at each other for a moment without

speaking. I thought, for a second, that he was about to reach a hand up towards my face. But then he took a half step back instead.

"Wow," he said simply.

Had he felt the same thing? Or was he just flattered by my enthusiasm? I couldn't tell. He had a way of masking his emotions when he wanted to. It was one of many small things I knew about him. But of course, he wouldn't know me as well. Aside from two conversations at his bedside, a couple on the phone, and a whole bunch of texts, he really didn't know me at all.

I had to remember that.

Take it slow, Kali. I begged myself. *You have time.*

"You *are* going to say something eventually, aren't you?" he asked good-naturedly, raising one eyebrow.

I realized I had yet to say a word.

My lips twisted into a grin. "You have a problem with nonverbal communication?"

His smile broadened, showing straight white teeth as perfect as the rest of him. "Oh, no," he corrected. "As of now, I'm a big fan."

The ice was broken.

I smiled back at him. Then I stepped away and pointed toward the longboard leaning against the picnic table. "Been ripping a few, have you?" I said lightly. "I was worried that you weren't fully recovered yet. I guess you must be feeling pretty good."

"I feel fabulous," he returned, picking up the board and tucking it under his arm.

Tanned biceps... oh, my.

"But I'm not 100% yet," he continued. "The doctors said it could take up to a year for me to get back into peak condition; I've been shooting for three months." He began walking toward the beach, gesturing for me to

follow. "Ordinarily, I'm a patient person. But come on...
it's *Hawaii*, you know?"

Did I ever.

"Just look at that," he said with reverence as we
reached the top of the rise. "I still can't believe I'm really
here."

Neither could I. I joined him in looking out over the
sweep of beach. Pale sand, blue water, funky lava rocks,
towering green peaks beyond. This particular stretch was a
familiar sight to me. But this time, something was wrong.

"What happened to it?" I cried.

He looked at me strangely. "What happened to what?"

"The waves!" I moaned.

He laughed out loud. "It's *June*, Kali. The big surf
won't get kicking again until fall. Summer's flat as a
pancake."

I knew that. "Oh, right," I said, not bothering to hide
my disappointment. "So what have you been doing 'out on
the water?'"

He shrugged. "Just paddling around. Getting the feel
of the breaks. Every once in a while, a two- or three-footer
will roll in. Most of all, I'm getting to know the locals.
There's a pecking order here — you have to respect it and
work your way up."

I looked out at the placid ocean. Not a single surfer
was in the water — at least not a live one. The beach was
nearly deserted except for a half-dozen walkers and two
girls in bikinis who were sunbathing on mats a couple
hundred yards away. Both girls appeared to be watching
us.

Or rather, they were watching Zane.

Had he met them already? I felt an uncomfortable
twist in my stomach.

"How about we walk down the beach a bit?" he asked,

heading in the direction opposite the sunbathers.

"Sure!" I agreed, a little too enthusiastically. I couldn't feel the girls' emotions at this distance, and I wanted to keep it that way. I slipped off my sandals and joined Zane. The warm, deep sand sucked down my feet and squished around my toes. The sun shone brightly from the afternoon sky, even as my brain expected a cool, gathering Wyoming dusk.

My head spun a little. It was all too surreal.

"So tell me about the move," Zane said cheerfully as we started off. "How does it work with the military? Did you fly commercial? How do you like your new house?"

I smiled. Always, he had taken an interest in what was going on with me — even the little things. I answered his questions gladly and slid in some of my own. My feelings of awkwardness disappeared, and with each step along the calm ocean I felt my spirits rise.

Until, suddenly, he went quiet and stopped.

"What is it?" I asked. I had not been paying the least attention to where we were walking, but now I also stopped and looked around. He was staring back into the houses that lined this section of beach. Specifically, he was staring at the rental condo in which my parents and I had stayed over break.

I felt a wave of giddiness. "What are you staring at?" I repeated.

He turned. "I was hoping you could tell me. It's been messing with my mind for weeks now. Is that where you were staying when we met?"

I tried hard not to smile. "What makes you think so?"

His mouth twitched a little. Clearly, he knew my game. "Because every time I look at it, particularly that back patio, I get a very weird feeling."

"Tell me," I begged.

His green eyes held mine. "It's a jumble of different feelings, really. I'd say excitement is the main one. Optimism. Laughter. But it's not all positive. Every once and a while I'll be looking at it, and then suddenly I'll feel... very sad."

"Bittersweet," I said softly. "That about sums it up. Yes, that's where I was staying. I would talk to you on the patio so my parents couldn't hear me. It was only sad because of your situation, and then... well, when we knew you were leaving." *And a few other awkward moments,* I didn't add. "Does looking at it make you feel anything else?"

His face changed slowly into a grin. "Maybe. But I'm pleading the fifth on that one. For now."

My cheeks flushed. *Stop that!* I ordered myself. I started walking again, and he followed me.

"Kali," he said seriously, "I can really use your help. These random feelings I keep getting all over the place... they're driving me crazy."

I couldn't help but chuckle. "Welcome to my world," I quipped.

"Tell me more about that," he asked. "Any progress with the blocking thing?"

We were a good deal further down the beach before I finished filling him in on everything that had happened since our last phone conversation at prom. He was as fascinated by my abilities as he had been the first time I'd told him about seeing the shadows; if possible, even more so.

"You can't tell what I'm feeling though, right?" he asked for the second time.

"I told you I couldn't," I said with suspicion. "But you never know, things may change."

He offered his sexiest smile. The effects were devastating, as usual. "I hope not," he replied. "Some of them could get me into serious trouble."

I tried really, really hard not to blush again. "No doubt," I said. I might have sounded cool, if my voice hadn't squeaked as I said it.

Now I did blush.

He pretended not to notice. "Kali," he said with a sudden earnestness. "I hope you were serious about the do-over, because I am."

My pulse went into overdrive. I wasn't sure what to say. I wasn't sure exactly what he meant.

"I want to go back over everything that happened before," he continued. "Step by step. I want you to take me there, tell me everything you remember. So I can match up all these crazy, random feelings I keep getting with something concrete. I can't move on with my life until I do." He stopped and looked at me. "I want to know everything *you* know... about what happened with us. Is that asking too much?"

Somewhere deep inside me, a little chord of fledgling hope twisted... then snapped. Of course he was eager to see me. I was his only link to the supreme mystery that was his out-of-body experience as a wraith. The only one who could give him answers, grant him peace. Once again, just as before, he was dependent on me — and me alone.

He had no choice.

"Of course it's not asking too much," I answered, my voice as bright as I could make it while I died inside. "You know I'll help you however I can."

So that you can "move on" with your life.

With me... or without me.

"Thanks, Kali," he said warmly, flashing another killer smile.

I felt another painful twinge in my gut, and looked away.

chapter 14

Kylee and Tara didn't often agree in their advice to me. But on this point they were united: I was overanalyzing. And if I didn't cut it the hell out, chillax, and enjoy myself, they were going to dog paddle across the Pacific and kick my pessimistic butt clear to Japan. So what if Zane felt grateful to me? So what if he needed my help? That didn't mean he *didn't* care. That he *wouldn't* want to be with me regardless. Where did I get off anyway, thinking so little of myself all of a sudden?

They had a point.

I missed them terribly.

I stood in front of the louvered window in our new living room, looking anxiously out into the street. It was nearly noon; Zane could be here any second. Today was the day, he had insisted as I drove away from the beach last night, that I would have my first swimming lesson. No putting it off.

"You make sure he comes in, now," my dad ordered, watching me as he tried to repair a coffee table beat up by the move.

"I will," I agreed, trying to unknot my insides. What guy would want to miss out on the world's most sphincter-tightening "meet the father" experience ever?

My dad was, for all his bluster, really quite a pushover. But no sane human meeting The Colonel in full intimidation mode would believe that. Even Tara and Kylee were still a little afraid of him, and they'd seen the man eating cereal in Darth Vader pajamas.

A small, beat-up sedan decked out with both roof and

bike racks pulled up the street and parked along the curb. My dad stepped up to the window behind me. "Not much of a vehicle, is it?" he commented.

I wasn't sure if that was a compliment or an insult. As much as my dad worshipped planes and most other giant means of transportation, ordinary-people cars had never held the same fascination for him. Our own were always the utilitarian type — boring but functional. I decided to spin it positively. "He told me that he didn't want to spend a lot of money on a car," I explained. "He's saving up for other things."

My dad's eyebrows rose. "Such as?"

"I'm not sure," I answered, watching as Zane hopped out of the car and headed for the front door. He moved easily, confidently. He looked amazing in a bright blue polo and new board shorts. "College, I guess," I offered, trying to think of the most parent-friendly answer. I really had no idea what Zane wanted to do with his money — I only knew that he stood to inherit a lot of it when he turned twenty-one.

The doorbell rang. My father grinned and hustled to beat me to it.

Kill me now.

I stood in the center of the room, trying not to collapse, while my father shook Zane's hand, introduced himself, invited him in. My mother appeared from the kitchen; there were more introductions. My father was being intentionally intimidating, standing practically at attention as he talked, while my mother was making a laughable attempt to pretend that she — as a respectable middle-aged married woman — was *not* completely gaga over the shock of Zane's unnaturally good looks. (I had told her several times; evidently she thought I was exaggerating.)

Among the four of us, only Zane seemed to be acting normal: relaxed and upbeat. In fact, after his first glimpse of my parents, when he seemed somewhat taken aback by what was probably a flash of recognition, he seemed even more cheerful than usual.

I had to wonder what feelings he associated with them.

I tensed as the first moment of conversational silence fell, and I could see my dad inhale, revving up for his first pitch. In the game of awkward questions, the man was a master. Historical highlights had been such gems as: "So, young man, how do you plan on serving your country after high school?" and the particularly cringe-worthy "What ideas do you have for how you'll support a wife and family?" (the last being famously delivered not to any date of mine, but to a friend of Tara's brother who happened to be giving us a ride to homecoming). Fathers who let things go with the classic "what are your intentions with regard to my daughter?" had nothing on Mitch Thompson, who had long-since exhausted that line on the bewildered young hosts of grade-school birthday parties.

But whatever mortifying question my father was preparing in his head, he never got a chance to ask it.

"I wanted to thank you," Zane said smoothly, making eye contact first with my father, then with my mother. "Both of you, for letting Kali fly back to the mainland and track me down at that hospital in Nebraska. Not many parents would have done that. But the fact is, if you hadn't trusted her instincts, I don't think I'd be alive today. The doctors said there was nothing else they could do for me — that I'd given up. But your daughter dragged me back to life again."

He turned to me, his eyes twinkling.

O.M.G.

I braved a look at my dad. He'd shrunk about two inches and his face had gone pale.

"You're welcome," my mother said finally, warmly. "We're just glad it all worked out okay." She cast an amused glance at my father, then turned back to Zane. "And we need to thank you for convincing Kali to be honest with us about what she's been going through all these years. We really had no idea."

Zane smiled back at her. "I have no memory of doing that, but hey — I'll take the credit."

My mother looked at him thoughtfully. "You don't remember anything from when you were... here before?"

He shook his head. "No events. Some things do seem familiar to me, though." He cast a glance at my dad, who was currently staring, glassy-eyed, out into space. "I do remember seeing the two of you before," he admitted.

My dad snapped suddenly back to attention. "Um... what was that?" he asked stiffly, as if he had missed a question.

"I was wondering," Zane said easily, obliging, "if you were still looking to surf the North Shore. Kali said you were interested before, but the surf was too rough. It's plenty tame now, though, and I've spent a lot of time talking to the locals, learning all the best spots for getting your feet wet without breaking your neck. I'd be happy to point them out to you sometime."

I watched as my dad's internal struggle played out on his tortured face. Zane's bringing up the topic of the supernatural had thrown him into a tailspin — he still couldn't acknowledge it, wouldn't discuss it, no matter what physical evidence stood in front of him in all its glory. The fact that Zane had brought the matter up so lightly and matter-of-factly only added insult to injury, particularly when, at this point, my dad had hoped to have the fine young man reduced to a quivering mass of jelly, rather than the reverse.

Then again, he had always wanted to surf. And this *was* Hawaii.

My dad's normal color returned. "Kali says you're staying up by Backyards? That right? What you got out there right now? One, two footers?"

And with that, the surfer talk began.

Slowly, I started to breathe again.

It took some time to get Zane herded toward the door and out, particularly after my mother started telling him embarrassing anecdotes about my previous fails at learning to swim — a subject Zane took way too much interest in for my liking. But by the time we left, there were legitimate smiles all around: my dad had a firm date to rip a few on the North Shore, and my mother seemed confident that — at long last — she had finally met someone who might actually be able to keep me from drowning.

I was just happy to be alone with him again. "That went well," I praised, buckling myself into the passenger seat.

To my surprise, Zane turned to me with an anxious look. "I hope my talking about your gifts didn't upset your dad too much," he said regretfully. "I didn't mean to make our first meeting awkward for him."

I looked into his earnest face and cracked up laughing.

I had texted Lacey to ask where she was lifeguarding; when we arrived at the pool, she was on a break and waiting for us by the gate.

We hugged each other like old friends, which was

pretty ironic, since really we were new ones. She looked the same as I remembered her, short and blond with a plumpish figure, pretty face, and sunny smile. I introduced her to Zane and was forced to watch as yet another female went wide-eyed at the sight of him. She recovered quickly enough, though, and within seconds was talking to me as though we had known each other forever.

Zane soon left us alone to catch up, claiming he was anxious to "warm up with a few dives." The second he was out of earshot, Lacey whistled out loud. "Are you kidding me?!" she joked. "Wow. Poor Matt never had a chance, did he?"

"It's not like that," I protested. "I mean, it's not like there was ever any competition, certainly not based on looks. I adore Matt, but... I met Zane first, and he and I are..." I sighed. "It's really complicated."

Lacey let out a sigh herself. "Talk to me about complicated."

I studied her face and could feel, vaguely, the conflict within her. She was irritated. Frustrated. At the end of her rope. But a broken heart was not in the picture.

Matt hadn't told her about Ty.

"So, what's up with you?" I asked gently.

Her blue eyes flickered with an internal blaze. "Well, I have a boyfriend who's never around," she answered, her voice sounding way more light-hearted than I knew she was. "But that's nothing new, is it? Other than that, all is cool. Job here's pretty good, and we're all psyched for senior year. So excited you're going to be there with us!"

I smiled back at her warmly. She meant it. She really was excited. "I can't wait, either," I said honestly.

A whistle sounded, and Lacey jumped. "That's me. Gotta get back to work. Damn, he's hot!"

I followed her line of vision to the deep end of the

pool, where Zane was executing a rather magnificent dive off the high board.

"Sorry, Kali," Lacey said with a chuckle. "Couldn't help myself. You two go play. I'll catch you later." She hustled off.

I looked out over the crowd and felt a queer fluttering in my stomach. It was a community pool, full of kids of all ages as well as adults. As Zane pulled himself up the ladder, shook out his wet curls, and walked around for another dive, he might as well have been a giant, candy-sprinkled donut. Every female over the age of twelve was staring at him with her mouth open.

I dropped my bag onto an empty deck chair, shrugged off my tee shirt and shorts, and plopped down on the edge of the shallow end to dangle my feet in the water. There really was nothing I could do about it, was there? It was bound to happen now, wherever we went. Correction: wherever *he* went. My presence didn't matter one way or the other.

I cried out suddenly as a hand appeared from nowhere and tickled the bottom of my foot. Zane arose from under the water, laughing. "Love the uniform," he said, his green eyes dancing. "You ready for orientation? Fair warning: You will get wet."

I grinned back at him. Never in a million years would I admit how much time I'd sunk into picking out this stupid swimsuit. It showed no more skin than a dance leotard, but its curvy vertical side stripes and open back did as much for my boyish bod as any one-piece was going to. "Wet!" I said with mock horror. "You didn't tell me I had to get *wet!*"

Two seconds later I was drenched.

"You knew that was going to happen," he teased.

"Yeah," I admitted, laughing. "I did."

"Come in with me." He extended his arms.

Oh my. On the one hand: Zane, bare chested, inviting me into his arms. On the other hand: waist-high water. The combination was too cruel.

He took my hands. "Come *on,*" he cajoled. "I'm not going to push you into anything scary, I promise. Just come and hang in the water with me for a while. Get used to the feel of it."

His hands, clasping mine, sent waves of warmth rippling through me.

Safe. With no further thought, I slid my hips over the side and slipped into the water. "It's cold!" I winced, surprised.

"It won't be for long," he assured, backing me away from the edge to a clear spot near the middle. For a moment, as we moved, I was struck by the feelings of the swimmers around us. But with a little effort I was able to bring the blind down again. I was really getting quite good at it, when I wasn't made vulnerable with an empty, drifting mind. Or a frightened one.

We were standing in water just up to my rib cage. It was deeper than I was used to, definitely deeper than I was comfortable with. Still holding my hands, Zane began to move my arms slowly back and forth under the surface, as if we were treading water. "Now, tell me about your other lessons," he urged. "Everything you remember. What they taught and what you did. What you liked and what you didn't like."

I raised an eyebrow. My pulse was racing. I really, *really* hated deep water. "You don't seriously want to hear all that?"

"I wouldn't ask if I didn't."

I studied his eyes and decided he meant it.

I have no idea how long we stayed like that, just

standing and waving our arms underwater, talking and laughing. All I know is that at some point, I stopped worrying so much about drowning and started to relax. The water did feel... interesting. It almost made my body seem light; which was strange, since I had always imagined myself sinking like a stone. I kept waiting for him to give me some impossible assignment, like putting my face down and blowing bubbles (to my child's mind, the equivalent of waterboard torture). But he seemed to enjoy just talking.

"Your parents looked so familiar," he mused. "It's funny to think that they have no memory of me, either."

"What did seeing them make you feel?" I asked curiously.

He thought a moment. "That was strange. It was a positive feeling, but at the same time, there was this weird vibe. Almost like... jealousy?"

I smiled sadly. "I think I get that. You were comparing my parents to yours. You were pretty impressed with the Mitch and Diane still-crazy-in-love-and-acting-like-kids show." Which was understandable, I thought to myself, given that according to him, his own never-married parents barely knew each other — either before or after he was born.

He looked thoughtful. After a long moment, he turned back to me. "Your dad looks Hawaiian. You're named after his mother, right? But you take after your own mother. Is she Italian?"

"Greek," I answered, the uncomfortable, slightly sick feeling I now associated with my ancestry rearing its ugly head again. "When my mother was born her family lived in California, but after the youngest kid went to college, my grandparents moved back to Greece. I don't see them much."

"That's too bad," he sympathized. "I wish I had more memories of my grandparents. Who was the Hawaiian girl at your house? Your cousin?"

I stopped my arm motions and stared at him, puzzled. "What Hawaiian girl?"

He looked surprised. "She was standing right there in the room with you. When I first came in. I thought your dad would introduce us, but then your mom came in, and she must have slipped out."

My eyes narrowed. "What did she look like?"

He shrugged. "I was kind of focused on your dad when I saw her, but... she was young and pretty and looked... well, Hawaiian. You seriously don't remember her?"

"Zane," I said heavily. "There was no Hawaiian girl in my house. If you saw her and I didn't, she must have been a ghost."

The shock on his face made me laugh out loud. "Don't look so surprised! You knew you could see ghosts."

"Yeah, *one*, but—" he gave his head a shake. "She didn't *look* like a ghost!"

"Well, they don't wear white sheets," I teased.

"Still," he protested, "I..." He stifled the comment. "I guess she did disappear kind of mysteriously, now that you mention it."

"Maybe she'll show up again sometime," I said lightly. The truth was, I didn't particularly care. I was aware of enough forms of "energy" already — not having to deal with this particular variety was fine by me. "So," I began, anxious to bring the conversation back to the present and the living. "Are you actually going to teach anything in this lesson, or do I get my money back?"

"I hadn't planned on it," he admitted wryly. "But if you're determined to jump ahead, you could demonstrate

those two moves for me. You know, the ones you said
you'd mastered already."

I should have kept my mouth shut. "I was thinking
more in terms of watching you demonstrate something."

"At these prices?" He smirked. "Not likely. Now, go
on. Show me what you've got."

I sighed and walked back toward the shallow end. As
we moved through the water together, I couldn't help but
become aware of two particularly watchful sets of eyes.
Two college-age girls sat perched on the side of the pool
near the stepladder. They were giggling and play-screaming
and pretending to be engaged in the most hysterical of
conversations. But what they were really trying to do was
catch Zane's attention.

I tried my best to ignore them. He seemed not to
notice them at all.

I held onto the wall and attempted a practice kick.
Both girls were, of course, wearing the skimpiest of two-
pieces.

My feet sunk to the floor. Embarrassed, I switched to
the other maneuver: a simple arm flapping thing any four
year old could do in a bathtub. The girls laughed out loud.

Water splashed in my face and I banged my hand on
the concrete pool rim. "Sorry," I said miserably. "I guess I
really can't do any of it."

"Don't apologize to me," Zane replied, swooping in
close with one of his more devilish grins. "The longer I
can stretch out these lessons, the more time I get to spend
with you in that swimsuit."

He lifted a hand and brushed a lock of wet curls away
from my face. His fingers grazed my bare shoulder, and a
rash of goosebumps swept up my arm.

The girls in the bikinis stopped laughing.

For one long, exhilarating moment, I thought for sure

that he was going to kiss me. But I was wrong. With an exhale that was not quite a sigh, he dropped his hand and took a half step back.

"Enough pool time for one day," he declared. "What do you say we get back to the beach?"

chapter 15

"And here," he said happily, pointing to the exact spot on the sand where we had enjoyed a picnic lunch our first full day out together. "This place is the best. Nothing but good vibes, here."

I smiled. "This was where we had the picnic. Of course, I was the only one who ate anything. You just talked surfing non-stop, except when you were asking me about dance."

"Tell me again," he insisted.

It had been the same process all up and down the shore, by car and by foot. When he stood in certain places, looked at certain things, the feelings those sights generated told him we had been there together. I knew that, as a wraith, he had had other experiences without me, some of them also positive. But if he picked up on those too, he didn't bother to point them out. So far, his instincts of where we had spent time together were dead on. He remembered being with me at the beach across from the Dillingham airfield. He remembered the snorkeling pool at Turtle Bay. He looked with frustration at the condo where I had stayed, wanting to walk up onto the deck and look around inside, but knowing the current residents would hardly appreciate it. Everywhere we went, he begged me to tell him everything I could remember. And I did try.

But sometimes, it got complicated. Zane knew that my father had arranged for the son of another officer to give me a tour of the island, and that this guy had also taken me to a dance at my future high school. Zane also knew that he had tagged along with us. But so far he didn't know much else, and since we hadn't been back to any of those locations, he had no visuals to spark any related feelings. Except, possibly, for the stretch of Sunset Beach where Matt and I had our evening walk the night after the dance — the spot where we had kissed. There was a moment, while Zane walked near there, when I thought I saw a flicker of something troublesome pass through his eyes. But I wasn't sure, and he didn't ask me about it.

I was conflicted. A part of me wanted to get everything out in the open right away, whether he remembered any feelings about the kiss with Matt or not. I didn't want to keep it from him; it was mutual history, after all, and he deserved to know. But having him know was one thing, and telling him about it myself was another. As much as I felt I should apologize for hurting him then, it was an incredibly awkward topic to bring up when I didn't know how he felt *now*.

I had sworn up and down that I wouldn't expect too much from him too soon... or at all. Yes, he had feelings for me before — when I was the only human he could talk to. But that was no fair test. What happened between us from this point forward was all that really mattered.

No pressure or anything.

"I wish I could put everything that happened in order," he said as we began walking down the beach again. We were heading toward his place to get back into the car and retrace the steps we'd taken during my dress-shopping expedition to Haleiwa. "It's hard to keep all these random stories straight. Can you start at the beginning again, and tell me what happened each day?"

I tried not to tense. I would simply stick to the same outline I'd given him before; and if he asked for more details I would give them, come what may. I started at the beginning with our first meeting. Then I looked down the beach and nearly groaned out loud. We were about to pass yet another set of prowling females.

Being a pro surfing mecca, the North Shore was usually populated with more men than women. But today, for whatever reason, we couldn't walk fifty yards without passing some tropically tanned girl or other, every one of them eyeing Zane with a look of invitation — as if I wasn't even there. Whether I had any claim on the guy or not, it was seriously getting on my nerves.

"And then you followed us to the Foodland," I was saying. "The next time I saw you was at the condo—"

The girls came up level with us. They had to be in their mid-twenties, but that didn't stop them from not-so-subtly throwing out their chests and flashing their best smiles. "How are you doing?" one of them said silkily, her dark eyes flashing.

"Hey," Zane said in a friendly voice, smiling back at her.

The girl actually stopped walking, even though Zane and I kept on. After a couple paces, I threw a quick glance over my shoulder to catch her frowning back at us. Her companion laughed and nudged her to keep moving.

I exhaled with a sigh.

"Go on," Zane urged.

I thought a moment. "I forgot what I saying."

He looked at me curiously. "Something wrong?"

I avoided his eyes, looking further down the beach instead. Naturally, another tigress was approaching. This one was alone and wearing a thong. I released another sigh.

"Kali," he insisted. "What is it?"

I did not want to have this conversation. But I wasn't the coy type. "You must get a lot of that," I said flatly.

"Of what?" he asked.

"Of girls, women even, looking at you like..." My mind flew to the most desirable thing I could think of. "Like melted chocolate."

He blinked back at me innocently. "Melted chocolate?"

"I mean flirting with you."

He shrugged. "They were just being friendly."

It was too much. I stopped and glared at him.

All at once he dissolved into laughter.

I groaned. He knew exactly what I meant. "You are—" I stammered, irritated.

" — Like melted chocolate?" he finished, his green eyes twinkling at me.

Thoughtful Zane was attractive, yes. But playful Zane was killer, annoying male ego notwithstanding.

"I am never complimenting you again," I stated, walking away.

He jumped back into step with me. "Ouch, that's harsh!" he grinned. "And you know how much I enjoy it."

The girl in the thong was nearly level with us, and I prepared to ignore another shameless mating display. But just as she began to arch her back and run her fingers through her hair, I felt Zane's arm snake around my own and clasp my hand.

My breath caught. It was crazy how strongly his touch affected me. Just having our fingers laced together shot a pang of longing through me like a thunderbolt.

The girl lowered her eyes to the ground and moved on.

When she was out of earshot, Zane turned to me. He did not release my hand. "Better?" he asked softly.

I swallowed, sure that my heart was in my eyes. "Much," I answered.

The main drag in Haleiwa was as lively and quaint as I remembered it. Old buildings, new buildings, outdoor markets, restaurants, shave ice, tropical plants, surfboards, one giant bus full of Japanese tourists, signs for a church barbecue, swimwear, art galleries, and roaming red chickens.

"Oh, look. What about him?" Zane asked, pointing to a heavy guy in his mid thirties who was enjoying a beer next to a store hawking seashell art. "Does he look familiar to you?"

I took as close a look as I cared to at the man, then pulled my empath blind back down again. I did not care to know his feelings regarding the half-naked girl on the swimwear poster in the opposite store window. "I don't think I've seen him before, either," I admitted. "You have to remember, you spent a lot of time out surfing with these guys when I wasn't around — or wasn't paying attention. You probably shared a board with half of them."

He frowned. "I guess I'll never know for sure. It's just so bizarre. I see that guy almost every time I pass by here, and every time I look at him all I can think is, 'He's an idiot.'"

I laughed. "Maybe you should trust those feelings."

We had been strolling up and down the main drag in Haleiwa for a while now, with Zane pointing out various spots and me trying my best to explain what had happened there. His association of different feelings with visual memories was uncanny, though of course there were some things I had no clue about, the seashell guy being one of

them. But I was touched when he remembered being
worried in the dress store — a feeling which puzzled him
until I explained that we had gotten separated and he had
searched for me for a long time. The weather was sunny,
mild, and picture perfect, and walking beside him now,
solid and alive, was so much like a dream come true I felt
giddy with the thrill of it.

"Are you getting hungry?" he asked finally, as the
increase in traffic announced the arrival of rush hour —
and dinnertime.

"Starved," I answered.

"Dinner's on me, then," he said cheerfully, steering me
into a nearby shopping plaza and around to the restaurant
in the back. "I love this place. You okay with Mexican?"

I looked up at the colorfully painted logo above the
restaurant's front door. *La Ola*. The place where Matt was
waiting tables this summer. "Mexican's fine," I said
uncertainly, cursing myself even as I hesitated. The whole
story had to come out sooner or later. It was *not* that big a
deal.

"You sure?" Zane asked, holding the door half open.

"Yes," I said firmly, stepping through it. My eyes
scanned the restaurant. It was about a quarter full already.
There was a hostess, and a bartender, and two other wait
staff that I could see. No Matt.

I breathed a little easier as the hostess seated us in a
booth and told us that "Bryan" would be with us in a
minute. But I still felt uncomfortable. The latest narrative
I'd given Zane still had gaping holes, and that wasn't fair
to him. I needed to fill in the details soon, whether he
asked for them or not. Today. Before he took me home.

"It's amazing what a difference twenty-four hours can
make," Zane said cheerfully. "These last few weeks I've
stockpiled so many questions I thought we'd never get

through them. But thanks to you, I'm already feeling closer to normal again."

"Normal?"

"As in, knowing my own life," he answered. "Having no idea what went on while my body was in that hospital bed, things *I* did and said thousands of miles away, was really freaking me out. But I'm finally starting to feel better about it." His eyes wandered to a point in space over my shoulder, and his face darkened. "Not that some things don't still bother me."

"Like what?" I asked.

His gaze remained elsewhere. "I'm not a violent person, you know. Never have been. I've always been the peacemaking sort. This is probably uncool to admit, but I've never even been in a fistfight. I've always been able to talk my way out of it. And I've been in some dicey situations, believe me."

My pulse began to race. Where on earth was he going with this?

"I don't hold grudges, either. Not my style. Don't cultivate enemies; don't want any. I try to see the best in people. That's why it's so weird."

"What's so weird?" I asked anxiously.

His gaze turned back to me. He tilted his head in the direction behind my seat. "That guy over there. I saw him here a couple nights ago, and he was nice as could be. Didn't know me from jack, but was plenty friendly. Good waiter, too. And yet..."

He leaned in toward me, lowering his voice. I leaned in too, though my pulse was now stratospheric and my appetite nonexistent. "And yet," he repeated, "every time I look at the guy, I have the most amazing urge to smash his face in. You have any idea why that might be?"

"Kali!"

My heart dropped into my shoes.

Matt hustled up to the table, loaded tray in hand, his voice jovial and his face beaming. "You made it! All right! You didn't come all the way out here just to give me a hard time, did you?"

It was all I could do not to liquefy and ooze under the table.

"Hey, Matt," I said as casually as I could manage, which was not very. "We just got moved in yesterday. Today Zane and I have been checking out the beaches. How's work?"

"Awesome," Matt answered, setting two glasses of water, a bowl of salsa, and a basket of chips down before us like a pro. "This isn't my table, but what the heck — I'll get #10 another spread in a second." He glanced at Zane. "Hey, weren't you in here a couple days ago?"

"Sure was," Zane said without expression. "You talked me into the enchiladas suizas."

"Yeah! Hope you liked them." Matt looked from Zane to me again, then startled slightly. "Oh, wait. So you're..."

"That's right," I said clearly, answering his unspoken question. Could this possibly get any more awkward?

Deal with it, Kali.

"Matt, this is Zane; I told you he moved out to Oahu just recently. Zane, this is Matt, fellow Air Force brat. He's the guy who gave me a tour of the island when I came out for spring break. He also talked me into going to Frederick High next fall."

The guys exchanged another nod of greeting. "A decision you won't regret," Matt said to me, his voice still easy. "Well, I gotta get back to it. You guys enjoy your dinner." He threw a friendly smile in Zane's direction. "Hey, if you're in the mood for beef, try the guisado de res. It's awesome tonight!"

He winked at me and disappeared back into the kitchen.

I let out a ragged exhale. "I'm sorry about that," I said miserably, forcing myself to meet Zane's eyes.

He studied me back with a curious expression. I couldn't read any more; he was too good at masking his emotions when he wanted to. "What are you sorry for?" he asked evenly.

"For letting you get blindsided like that. He told me he worked here; I just didn't think about it until it was too late."

Zane took a sip of his ice water. "So, that's it."

I didn't want to know. But I asked anyway. "That's what?"

He smiled at me, but it was a small, sad sort of smile that twisted my stomach into a knot. "Where the face-punching thing comes from. He was into you, and vice versa, and I was a walking corpse. I get it."

But he didn't. "Matt liked me, yes," I explained. "And I started to like him, too — he really is a good guy. You were there for the tour, the dance, everything. I asked you to come with us and you agreed, but you said you didn't want to interfere."

"How very noble of me," he said dryly. "Did I keep my promise?"

He had let his guard down. Despite his efforts to seem poised and casual, I could see the pain in his eyes. The sight hurt me every bit as much as it had the first time, and I felt a spurt of righteous anger that we had to go through this twice.

"Of course you did. Neither of us thought there was any chance for us." I steeled myself. "But after the dance, Matt and I kissed goodnight, and you—"

"On the beach," he interrupted. "I saw you, didn't I?"

I nodded. "I thought you might be feeling something at that spot when we were there earlier today. I should have just told you all this then. I'm sorry."

He sat back in the booth. "Then what happened?" he asked.

I swallowed. This was the hardest part. "Then you told me that you were leaving. You said you couldn't stand to watch me fall in love with some other guy."

His eyes locked on mine. "And what did you say?"

A booming voice erupted. "Hey, guys! I'm Bryan. I'll be taking care of you tonight, although I see Matt's already got you started off with some chips. Can I get you some drinks?"

Somehow, mechanically, Zane and I both managed to place our orders. It seemed like years before we were alone again, but the delay was useful. I now knew exactly what I needed to say.

Feeling a surge of boldness, I reached out and took one of Zane's hands in mine. Another ripple of heat surged up my arm. "Here's the truth. The second I realized you had feelings for *me*, I never thought about Matt again — not in that way. Even though it still looked hopeless for you and me, I let myself fall for you. Totally and completely. And when you faded away, it hurt like hell."

My voice wavered. "And for what it's worth," I finished, "I wouldn't have gotten back to you in Nebraska as soon as I did if Matt hadn't driven me to Honolulu in time to catch the next plane out."

Zane's face had gone unreadable again. He raised an eyebrow. "Matt drove you to the airport? How'd you manage that?"

"I told him the truth. Or at least as much of it as could possibly make sense to him. That I had to get back to see another guy I cared about that might be dying. It was awkward."

Zane sat forward once more, adding his free hand to our joined ones. "Wait. You had just kissed this guy, like, two days before, and then you told him you needed a ride to the airport to go see some *other* guy, whom he had to think you were already involved with before you met him, and he said yes?"

"I said it was awkward."

At long last, the twinkle returned to his eyes. He massaged the backs of my hands with his thumbs, sending tremors all the way to my spine. "You know what?" he said warmly. "I think you're right. I think this Matt character really is a good guy."

I smiled with relief.

He gave my hands a squeeze, then released them.

"Wish I'd known that five minutes ago," he said lightly. "I would have ordered the guisado de res."

chapter 16

Zane and I were about to walk out of the restaurant when Matt hailed us and stepped over. "I wanted to ask you, Kali," he began with a note of seriousness. "Have you talked to Lacey since you got here?"

"We saw her this afternoon at the pool. Why?"

His hands fidgeted with his apron. "I was wondering how she seemed to you. If she was... you know... upset."

His eyes met mine, and I understood. "Not particularly," I answered. "She complained about Ty not being around, but she didn't seem any more upset than the last time I heard her say that."

Matt looked at me with disbelief for a second. Then his blue eyes flashed fire. "He didn't tell her," he growled. "He *swore* to me he would! I'm going to kill him."

"Forget him," I urged. I didn't think that Matt was quick to anger, but this particular grievance had been brewing for a while. "Just focus on what's best for Lacey. Tell her yourself."

He looked away from me. "I thought it would be better coming from him."

"Maybe it would," I agreed. "But is that ever going to happen?"

He growled once more. "I'll take care of it," he said gruffly. Then he raised his eyes, looked from me to Zane and back again, and forced a smile on his face. "Come back again anytime, you two. I'll throw in some extra guacamole."

He clapped me gently on the back, gave Zane a nod, and left us.

Zane and I walked away together toward the spot where he had parked his car. I kept expecting him to ask for an explanation. But he just walked silently, seeming thoughtful. "Zane," I said finally, "If you ever want to know something, *anything*, all you have to do is ask me. I'll tell you the truth."

His eyes met mine, first with surprise, then with a tenderness that was tantalizing. "Do I have anything to worry about with this guy, Kali?"

I smiled back at him, my limbs feeling like rubber. It was no confession of undying love, but whatever it was, I would take it. "Absolutely nothing," I assured.

His knee-weakening gaze continued a moment more, then abruptly he broke it off, opened my car door for me, and walked around to the driver's side. "We'd better head back to Honolulu," he said regretfully, hopping in. "I believe you have a date with a packing box."

I groaned. "Yes... about sixty of them." *Why* had I promised my parents I would get back early enough to help out some more? The day had flown.

We drove out of Haleiwa and got back on the highway towards town. "So tell me," Zane asked finally, "who exactly is Matt going to kill? Euphemistically speaking, of course."

"Of course," I confirmed. I gave Zane a summary of the situation with Ty and Lacey, but even as I defended Matt's peaceful nature, the heat of anger I had seen in the football player's normally gentle blue eyes disturbed me. Then all at once, I understood it.

"So," Zane was asking, "do you think he'll tell Lacey himself?"

I turned to him. "Don't you think he should?"

"For her sake, sure," he agreed. "But she's going to hate him for it. At least for a while. Tough way to lose a friend."

"He's going to lose her as a friend anyway," I predicted, smiling smugly to myself.

Zane threw me a puzzled look.

"He's in love with her," I explained. "He just doesn't know it yet."

———✿———

"Hey, check it out," Zane said with amusement, looking across me and into the front windows of my house, where my parents were dancing the foxtrot in plain view of the entire neighborhood. It wasn't even dark out yet.

"I don't need to, thanks," I replied. "I live with it 24/7."

"But it's so great!" he said fondly. "How long have they been married?"

"Thirty-something years. I was what you'd call a 'midlife surprise.' And yet, as you can see, they still act like honeymooners. It can get pretty embarrassing sometimes."

He studied me. "And when I witnessed all this before, and you said something like that, did I tell you you're an ungrateful brat not to appreciate having parents who are so obviously in love with each other?"

I grinned at him. "Not exactly. What you said was that you wanted what they have."

His eyes left mine and drifted back to my parents. Maddeningly, he made no response.

"Do you want to come in?" I asked finally.

He smiled and pulled his keys out of the ignition. "I thought you'd never ask."

An hour later, we were sitting together on the floor of the living room after having managed to unpack, untangle, and reconnect the six billion cords and cables that controlled my mother's computer workstation. She had made us cups of her famous spiced tea; my father was boring Zane with talk of his days as a fighter pilot. Or at least he was boring *me*. Zane appeared to be fascinated. Then again, he was an excellent actor.

I was just about to finish the job by figuring out which port my mom's ancient mouse plugged into when I felt Zane's hand nudge my leg. I looked up at him, but he seemed absorbed in whatever my dad was saying and I couldn't catch his eye. Assuming it was an accident, I buried my head back under the desk. He nudged me again. I plugged in the mouse and sat up straight. My dad was still talking a blue streak; but this time, Zane's eyes flickered toward me ever so briefly. Then he gave a slight nod of his head towards the window.

My dad noticed none of this. My mom was still working in the kitchen. My eyes followed the direction Zane pointed, but I saw nothing interesting either in the room or out the window. The car was parked where he had left it. I looked back at Zane. And then I knew. He was seeing *her* again. The ghost of the Hawaiian girl.

I looked at the space and concentrated, but could see nothing at all. I opened my senses and tried to feel, but all I picked up was the shadow of the sad woman by the front door. I'd found three shadows in the house so far; thankfully nothing I couldn't handle. I pulled the blind back down and the woman's sadness evaporated.

I shook my head as a signal to Zane. He wasn't looking directly at me, but I knew he would pick it up. *No, I can't see her.*

My mother walked in from the kitchen. "Mitch, can you come help me with the deck chairs?"

I smiled up at her warmly. *Translation: Mitch, would you*

shut up and leave them alone for a while?

My dad was not unaware of the ploy. He gave her a wry look and rose with a sigh. "As you wish."

I exhaled with relief. I knew I should appreciate Zane's willingness to get to know my parents, and vice versa, but I was impatient to be alone with him again. "The Hawaiian girl?" I whispered as soon as they were both out of sight.

He nodded, seeming troubled.

"Is she still here?"

"No. I could only see her clearly for a couple seconds." He rose from the floor and went to stand where the ghost had been.

I followed. "What's wrong?"

"She wants something, Kali," he insisted, moving his hand through the space as if trying to feel what he could no longer see. "She was... really upset. I felt bad for her."

I sighed deeply. We had had such an amazing day. This was hardly the ending I had been hoping for. "You can't let it get to you, Zane," I pleaded. "Believe me, I know. You're probably going to see lots of them from now on, and you're never going to figure them all out, much less be able to do anything for them."

"I helped out the guy at rehab," he argued. "Or at least I hope I did."

I knew I was being selfish. I didn't care. Couldn't we, for one full day, be happily alive together and free of spooky, creepy things that weren't?

"But that guy could talk," he continued, as much to himself as to me. "Maybe that's because he hadn't crossed over yet. You think this girl could be one of the other kind, the ones that have already gone into the light and are trying to come back? It makes sense that it would be more difficult."

My shoulders slumped. He wasn't going to let it go.

"The first time I saw her, she looked just like anyone else," he went on. "She did this time too, at first, but then she started fading out. It was like she couldn't keep up the effort. She tried to talk, but there was no sound, and whenever she moved, she got blurrier, so I couldn't read her lips, either." He ran a hand through his blond curls. "She was trying so hard to tell me something, Kali. But I just couldn't get it!"

"If you want, I could ask Kylee's grandmother," I heard myself say. "About how to communicate with them, I mean."

He looked at me gratefully. "Would you? She just seemed so... desperate."

I studied his ridiculously handsome, concerned face, and despite my frustration, my heart melted all over again. How sweet was it that he cared so much about a random ghost?

"I'll call Kylee tomorrow," I promised. "But can we forget about it for now? I was thinking maybe, after we finish the computer, we could take a walk around the neighborhood—"

But no, I had lost him again. His eyes had locked on the bookcases, and he was walking towards them. He stopped at the shelf my dad had filled with the family wedding portraits.

I stepped over to join him. "Those are my Greek grandparents," I began, offering him a tour from left to right. "And that's my mom and dad, of course."

"And this?" he asked, picking up the frame to the right and extending it toward me. "Who is this?"

I looked at the picture and got a sinking feeling in my gut. "That's my grandfather Albin. And my grandmother Kalia."

I didn't need to hear his next words. I could tell what

he was going to say from the look on his face.

"The Hawaiian girl," he said in a whisper. "It's her. Your grandmother Kalia."

—◆—

The set up *could* have been perfect.

Zane and I were sitting in folding patio chairs on my lanai. The sun was setting behind us, and purple shadows fell slowly over the green peaks to the northeast. A few gray clouds rolled lazily toward the windward side, but the balmy breeze was mild.

We could have spent the last hour getting to know each other better — the real me and the real him, as we were now, in the present. Instead, both our minds were mired in the past again.

He held my DNA analysis results in his hands. I had told him everything.

"So what do you think she wants?" I asked weakly, slumping in my chair. I wasn't sure how a person was supposed to feel upon finding out that the ghost of a long-dead relative had been hanging out in their living room. But it certainly seemed like I should feel positively toward the soul of a woman I had spent my entire life idolizing.

Instead, all I felt was aggravation.

"I wish I could answer that," Zane said sympathetically. "She was standing so close to your dad — hovering, almost. Her body language was very protective. I thought that was weird, but it makes sense now. He's her son. She loves him."

His words made me uncomfortable. I had no idea why. "You said she seemed desperate. Desperate how?"

He leaned back in his own chair and closed his eyes. "I'm trying to remember. The way she looked at him, and

then at me... it was like she was afraid of something."
After another moment, he opened his eyes and sat up.
"She wanted me to do something, Kali. I just can't imagine
what."

Afraid of something.

Kylee's grandmother had spoken specifically of the
ghosts of loved ones returning. What had she said?

My Tien appeared to Kylee to save her from death.

Death!

I felt the blood drain from my face.

"Kali?" Zane said quickly. "Are you all right? What is
it?"

I couldn't answer. I didn't want to think what I was
thinking. But knowing what had happened to Kylee, what
had *almost* happened to her, how could I ignore it?

"Kali?" Zane repeated.

I sprang up from my chair. I had no idea where I was
going. My legs felt weak. My head swam. I think I began
to sway.

The next few moments were a muddle. One second I
was sure my knees were going to buckle, the next I was
enveloped in the most soothing warmth imaginable. Zane
had me; he was holding me against his chest. The same
magnetic, irresistible force pulled me closer to him, and
without thought I buried my face in the crook of his
shoulder and inhaled the scent of him. I was safe and all
was good, and time was standing still...

If he hadn't set me back down in the chair, I would
never have let go of him.

"Sorry about that," I croaked, my former panic
returning immediately.

"What scared you so much?" he demanded, crouching
beside my chair. "Tell me!"

"It's my dad," I answered weakly. "I'm afraid he may

be in danger. I think that's what Kalia is trying to tell you."

"What sort of danger?"

I shook my head. "I have no idea."

I told him everything I could remember about my conversation with Kylee and her grandmother. He told me everything he could remember about Kalia's ghost.

Neither one of us had the faintest idea what we could do about it.

"There has to be more," Zane said finally. "Think about it. She didn't appear just to worry you. She wants us to do something specific, but she hasn't been able to communicate it yet. Maybe she's trying to gather strength. Maybe she needs more time to make her message clear."

"Does my dad *have* time?" I asked miserably.

"He must," Zane said firmly. "Or she wouldn't be doing it like this. She knows things we don't know... I think we just have to trust her and wait for more."

"Well, I *don't* trust her!"

The hostility in my voice rang in the air like a pistol shot. Embarrassed as I was to have Zane hear that anger, I knew I couldn't hold it in anymore. "I guess all this DNA stuff has had more of an effect on me than I thought," I admitted.

"What do you mean?" he asked gently.

"I wasn't just named after Kalia," I tried to explain, my eyes tearing up. "When I was growing up, she was my hero. It was such a sweet, sad story. She was so young and beautiful, but she came from a large family that was so poor she was sent out to work while she was still in high school. She fell in love with a tall, dashing Air Force officer, they got married, my dad was born, and she died tragically when their son was still too little to remember her. But my grandfather never stopped loving her — even after he remarried, he made sure that my dad always kept their wedding picture out to remember her by."

I drew in a shaky breath. "But it was all a lie."

Zane was silent a moment. "You don't know that."

"Don't I?" I said sharply, swiping away the tears on my cheeks. "I remember my grandfather. He was the sweetest, gentlest man alive. He used to let me take my afternoon nap cuddled up in his lap in the big armchair while he watched TV. I would ask him about the Kalia I was named for, and he would tell me how beautiful she was, and how smart, and how loving. And he would tell me he was sure I would grow up to be *just like her!*"

I gave up fighting the tears. "She and my grandfather met at Christmastime," I continued bitterly. "They dated for months before my dad was conceived. *Months!* Albin loved her so much. And she let him think the baby was his! She *married* him, for God's sake. She let him raise my dad as his own — she made them both live a lie!"

"You don't *know* that," Zane repeated, this time more firmly. "I know it looks that way, but you're making a lot of assumptions, and all of them for the worst. There are other possibilities."

"Like what?"

"I don't know," he answered. "But can't you give her the benefit of the doubt? There's one thing I do know, because I saw it with my own eyes. She loves your father very much."

I tried to get a grip on my emotions. Really, I did. I had never been a crybaby and I certainly didn't want to start now, at the end of such an otherwise amazing day. But I had bottled up my feelings about Kalia for too long, and now that the dam had finally burst, I couldn't stop the flood. I struggled, and lost, and cried, and struggled again. "Could you please just smack me or something?" I said with a hiccup.

Zane chuckled. "Sorry. Not happening." Instead he rose, disappeared into my room, and returned with a handful of tissues. "Here."

I accepted the offering and made another effort to pull myself together, this one mighty. I could not let the day end like this. Zane had all the answers he wanted from me now. Unless his feelings for me were turning into something more than just memories, he had no further incentive to humor me, particularly not now that I had turned into such a blubbering idiot. I opened my mouth to apologize, but before I could get the words out, he interrupted me.

"So, what time would you like your swimming lesson tomorrow?" he asked. "I was thinking we'd go back to Turtle Bay this time, if the surf's calm enough."

Tomorrow.

I sniffled. "What time works for you?"

"How about noon again?" he offered. "I'll pick you up. And I really hate to say this under the circumstances, but I've absolutely got to get out of here — like *now*. It's getting late, this lanai is technically part of your bedroom, and I'd hate to start off on the wrong foot with the Colonel." He pulled his keys from his pocket.

Start off?

I liked the sound of that. "You want me to walk you out?" I asked, rising and following him back inside.

He smiled at me, amused. "Um... no offense, but I'd rather you didn't. If we went downstairs together with you looking like that, I might not get out alive."

I looked in my mirror. My hair was wild, my cheeks were streaked with red, and my eyes were puffed up like sausages.

I laughed out loud. "Wuss!" I accused.

"Guilty as charged," he agreed, moving towards the

stairs. "I'll see you tomorrow. And about your dad — try not to worry too much. We'll figure it out, I promise. Goodnight, Kali."

There was no question of a goodnight kiss. He was standing six feet away. I wasn't surprised or disappointed, since the mood obviously wasn't right. But there was something about his expression that encouraged me. He looked... well... almost *nervous*.

What exactly had he felt when he caught and held me? It had been the first time since our reunion hug that we'd touched any more than holding hands. Did he feel the same heady, nearly overwhelming pull of attraction? Is that why he'd dumped me so quickly back in my chair?

I had no way of knowing. But a girl could dream.

"Goodnight," I returned, smiling.

chapter 17

That night, exhausted, I dropped off into a deep, dreamless sleep the minute I crawled into bed. It was not until morning, when the warm rays of tropical sunshine began to stretch through the glass door to my lanai and fall upon my pillow, that my brain began to stir again. My mother was in the room.

"I'm getting up," I said lazily, only reluctantly opening my eyes. "I know, I know... I promised I'd get back to work early. What time is it?"

My sight came into focus, but my mother wasn't there. Why had I thought she was? I could hear the television downstairs; the air smelled of bacon, toast, and coffee. I sat up and stretched. Maybe she had called up the steps for me.

My head jerked suddenly to my left. Someone was watching.

No one was there.

I stared into the empty space. And then, in an instant, I knew.

"Kalia," I breathed.

No human form was visible to me. At most, what my brain translated from my eyes was a mild disturbance in the air — like a video with one area pixelated. But I was aware of her presence. It radiated with an aura I could only classify as "maternal." The breakfast aromas from below became mixed with the scent of ginger.

"What do you want?" I croaked, my insides churning with conflicting emotions. "Is Dad in danger? Show me!"

The presence shifted. It moved from my bedside to the

far wall of the room, then hovered over a stack of still-packed banker's boxes. I rose and walked to them.

I lifted the lid of the box on top, my arms actually sliding through the presence to do so. I couldn't feel her like I could feel the shadows. But still... there was something. Reading her feelings was like trying to watch a movie in a foreign language: the words were gibberish, but sometimes, if you were paying attention, you could get the gist.

She was insistent. Practically frantic.

It was *her* box. The box of her memories and mementos. I pulled out what I knew to be lying tucked in the folds of her wedding dress ever since I had stashed it there last night: my DNA results.

"I know Albin wasn't my biological grandfather," I said stiffly. "But how does that put *my* father in danger?"

The presence grew agitated. The pixilations seemed to grow denser; I could no longer see through her clearly. But neither could I make any sense of her image.

"Look," I said, getting frustrated myself. "If all you're worried about is him finding out, then forget about it. I don't plan to tell him. It would destroy him, as you should know!"

The blurry area became still thicker, creamier. It seemed almost to bounce upon the box. I heard nothing with my ears, but I was certain the presence was screaming.

"Stop!" I ordered, feeling a reluctant tug of sympathy. She was trying so hard... but it was never going to work. "I can't see you!" I explained, suddenly unsure whether she knew that. "Zane can see you, but I can't. All I see is a blur! Save your energy for him — maybe he can understand you."

She disappeared as quickly as a soap bubble popped.

The image, the scent, the presence, the feelings... *gone.*

I collapsed on my bed.

"Kali?" my mother called up the stairwell. "Who are you talking to up there?"

"Nobody living," I called back.

There was a pause. "Breakfast is ready."

I chuckled at the absurdity that was otherwise known as my "gift." It was either that or cry, and I had done more than enough of that already.

I dressed quickly and joined my parents downstairs. My dad was in uniform. For them, the moving "vacation" was over. Today they went back to work.

"Kali," my mother began, her voice tired. The creases of tension in her forehead were deeper than usual. "I know you were planning to start putting job applications in soon, but... I have a proposal for you."

My eyebrows rose.

She sighed. "This house is going to take a lot more work than we thought to make it livable — and I just don't have the time to deal with it right now. We're not even through unpacking, and I've got to get back to the textbook project or I'll never make my deadline. So since you need spending money anyway..."

My hopes climbed.

"Your dad and I have discussed it, and we'd like to pay you to work on it. Nothing too complicated — just cleaning, unpacking, sorting, reorganizing, figuring out *some* way to save some more space... and then the repainting, and every stitch of carpet needs to be torn out and the floor cleaned before we put in new—"

"Deal!" I answered, short-circuiting the rest of the list. I didn't care if they wanted me to scrub the tile grout with a toothbrush, so long as I could set my own hours and spend the maximum amount of time possible with Zane.

My father threw me a questioning glance. "That easy, huh? And what about your surfing friend? Does he plan on getting a job anytime soon?"

My hackles rose. I knew that a lot of people viewed surfing as a pastime for loafers and druggies. I didn't care what most people thought about most surfers, but I did care what my dad thought about Zane. "Dad," I said heavily. "Zane has worked some job or other, year round, since he was fifteen years old. For a while there, he was essentially supporting himself. And after the accident he went straight into PT — doing two and three times as much workout as he was supposed to, just so he could get better faster. When he moved to Oahu, Craig and Trina — that's the lawyer and his wife — made him promise he would take a couple months off to chill out and relax before starting college in the fall. The doctors and therapists at rehab all told him the same thing. Which is—"

My dad raised his palms in surrender. "Down girl, down!" he mocked, grinning at me. "I was just asking, after all. Where is he going to college?"

"University of Hawaii Manoa."

"To study what?"

"Engineering."

My dad humphed in reluctant approval.

My mom chuckled. "Anything else, Mitch? Think quickly now."

My dad straightened. "They have engineering at the Academy, you know."

My mom and I groaned out loud.

"Fine then!" he said with good humor, rising. "I know when my opinion isn't valued. I'm off to the base."

Fear stabbed suddenly at my insides. Was he in danger, or wasn't he? Would he walk out the door only to be mown down by the bus he planned to ride? Would an airplane drop out of the sky on top of him? I was halfway out of my seat to prevent his leaving when I stopped and slowly sank back into it. With no specifics on whatever threat might loom, what could I do? Who was to say that if I prevented his going to work, the roof of the house wouldn't collapse?

"Goodbye, Dad," I managed.

"Goodbye, darlin'," he returned, kissing my mother and heading for the door. He was halfway through it when he turned around and popped his head back in. "Oh, and by the way," he said with a smirk. "I do like the boy."

He whirled back out and shut the door behind him.

My second swimming lesson took place in the sheltered snorkeling area at Turtle Bay. The ocean water was crystal clear and teeming with brightly colored fish. The sky was blue and the air was warm. Gulls and the occasional giant frigatebird soared overhead, and a brisk wind twirled the tall white turbines of the wind farm on the green peaks nearby. Children splashed in the shallow water all around me. Zane was helpful and instructive and patient and kind.

His student sucked.

"You're getting it," he insisted.

"Ah erm mnot," I argued, pulling seawater-soaked curls out of my mouth. I was supposed to have been keeping it closed. I was nervous, like I always was when large bodies of water were involved, but this afternoon was worse than usual for me. I couldn't focus.

Zane looked at me thoughtfully. "You're worried about your dad, aren't you?"

I looked back at him, then exhaled with a sigh. Yes, I was worried about my dad. When Zane had come to pick me up, we'd walked around every inch of the house looking for Kalia, but the ghost had been AWOL. I still had no idea what her problem was, no idea how to protect my dad, and no clue how to deal with my own conflicted feelings about my grandmother.

But that wasn't the only reason I was out of sorts.

"Yes," I answered. "Maybe we should call it quits for today? Before I drown?"

His killer green eyes blinked at me, affronted. "I'm not going to let you drown, Kali."

I looked at him standing there in the waist-deep water, his bronzed torso glistening with drops of seawater, his blond curls shining in the sun. It would almost be worth it to inhale a lungful or two, if it meant he would actually touch me.

So far today, he'd been doing just about everything to avoid it. When teaching someone to swim, that took effort.

"But if you're not feeling it," he continued. "We can try again tomorrow."

We walked up out of the water together, and as his gaze drifted back over the open ocean, I could see the spark of excitement in his eyes. The waves had been growing steadily higher all afternoon.

"Zane," I chuckled. "If you want to get out there, don't let me stop you. Park me on the beach and I'm good. In fact, I'd like that. I could use a couple hours to just sit on the sand and chill. I love to watch you surf."

His face, first lighting up at the suggestion, darkened at my last few words. He seemed suddenly deep in thought. "I do want to get out there," he replied as we collected our things and headed towards his car. "Maybe in a bit."

He said no more, and by the time we reached the parking lot, I had had all I could take. There were only two things that explained his bizarre behavior. Either he had decided he wasn't into me after all — a reasonable decision given the baggage I'd revealed over the last twenty-four hours — or we had some kind of major misunderstanding going on. If he wasn't into me, I'd rather know now. As for misunderstandings... I didn't do them. Life was too short.

We dumped our stuff in his backseat. But before he could get in the car, I stopped him.

"You're afraid to touch me and you don't want me to watch you surf," I said. "Would you tell me why? Please?"

I had startled him. But only a little, thank goodness. If he couldn't handle directness, he would have dumped me in Nebraska.

"You're very perceptive," he said softly.

"Off topic," I replied. "Let's do one at a time. Why don't you want me to watch you surf?"

His eyes left mine. "Kali..." he said with discomfort.

My heart began to crack wide open. "Zane," I interrupted, forcing myself to say the words, to get it over with. "You don't owe me anything. You're not obligated. I helped you get your memory back and you gave me two swimming lessons. We're even. There's no need to pretend anything you don't feel anymore. All you have to do is—"

"What are you talking about?" he broke in. "Are you kidding me? You can't possibly think—" He ran a hand through his curls and turned away. Then he blew out a breath and turned back. He started to reach out toward me, then abruptly withdrew his hands. "This is impossible!" he said with a groan. Then he faced me squarely.

"Just listen to me, Kali. I know you think you know

me already — that *I'm* the one who needs to get reacquainted with you. Well, I've done that. It took about thirty seconds. I'm as crazy about you as I ever was, could possibly ever have been. How you could be so perceptive about everything else and not see *that*, I have no idea. But what you don't get is... *you* don't know *me*."

My knees were getting wobbly again. My heart, newly repaired, was now pumping blood so hard I was afraid my cheeks would explode. "Of course I do," I argued.

"No, you don't," he insisted. "Kali, the guy you fell for before... he wasn't real. He was like some kind of superman. He could disappear; he could reappear. He could walk through walls. He could walk on water. He could jump off the wing of an airplane and hang suspended in the air. He could *surf the pipe!*"

His voice nearly broke. "I can't do any of those things," he said roughly. "It's taken months for me to get back to anything even close to the guy you remember. But even in the best of shape, I'm no great surfer. I'm nothing but a rank amateur from Hackensack, New Jersey." His eyes held mine. "I can't defy physics anymore. I'm not that guy. I'm just... *me*."

I thought about what he said. I thought about it for about two seconds. Then I backed up about five steps, ran forward, and jumped on him.

He caught me against his chest, solid and firm. I surprised him so that he nearly stumbled, but of course he didn't; he shifted his weight, clutched me tightly, and broke my fall.

He lowered me back down slowly, his breathing rapid. "What was *that?*" he demanded.

I grinned at him, not loosening my own hold in the slightest. "Did it ever occur to you that I might not *want* a guy who can walk through walls? That I might, just possibly, prefer a guy who can keep me from doing a faceplant on the asphalt?"

I watched, my heart thudding pleasantly, as his expression turned slowly into a smile.

"I can do that," he whispered.

Oh, my. It was the sexy whisper. The one I had zero control over. He still held me, and I held him, and the insane, ridiculous pull between us was so warmly, wonderfully powerful that this time I felt sure I would drown in it.

He drew in a ragged breath. "Do you feel that, Kali?"

"Yes," I answered.

"I don't think it's... normal."

I chuckled. "I wouldn't know. But nothing else between us has been, has it?"

He smiled at me. "Good point."

I was sure he would kiss me. But I was wrong.

"Does it scare you?" he asked.

"No," I answered easily. "Does it scare you?"

He hesitated. "Oh, yeah. *Bigtime.*"

My heart leapt all over again. He had just answered my second question.

"Well then," I replied with a smile, continuing to hold him. *"Get over it!"*

He laughed, his green eyes sparkling. He ran a hand gently up my back. Slowly, his head leaned down toward mine.

A truck horn blasted six feet from our ears.

"Hey lovebirds!" a middle-aged local man yelled out the driver's window. "You moving into that spot, or what?"

We looked up to see an open-bed pickup filled to overflowing with men, boys, and surfboards. The driver was waiting to pull into the spot next to Zane's car — the only otherwise-empty spot in the public lot. The surfers, to a one, hung over the sides of the bed, leering and grinning at us.

We broke apart laughing.

chapter 18

Zane spent the rest of the afternoon on the ocean. I spent it on the beach, alternating awkwardly between angst over my dad and joy at watching Zane surf again. Apparently, having even a half-decent swell hit the North Shore at this time of the year was enough to entice every human with a surfboard to flock to the beaches immediately, so all the best breaks were crowded to capacity. Even at the less desirable spot Zane chose to stake out, competition for waves was fierce. In two hours of paddling and drifting he managed to catch fewer than a half-dozen waves, most of those barely surfable. But at last, he got lucky. He ended his run with a beautiful ride on a perfect waist-high wave that he was able to ride nearly all the way back to the beach.

I stood up and applauded wildly. He was nowhere near ready to rip with the pros, true. But it was clear that, as I suspected even when he was a wraith, the guy had natural talent.

He came off the water totally stoked and insisted on buying us a celebratory pair of barbecue plates at Ted's Bakery (chased down by two amazing pieces of pie), where between forkfuls he went on to deconstruct the entire session in detail. I didn't have the heart to tell him I didn't understand half of what he was saying. I was enjoying his enjoyment more than I could say.

We were on our way back to my house, and he was bragging to me about how dedicated the surfing community was both to protecting the ocean environment and to improving the lives of poor people near the world's best breaks, when my phone rang. It was Kylee. I had been waiting for her call all afternoon.

"What did your grandmother say?" I asked as soon as the hellos were over. Kylee had assured me, on my last call, that I shouldn't assume the worst — that if a loved one were in imminent danger of death, Kalia would have acted more directly to stop it, like Tien did. But we both wanted to hear that from her grandmother.

"Well," Kylee began, "since Kalia almost certainly never lived in the house you just bought, what she's attempting isn't really a "haunting," but a targeted visible manifestation — which is much more difficult to do. *Ba noi* says that Tien could probably not have appeared to me so far from where she died if it weren't for all the family around me at the time... a family's love has incredible strength, and a spirit can tap into that, if their motives are good. Kalia isn't as far from where she died, but still, appearing so solidly to a stranger like Zane, even for a couple seconds, is a pretty amazing feat. He must be very sensitive, for a newbie."

"Don't praise him too much," I warned, grinning at Zane. "You're on speakerphone, and his ego is big enough already."

"Hi, Kylee," Zane said.

There was a pause. In the background, I knew, Kylee was silently squealing. "Hi, Zane," she replied. "Anyway, Kali, don't expect too much from her. She's bound to be exhausting herself, and you'll need to help her any way you can."

"Like how?" I asked.

"*Ba noi* says you need to give her options — almost like multiple choice questions. If she can gesture but not talk, you've got to give suggestions and then give her an easy way to answer you, like by pointing at something."

"Check."

"And if it's easier for her to appear to Zane, make sure she has enough opportunity to do it. She may find enough strength only intermittently, and you can't know when that will be."

I looked at Zane. "I don't suppose you want to spend another frolicking evening unpacking dusty binders, Christmas decorations, and vinyl records from the seventies?"

He smiled back at me. "Sold. You think this time I can get your dad to tell me about his days at the Academy?"

"Don't you dare," I threatened. "Okay, Kylee. We'll do it. Anything else?"

"Just that..." she hesitated. "Well, she says not to judge Kalia too harshly. You don't know the whole story, and... well, any kind of negative feelings from you could make it harder for her to appear. You understand what I mean?"

My teeth clenched. I felt falsely accused and guilty at the same time. "I get it," I answered.

"Kylee," Zane asked, his voice suddenly sounding odd. "Is it possible for Kalia to appear other places besides the Thompson's house? Like random places where Kali and I might be?"

"It's easier with more family around, but sure," Kylee answered. "Why?"

I slid in my seat as Zane made a sharp swerve onto an exit ramp.

"Because I just saw her on the side of the road," he answered. "She pointed to the exit. I think she wants to lead us somewhere."

My pulse sped up. Lead us *where?* "We have to go, Kylee," I said quickly. "I'll fill you in later, okay?" I got the distinct feeling, as Kylee reluctantly said goodbye, that it was not okay. She would have preferred I leave the speakerphone on all day and tote her around like a caged cricket. But I had to focus.

"Have you seen her again?" I asked anxiously.

"No," Zane answered, straining to scan the crowd at every intersection. We were into the city of Honolulu now. "But she definitely wanted us to go this way. I guess we should just keep going straight, until she shows us otherwise."

Tense minutes passed. He had to be wondering if he'd imagined the whole thing, but he made no move to turn around. The traffic was terrible.

"Wait," he said sharply. "There she is!"

I looked out, but naturally I saw nothing.

"It was just for a split second," Zane explained. "I hope I'm catching everything." He made a right at the next light. "And there," he said a few moments later, turning again. We were past Waikiki now, heading toward the cone of the extinct volcano Diamond Head. Zane made a couple more turns, then abruptly pulled off the road and stopped. "Okay, Kali," he said tightly. "Here we are."

I looked out the window at the small white-painted office building that rose up on my right, guarding entry to a large, flat field beyond. The field was bathed in well-tended green grass and dotted with floral arrangements.

It was a cemetery.

Oh, no.

"Do you know anyone buried here?" Zane asked.

I nodded grimly. "Kalia is buried here. My parents looked up her grave when we came in March, but I wasn't with them." Because they knew I hated cemeteries. Already, I struggled to block the intruding feelings. I could see countless shadows standing about the grounds, and the edges of my mental blind kept stubbornly rolling up on me. *Sadness. So much sadness...*

"Are you going to be able to do this?" Zane asked, watching me closely. "Maybe it would be better if I went in alone. Maybe it's something she can show me—" His gaze moved suddenly upward, out the windshield. He exhaled with a sigh, then turned back to me. "She says no, Kali. Whatever it is, she needs you to see it."

My stomach cramped. As well as I had been doing with the blocking techniques, a shopping mall was one thing and a cemetery was another. The dozen or so graves at Striker's Schoolhouse were nothing compared to the hundreds and hundreds in the memorial park ahead... and once I was inside, there would be no running away. The shadows would be everywhere, encircling me. And they would all be in horrible pain. If the experience hadn't been highly emotional for the people the shadows represented, the shadows wouldn't be there.

"It could be," I said slowly, making a lame attempt to sound brave, "that what she's trying to show us is a shadow." I swallowed. "A shadow at her own grave. So yes, I have to go."

You have to, Kali. Now get a grip!

I took a deep "cleansing breath," as the other empaths in San Jose had recommended. Then I brought down the blind and pulled it tight. "Okay, go ahead and drive in."

Zane began navigating the car slowly through the park, and although I would have preferred to shut my eyes, I forced myself to stay watchful. In other circumstances, it would have been a beautiful, peaceful place. The stones were all flat to the ground, flowers were everywhere, and the lanes wound through tropical trees, all in the shadow of the towering mound of Diamond Head. If only that was all I could see. But to my eye, the acres were packed full of semi-transparent grief-stricken mourners, each and every one of them radiating bitter anguish.

Blind down. Blind down. Blind down...

"Here?" Zane said aloud, though not to me. "Okay... we'll do the rest." He cast a concerned glance in my direction. "Are you still okay?"

No. Even focusing as hard as I could, the blind couldn't stop it all. The accumulated weight of grief was too heavy, and I was too inexperienced. But the pain that wracked me from all sides was at least reasonably bearable — as opposed to what I had endured at Pali Lookout. I could do this. I had to do it. "I'm good," I said unconvincingly.

Zane walked around, opened my car door, and helped me out. "Here," he said, taking my hand and locking his arm firmly around mine. "Maybe this will help."

Warmth. Safety. Peace...

"It does," I said gratefully. "Thanks. Let's just do this thing, okay?"

We walked around in the vicinity of the car, looking for a relatively new floral arrangement. I thought I remembered my mother saying she had bought silk roses. But it was not the flowers that ultimately attracted my eye to a plot about fifty feet from where we had parked. It was the shadow.

I stopped in my tracks, holding onto Zane's comforting, solid hand with both of mine. The sadness and grief were everywhere; deep, pervasive, so very painful... but his touch was like a campfire in a snowstorm. "That man," I said weakly, pointing toward the shadow ahead. "He's my grandfather."

I opened myself up, ever so slightly, to perceive the shadow's presence more fully. Instantly I was hit with a sensation of grief so intense my whole body trembled. Zane dropped my hand and put his arm around my shoulders, hugging me close to his side. Soothing waves of warmth spread through me immediately, and the trembling stopped. "Have you ever seen the shadow of a relative before?" he asked gently.

I shook my head. "I've never been this far inside a cemetery before. And I... I couldn't do it without you here. Thanks."

He continued to hug my shoulders, rubbing the outside of my arm briskly as if he could feel the chill inside, despite the bright sunshine beaming down on both of us. "Are you able to go closer?" he asked.

"I'm not sure," I said honestly. "But I need to try."

The shadow had disappeared now. But slowly, step by step, I pulled Zane with me toward the spot where it had been standing. I wanted terribly to keep the blind down, but I knew I couldn't, not if I was going to pick up whatever Kalia wanted me to pick up. I would have to feel and hear the shadows as well as see them. When we reached our destination, a couple feet away from where I had seen my grandfather, I stopped and took another deep breath.

Zane loosened his hold on me. It was only for a second, and probably only because he was shifting positions, but the instant I lost contact with his side, a rush of bitingly cold pain belted me like a blizzard.

"No!" I shouted, pulling him back toward me.

"Sorry, sorry," he apologized, rubbing my arms again. "This really helps, then?" he asked doubtfully.

I looked up at him with the closest thing to a smile I could manage. "Zane," I said wryly, "You're like a freakin' space heater."

His eyes twinkled. "I've been waiting my entire life to hear a beautiful girl say that to me."

The joking helped. I looked around.

My grandmother's flat, rectangular memorial stone lay

on the ground before us. *Loving wife and mother. Kalia H. Thompson.* Born in 1935; died in 1956.

"Barely twenty-one," Zane said sadly, keeping his arm tight about my shoulders. "Your grandfather must have been devastated." He looked at me closely. "Do you still see him?"

I shook my head. But even as I did, a swirl of shadow erupted at our feet. I pulled Zane backwards with me.

"What is it?" he asked.

"Another shadow," I answered. I opened my senses again, only to be struck — harshly and immediately — by the full force of this new shadow's anguish. He was a young man, and he kneeled before Kalia's stone on the ground, nearly prostrate, his head and thin shoulders heaving with convulsive sobs. He was dressed shabbily; he carried nothing. He said no words that I could make out. His grief was beyond intense — it burned with a fury, a fury against injustice and unfairness. But there was also shock. He couldn't believe what he was seeing. He couldn't *bear* it. It was not to be borne...

Both of Zane's arms were now wrapped around my middle; I was leaning back against his chest. My knees had almost given out on me. "Sorry about that," I whispered.

Would the shadow never disappear?

In an instant, it had company. My grandfather stood not four feet from me, tall, young, and hauntingly handsome in his crisp officer's uniform. I would know him anywhere, despite a face still puffy from recently shed tears and strong muscles that, by the time I knew him, had wasted away from age and illness. He stood straight and tall as a tree, almost as if at attention, showing the world a man of steel even as his heart was breaking. And it *was* breaking. I could feel the pain in him every bit as strong as that of the sobbing man not far from his feet, and my defenses were now nearly worthless — the only thing keeping me from flight, from collapse, or both, was the equally incredible, soothing warmth that Zane's touch radiated into my body.

"My grandfather's here again," I squeaked. "He and another man are mourning her. They're miserable. Horribly miserable. And they're both so... so *angry.*"

I looked more closely into my grandfather's eyes. He was not looking at the grave. He seemed to be watching or listening to something else — quite possibly a minister at a service. But even as he pretended attention, his eyes swept around the area, looking for something. For what? His eyes passed over the weeping man. He made no response to the other shadow, but as his gaze returned to what had probably been the speaker, his jaws clenched suddenly. *Anger.*

He was furious. The shadow on the ground let out a particularly piercing wail, and my knees weakened again, a faint moan escaping my lips as I felt Zane's grip tightening. In another second, my feet were off the ground. He was carrying me.

"That's enough," he said firmly, moving me away from the grave.

"No, wait!" I protested as the pain lessened. What was I missing? Zane stopped a moment, and I looked back at Kalia's grave, but the shadows were gone.

"They've left now," I said. "You can... put me down. I'm okay."

I didn't want him to put me down. I wanted to stay in his arms the rest of my natural life — and beyond. But between the warmth I felt from being so close to him and the protection of the blind I could now pull fully back down... I really was all right.

He looked at me skeptically and continued walking.

"You don't look okay. But let's not talk about it yet. I want to get you away from here first."

I didn't argue. All too quickly, he reached the car and bundled me inside. As he let go of me to walk around and get in himself, I missed his touch horribly, and only when he drove out of the cemetery and back onto the street could I force myself to let him have his right hand back.

The misery of the mourning shadows was gone now, and I sighed with relief.

"Better?" he asked.

"Much," I answered. "Thank you."

He smiled at me. "You're a brave one, you know that?"

It occurred to me that there were probably any number of girls who would gladly go through everything I just went through if it meant that a guy like Zane would sweep them off their feet and carry them away to safety. But I didn't tell him that. I was pretty sure he already knew.

"I didn't feel so brave at the time," I argued. "But thanks."

He turned the car towards home, and for a while we drove in silence as my mind replayed the scene I had just witnessed.

"Do you feel like talking about it yet?" he asked finally.

I felt a twinge of guilt, having completely forgotten that although he was the one being guided by Kalia, he wouldn't have seen or felt anything at her gravesite.

"There was another man there," I began, "besides my grandfather." I described the scene as completely as I could, and realized, as I tried to process my own story, that I had no more answers now than I'd had before. I only had more questions.

"I understand that anyone would be angry at Kalia's dying so suddenly, and while she was so close to having another child," I said, thinking out loud. "But with the shadows, both of them, it was more than that. They were angry at other people, I think."

"Were they angry at each other?" Zane asked.

I remembered my grandfather's cool stare, which swept right over the weeping man's figure. "I don't think so," I answered.

We were quiet for a moment. "Do you think the second man could be your biological grandfather?" Zane asked.

I blew out a long, slow breath. I had not gotten a good look at the man because his head was low to the ground and buried in his hands. His hair had been dark and wavy, and from what I had seen of his face I would guess he were at least part Asian or Hawaiian, but details like skin color were hard to read in a shadow. I got the impression he was young, but I wasn't sure why. He had looked so unkempt, so very world-weary. Only one thing I knew for sure. He had loved Kalia H. Thompson with all his heart.

"I think it's possible, yes," I answered.

"If he looked Hawaiian," Zane suggested, "there is another possibility. He could have been one of Kalia's brothers."

I thought a moment, then shook my head. "Maybe, but I've always been told that none of Kalia's relatives went to her funeral. That was one of the reasons my grandfather decided to leave Hawaii. Kalia's mother adored the baby when she was alive, but she died before Kalia did. No one else in the family seemed to care that Kalia had left a son behind, so Albin had no support system here. The fact that none of Kalia's brothers even bothered coming to her funeral left my grandfather so hurt and furious, he never made any other—"

I stopped in mid-sentence. "That's why he was so

angry!" I explained. "He was at the funeral when I saw his shadow."

"That makes sense," Zane agreed. "Are you sure you didn't feel any hostility between the two men?"

I considered. The weeping man seemed aware of nothing beyond his own grief. My grandfather had looked at him, but I sensed no particular reaction. "I'm not sure my grandfather knew who he was," I said uncertainly. "If he knew that man to be the father of his wife's child, surely he would have *some* feeling about him."

"Uh... for sure," Zane said heavily. "But if Albin *didn't* know his identity, wouldn't he at least be curious, considering how upset the man was?"

My eyebrows knit with confusion. "I didn't feel curiosity," I explained. "I only felt... a cool indifference."

Zane shook his head. "Well, I've never been in any of those situations, but Kali... I don't think your grandfather could do that. I don't think any man could. Seriously... he *loved* her. He loved the baby. Indifference? No way. There's got to be some piece we're missing."

I pictured the scene again, from start to finish. It didn't help. "None of it makes sense!" I cried with frustration. "If that man *was* the father of Kalia's baby, and he loved her so much, why on earth did she marry my grandfather Albin in the first place?"

Zane looked suddenly uncomfortable, and I knew he was thinking the same thing I was. But he didn't say it out loud, and I didn't want to either. *Because he was poor, shabby, and miserable, and Albin Thompson was an Air Force officer.*

The familiar sick feeling returned to my stomach.

The life of the party.

—⟋⟍⟍—

Zane and I stood together in a sheltered area just inside my carport. Sheltered, at least, from the prying eyes of anyone trying to look out the front windows of my house. I didn't know any of the other neighbors yet, so for now, they didn't matter.

He was about to drive back to the North Shore, and we were saying goodnight. We had delayed his departure as long as possible, trying to give Kalia a fair shot to clear up some of the hopeless confusion I considered her to have started. But the ghost did not appear. I had called Kylee back with the promised report, and her opinion was that we shouldn't be surprised. Kalia's street-corner appearances had probably cost her plenty, and she needed rest. Unfortunately, my parents needed rest too, which meant that despite another lovely evening of unpacking, sorting, and organizing to the tune of six thousand of my dad's stories about his and his buddies' hijinks at the Academy (I would get Zane for that), my guest had been politely kicked out for the night.

"I think it's all pieces of a bigger puzzle," Zane assured as we went over everything once more. My dad's day at work had been uneventful, and we had no reason to believe he was in immediate danger aside from the fact that Kalia had appeared beside him in the first place. That she feared *something*, was desperate to protect him from *something*, was clear. But the more clues she delivered, the more sure I became that the threat hovering over my father was no out-of-control SUV.

"We just have to be patient and let her tell us more," Zane continued. "Probably the scene at her grave won't make any sense until then, no matter how many times we go over it."

"You're probably right," I agreed.

His tone brightened. "So, where shall we go for your swimming lesson tomorrow? Back to the pool, maybe? It's the safest place to get out into deeper water."

I groaned. Now was as good a time as any to break it to him. "Zane, you're a very good teacher, but in my case, that's irrelevant. It isn't going to work. Didn't today's lesson prove that to you? I'm a failure. I can't do it. I'm never going to be able to do it."

"My, my," he clucked, "Such unbridled negativity! What a mystery you don't get better results."

"I *suck* and you know it! I can't do any of it."

"Actually," he said seriously, "You can do all of it. You've done all of it already. Just not at the same time. If you would only put that freestyle stroke into gear the same time as your kick, you'd be tearing across the water. The only thing you lack is self-confidence."

"I appreciate your efforts. Really, I do. But I can lead a perfectly full life without ever learning to swim."

"And motivation," he said sadly. "You lack that, too."

He looked so disappointed. Maybe some of it was put-on, but he was such a blasted good actor, I couldn't tell. "Oh, fine!" I conceded, unable to bear it either way. "Let's go back to the pool, then. As long as we get you back to the beach after. I heard some guy at Ted's say the forecast was for knee to waist high tomorrow."

His eyes twinkled again. "Deal."

He looked so handsome, standing there in the dim light of the streetlamp, I could almost not control myself. It had been such a long rollercoaster of a day — in parts magical; in others, horrific. But he hadn't touched me once since we returned from the cemetery, and sometimes, a girl just needs a hug. If he didn't pull me into his arms in about two seconds, I was to going to scream.

Nothing happened.

Oh, to heck with it!

I launched myself forward and wrapped my arms around his waist, burying my head in his shoulder. Ripples of warmth, serenity, and security — and something else — shot through me from head to toe. "That's better," I said contentedly.

His arms had gone around me reflexively, but still, I could feel him pull back a bit from the shock. He remained tense. "Kali," he said gruffly, "You're making me crazy, you know that?"

"Mm..." I murmured, my head still buried. He smelled of seawater. *Divine.* "Sorry," I replied.

"You are not."

I chuckled. "Nope." I raised my head and looked at him. "Is this so terrible?" I teased.

His jaws clenched. "You know it's not terrible. It's... amazing. But it's also scary intense."

"Don't make me call you a wuss again," I said dreamily, reburying my head.

Eventually, he relaxed a little. "I suppose I could get used to it," he confessed.

I raised my head again. His green eyes met mine, but his head didn't lower.

"What happened when I tried to kiss you before?" he asked.

I swiveled to face him fully. "What makes you so sure you *did* kiss me?"

He grinned. "I may have been bodiless and not technically alive, but I was still *me*. Now answer the question. What happened?"

My return smile died on my lips. I didn't like remembering that time. "It didn't work too well," I answered. "You were nearly faded away by then. Neither one of us could feel anything."

He looked thoughtful for a moment. "I see."

"I'm pretty sure it would be different now," I said hopefully.

"No doubt," he said grimly.

I bridled. "Why do you say it like that?"

His gaze was earnest. "Aren't you the least bit worried about what could happen?"

He was losing me. I blinked back at him, confused.

He groaned with frustration. He raised a hand and slid it gently down my cheekbone. Then he smiled a little. "I don't know what's going on with us, Kali, but if just holding you makes me this... insane, there's no telling what would happen if I actually kissed you. Who's to say our hair wouldn't catch fire? For all we know, we're two nether beings accidentally meddling with some funky cosmic vortex that's about to blow the top off Diamond Head again."

I cracked up laughing. Then I moved in closer and tilted my head toward his. "I'll risk it."

His eyes blazed. But still, he held back. "You really want me to kiss you, don't you?" he asked, sounding surprised.

"Well, *duh,*" I responded, laughing again.

A smile spread slowly across his face. But it wasn't his typical open, friendly smile. This one was downright conniving. "All right, then," he said, shifting suddenly into that knee-weakening sexy whisper of his. "I'll kiss you."

He leaned in toward me, tantalizing close. But he stopped with his lips just short of mine, his green eyes twinkling devilishly.

"Just as soon as you learn how to swim."

chapter 19

Sleep wasn't in the picture for me. I tossed and turned until the wee hours of the morning, and even then the best I could do was to fall into some weird semi-conscious state where I moved from one crazy dream to another. Zane was a wraith again, cruising through the Pipe. Then he popped out of my birthday cake in a devil costume and told me that refined sugar was bad for my teeth. My dad was a little boy, romping around the cemetery in the shadow of Diamond Head. Kalia came and took his hand, and told him to watch the fireworks, and the volcano erupted. But instead of fire and ashes, it spewed cardboard. The jig-sawed pieces held the answers to the riddle I was trying to solve, and I tried to gather them up and put them back together. But the skies darkened and opened up with rain, and the pieces in my hand turned soggy and unreadable, and I could see Kalia through the haze, holding my infant father and laughing...

Holy crap! I sat up straight in bed. My nightshirt was damp with sweat.

It was hot in my bedroom. There was no air-conditioning, of course — the old house didn't even have central heat. Ordinarily my room was kept cool enough by the breeze; but tonight, the wind was sickeningly calm.

I rose and opened the door to my lanai. It was cooler outside.

Doing my best to put the idiotic dreams out of my mind, I dropped down on the floor of the lanai and started a stretching routine. I was getting out of shape. I needed to find a dance studio soon — see if I could enroll in a summer program. It was only one of a long list of "to do" items I had so far ignored. But I shouldn't be too hard on myself. Even though it seemed longer, we had only been on Oahu for three days.

I had just finished my lunges and downward dogs and was about to move on to my splits when my mom came out to check on me.

No, not my mom.

I blinked back at the empty doorway. Then I rose. "Show me quickly," I whispered.

Nothing was visible to me, yet I knew Kalia was there. I knew when she went inside my room. I knew she was hovering near the box again. *Her* box.

You need to give her options — almost like multiple choice questions.

I practically tripped over my bed. I reached the box and took off the lid, then scrambled to strew its contents about the room, each piece in a distinct location. "Which one?" I whispered again, my breathing heavy. "I've looked at it all before; if I missed something, show me!"

I could see nothing still, not even faint pixilations. She was around the dresser somewhere, but I couldn't narrow down which piece she was indicating. Then she seemed not to be present at all.

"Kalia!" I squeaked, "Please! Try again!"

My frustration peaked, and Kylee's words came back to me like a kick on the backside.

Negative feelings from you could make it harder for her to appear.

I closed my eyes a moment. It wasn't Kalia's fault, was it? It was mine. *Innocent until proven guilty, Kali.*

I concentrated on the old days, the feelings I'd had for Kalia when I was a child. Many times I had taken her picture down from the shelf and sneaked it away to my room, where I would gaze at it while making up all sorts of wonderful, fanciful tales. My grandmother, I would pretend, had secretly been a princess. A Hawaiian princess. Beautiful and noble and loving and good... and someday, I would grow up to be just like her, because my grandfather said that I would. I wanted that so much. I loved her so much...

I opened my eyes. A creamy column of vapor hung directly over the fat envelope of correspondence.

"Good! Perfect!" I cried. I pounced on the envelope and emptied its contents, spreading the cards and notes as thinly across the floor as I could. But there were so many! I stood back and watched, but the column remained stubbornly over the envelope itself. I picked it up again and looked inside, but saw only a littering of torn scraps and crumbled off corners stuck in the bottom. Still, I cracked the envelope open wide and shook out every last bit of paper on top of my bed, spreading the scraps with my hand.

My eyes caught a small, discrete blur, just over a yellowed piece of newsprint. I snatched it up.

The piece of paper was small — just a column wide, less than a dozen lines long. It had shrunk and grown brittle with age. I didn't remember having seen it before, but I knew, as I began to read, that even if I had noticed it among the rubbish in the base of the envelope, it would have held no interest for me. Nor, for that matter, would it have meant anything to my dad.

Now, it meant everything.

```
Pfc. Emilio James Lam, son of Josefa Lam and
the late David Lam, of Waianae, has been
killed in action in Korea, the Defense
Department notified his mother Monday by
telegram. Pfc. Lam, aged 18, had sent a
```

letter to his mother dated June 21
indicating that his unit had shipped to
Korea and was participating in the Korean
fighting. Pfc. Lam was an only child and
recent high school graduate.

I flipped the clipping over. The back showed part of an advertisement. My sleep-deprived brain attempted to run the numbers. My father had been conceived in May of 1953, right around the time of Kalia's high school graduation. If this man... this *boy*, really... was the father of Kalia's baby, they could have been classmates. The clipping wasn't dated as to year, but its tone indicated that the Korean War was still going on. When exactly had it ended?

My breath caught. I couldn't be sure about the timing. But the scenario springing into my head did make sense. Kalia could have sent her high school sweetheart off to war, not realizing she was pregnant until after he had been drafted and had shipped out. Maybe not until after he had been killed. And her response had been to marry my grandfather.

Did Albin know?

I looked around the room. Kalia had gone.

"Emilio James Lam," I read out loud, softly. "My biological grandfather."

And he loved her. In my mind I saw again the wailing figure at Kalia's grave. I smiled sadly. He looked like an Emilio.

In an instant, my reverie was broken. At Kalia's *funeral?*

I stared again at the clipping. It wasn't possible. If the two were classmates, Emilio would have died nearly three years *before* Kalia.

So who the hell was the man crying at her grave?

I groaned out loud and dropped my forehead onto the

mattress.

"Kalia!" I said miserably. "Please! I need more! Why did you even take us to the cemetery?" I raised my head and looked around the room again. But she was definitely gone.

I picked up my phone.

It took Tara forever to answer. "Kali?" she said groggily.

Oops. What time was it in Cheyenne? I hadn't even thought about it.

Tara yawned. "My alarm doesn't even go off for, like, an hour. And for you it's the middle of the night..." Her voice cleared quickly. "What's up? Is something wrong?"

"Yes and no," I answered. "I'm sorry to wake you up. It's just that, well, Kylee's told you what's been going on with my grandmother appearing, right?"

"Yes," she answered. "At least up through the cemetery visit."

They were definitely keeping close tabs on me.

"I know what you're thinking," Tara said. "You're thinking we must have nothing better to do here at the home base than to live your adventures vicariously. Well, you're right. It's been boring as dirt since you left. Kylee and I can't even think of enough things to argue about."

I grinned. "That's awful. Maybe I could text you a list of suggestions."

"That would be great," she deadpanned. "Now, enough about us. Tell me why you called."

"You have something to write with?"

I gave Tara the whole story, reading the newspaper clipping aloud.

"The Korean War ended in July of 1953," she said offhandedly, as if it was a fact anyone with half a brain should know. So your theory makes sense. Of course, the

clipping could have come from an earlier year in the war
— but only if Emilio isn't your grandfather, in which case,
why would Kalia insist you see it?"

"It's him," I said, feeling sure of it now, even with all
of the outstanding questions. "Tara—"

"Wait a minute," she interrupted. "I'm checking
something."

I heard a keyboard clicking in the background. "It fits,
Kali," she declared. "The names: Josefa and Emilio.
They're most likely Spanish or Portuguese. And there are a
lot of Portuguese people in Hawaii. That would explain
your Southern European roots. Emilio's father could have
been a mix of Asian and native Hawaiian. It fits your
profile almost... well, perfectly."

I rubbed my free hand over my face. "That's
fabulous," I said with frustration. "But it still doesn't tell
me what Kalia wants, and what kind of danger is looming
over my dad. Ghosts don't appear just to clear up
paternity suits, you know? And even if they did, what good
would it do to tell my dad now that he isn't who he thinks
he is? His biological father is dead. His grandmother
Josefa is bound to be dead. And it says Emilio had no
brothers or sisters. We don't even know under what
circumstances Albin married Kalia — and I'm telling you,
if there was any deception involved, it would drive my dad
out of his tree. It would destroy his image of his mother."
Just like it did with me. I bit my lip. "I can't do that to him."

"Of course not," Tara agreed. "And I'm sure that's not
what Kalia wants either — at least, not by itself. There's
more we haven't figured out yet."

I said nothing for a moment. I was too discouraged.

"Kali," Tara said gently. "Is your dad still... you know...
ignoring what's going on with you?"

"Oh, yeah." I sighed. "Zane brought it up once in

casual conversation and the Colonel nearly passed out on the floor. My mother keeps saying he'll be okay with it in time, but I'm not so sure."

"It's hard for him," she said thoughtfully. "Believe me, I get what he's going through. But it's going to be tough on all of you if whatever disaster Kalia is trying to avoid can only be avoided with his participation."

I drew in a ragged breath. "I hadn't even thought about that."

My forehead banged on the mattress again.

"Listen, Kal," Tara said after a moment. "You and Zane just keep doing what you're doing — waiting for more messages from Kalia. I'm going to take these names and research the bejesus out of them. There are genealogy sites that can give you access to military records and a bunch of other public databases that a regular internet search won't pull up. Maybe I can find something interesting. Or helpful. Hopefully both."

I smiled into my sheets. "That would be great, Tara. Thanks."

"Don't thank me," she said morosely. "I'm stuck at home on demon watch all day. What else am I going to do, analyze dryer lint?"

My swimsuit was still clammy. Probably because instead of hanging it up yesterday, I had wadded it into a ball and thrown it into a corner of my room. I hadn't thought I would need it again. But despite my pleas over the phone this morning, Zane was still refusing to let me quit the swimming lessons. At least for now. I refused to take his resolution about the whole kissing thing seriously — he was a guy, after all. And since I would not, in fact, ever learn to swim, he would have to break down sometime.

Still, it was annoying.

Instead of putting the suit on, I stretched it out and threw it in my beach bag. Maybe I could talk him into going surfing first.

I changed from my work clothes into a bright colored tank top and shorts and headed back downstairs to watch out the front window for Zane. My mother was taking her lunch break in the kitchen. "I finished organizing all the yard tools and stuff," I told her. "They fit in the shed okay. But there's nowhere in the storage room to set up Dad's workbench. I think we need another shed."

My mother sighed. "I know. We'll look for one over the weekend." She turned to me with a serious expression. "Did you sleep okay last night?"

I tensed. "Not great. It was pretty hot upstairs. Why?"

She looked uncomfortable. "I could hear you talking up there again. Do you want to tell me to whom?"

"Not really, Mom," I answered. "At least not yet." It occurred to me, suddenly, that she might be more worried about a certain flesh-and-blood visitor than she was about the shadows. Which would be a normal motherly reaction, I suppose. Little did she know that her obviously lovesick seventeen-year-old daughter had found the one and only eighteen-year-old guy on the planet who absolutely refused to kiss his own girlfriend. "Like I said," I repeated, "it's nobody living."

"All right," she replied. "But you can tell me, you know, if you want to."

I smiled. "I know. Thanks."

My mother sighed again. "Your father had a rough night."

My pulse sped up all over again. I hadn't seen my dad this morning; he had left early, before I got up. "Oh? How so? Too hot?"

She shook her head. "No, the heat doesn't bother him. He was having... strange dreams."

"Strange dreams?" I repeated faintly.

"Yes," she replied. "Ever since we moved here, really. But last night was the worst. It really seemed to bother him, and he's not usually bothered by such things. Usually he gets up and shrugs it off. But this time..." She paused and looked at me. "He says that he keeps dreaming about his mother. And that she's upset about something."

I swallowed hard. Perhaps Kalia had been busier than we'd given her credit for. "What is he dreaming, exactly?"

"Disconnected, vague things," she answered. "Brief scenes where she's trying to lead him somewhere. But he isn't able to follow her." She stopped and sighed. "Ordinarily, I wouldn't think it meant anything. I would figure he was just thinking about her more because we're in Hawaii. But... you remember my friend Julie, from Maine? The hospice nurse?"

I nodded.

"She used to tell me how her patients would sometimes claim to see family members who had passed on. And it was—" her voice faltered a little. She steadied it and continued. "It almost always happened just before they died."

She turned to me, her soft gray eyes boring into mine. "*Not* that that's what happening here — I don't think this is the same thing. Your father is only dreaming — not seeing her while he's awake. But still, it seems very disturbing to him, and... I just don't know what it means. I don't want to scare you and I wouldn't mention it at all except... given your gift, I wondered if you had... noticed anything unusual."

Oh my. For a very long moment I stood looking back at her, my mouth opening and closing like a fish. I had no idea where to begin. But I had to begin somewhere. She knew I knew something.

Cleansing breath.

"Kalia is trying to send us some sort of message," I said carefully. "But I don't know what. Zane has seen her ghost — here in the house, and around the city. He can see her more clearly because he nearly died himself. I can't see her, but I can sense when she's around."

"Last night?" my mom asked quickly.

I nodded. "I was talking to her. But she can't talk to us — not in words. We're trying to piece together her message in other ways, and we're getting close, but we're not there yet."

"Is your father in danger?" she demanded, her voice rising.

"Not immediately, we don't think, no," I answered, trying to soothe her. I heard a car door slam. Zane was out front.

"You have to tell me everything," she insisted.

I glanced out the window again and was surprised to see Zane stop in his tracks halfway down the walk. He stared into the air for a moment, then made for the door in double time.

"He... saw her again just now," I announced, rushing to answer it. "Zane, what did—"

"Are you ready to go?" he asked anxiously. "She wants to lead us somewhere in the car. And she means *now.*"

I cast a glance back at my mom, who had gone completely pale. Zane hadn't realized she could overhear, but of course it hardly mattered now.

"We need to go," I told her. "But please don't worry.

We'll tell you the whole story as soon as we know it. We're going to figure it out... *today*. And Dad will be fine."

I looked back at her stricken face.

"I promise."

chapter 20

Zane wasn't speeding. In the "safe driver" category, my parents couldn't have asked for better. But I could tell from every facet of his body language that he was in a hurry.

"Left here," he said mechanically, turning. The muscles of his arms were tight with tension, and his mouth was set into a grim line.

"Is there something you're not telling me?" I asked.

He shook his head. "No. It's just... a feeling. You can't see her face, Kali. Every time I've seen her, she's looked upset. But at your house just now... Well, she seemed almost to be losing hope."

"But that doesn't make sense!" I argued, frustrated. "We're making progress, we're closer than ever! I even know his name, now. What else can she want?"

"Maybe it's not about what's happening with us," Zane suggested. "Maybe something else is happening, with *somebody* else, and Kalia feels like she's running out of time. This exit."

I looked at where we were, and my stomach flip-flopped. "Not the base!" I exclaimed. *Oh please, anywhere but there!* How could I possibly relive the bombing of Pearl Harbor today? Even with Zane beside me, the grief and terror of battle, the sum total of every single person's fears and agony and pain —

"No," Zane interrupted, turning again. "Not the base. We're going the other way."

I sighed with relief. I would do whatever I had to do to see this through, but it would be nice to be sane at the end of it. "Where are we going then?" I asked.

He didn't answer for two more turns. Then he took a deep breath and pulled off. "Moanalua Gardens," he answered.

We were in the lot of a public park. A small brown building ahead sported a sign for an upcoming hula festival. Beyond the building lay an inviting expanse of level green lawn and giant monkey pod trees. "Why here, I wonder?" I asked, as we stepped out of the car.

Zane looked around. "It's an old park. If it was here in the fifties, your grandparents might have come here... for a picnic or something. It's not that far from the base."

We walked out on the lawn, and all at once, I felt like smiling. Shadows were everywhere. And in this place, almost all of them were happy. "It's definitely been here since the fifties," I said confidently, catching sight of many shadows in traditional Hawaiian dress along with several men wearing fedoras and women wearing long dresses with corsets. There seemed to be shadows from every era — mostly playing, picnicking, and celebrating — and their emotions were so predominantly positive that I was able to leave my blind open. "Let's just walk around," I suggested, doing so. "I'll look for them."

A little stream flowed through the gardens, and I began walking toward it. If I was wasting time, Kalia could redirect me, but as emotional moments in beautiful places went, there was nothing like a picnic lunch along a stream. Shadows — as well as several other living people — milled about in every direction, and my eyes hunted through them for a familiar face. It was noisy, if I cared to listen. The shadows generally made sounds, and I had experienced entire conversations more than once. But unlike their feelings, which seemed to radiate from their bodies whether I liked it or not, the sounds they made didn't usually rattle my eardrums unless I made some effort to pay attention — perhaps because they were not real sounds at all, in the physical sense. However it happened, I was glad of it. The world had enough noise created by the living.

I was so blissfully absorbed in the feelings of excited children and canoodling lovers that when I spotted my grandfather, I had almost forgotten what I was looking for. But the sight of him, once again strikingly handsome in his officer's uniform, brought me quickly back to reality. "Here!" I called to Zane.

I hurried toward the image of Albin, who was leaning forward with one knee perched up on something invisible to me — most likely a bench or the seat of a picnic table. But when I saw the woman sitting beside him, I stopped cold.

It was Kalia. The young, vibrant, three-dimensional Kalia that my own eyes had never seen. She was stunning. Her glossy back hair hung loose over her shoulders, framing both a face and figure fit for Hollywood. Her cheekbones were high, her small nose pert, her mouth as perfectly formed as something from a lipstick commercial. Her large dark eyes were framed by thick, black lashes, and as they peered up at my grandfather, I could see in their considerable depths a woman who was every bit as intelligent as she was beautiful.

Unfortunately, she was also miserable.

I stepped closer.

"I *have* thought about it Albin," Kalia proclaimed, her voice strained and shaky. "I've thought of nothing else all day. But I *can't.*"

"Why not?" my grandfather countered. He was tense, earnest, nearly bursting with a volatile combination of hope and fear.

"Because it wouldn't be fair to you!" Kalia insisted.

"Is it fair to you that Emilio is dead?" Albin fired back. But then, seeming upset with himself, he gentled his voice. "Life isn't fair, Kalia. None of it. And I appreciate you worrying about what's fair to me. But you're wrong if you think I'm sacrificing a thing. I love you. I've loved you since the first time I saw you. I think you know that."

Kalia stood up. "I'm sorry, but I don't love you, Albin." She gulped in a breath, her eyes tearing. "You know I'm terribly fond of you. You're the sweetest, kindest, most charming, most... *selfless* man I've ever known." She swallowed painfully. "Including Emilio. That's why you deserve better than me. You deserve to be loved!"

Albin was close to panic now. "Your mother isn't well, Kalia," he said steadily, concealing his angst. "*His* mother won't even acknowledge the engagement—"

Kalia interrupted him. "It wouldn't matter if she did, now. She hates me; I wouldn't let her near this baby!"

"All the more reason to think about how you're going to raise it," he insisted. "You're going to need help." He took hold of her shoulders, gently, and sat her down again next to him. "Listen to me. However I may feel, I'll always be your friend. If you don't want to marry me, I'll still help you all I can. I'm not rich, but I could make things a little easier for you."

Kalia started to speak, but he silenced her with a finger to her lips. His face was very close to hers. He meant every word that he had just said. Still, his heart pounded with hope. "But if you will marry me, I promise I'll do everything in my power to make you happy. I'll raise the baby as my own. If we marry soon, no one outside your friends and family will even think to question it. I would love the child, truly. And maybe someday, you'll feel differently about me. But I'll never pressure you. I swear it."

Kalia was caving. I could feel her heart breaking. And I knew, in that moment, that although her feelings toward him were not romantic, a part of her already did love him. She might not believe she could ever be happy; but she did want him to be.

"I *want* you to be my wife, Kalia," Albin finished. "And there's nothing sacrificial about that. I'm not selfless. Right now I feel pretty damned self-serving, considering the fix you're in. But I'm asking you anyway. Please. *Marry me.*"

Kalia's eyes overflowed with tears. Her chest heaved. She made one tiny, affirmative nod of her chin. Albin lurched forward and folded her into his arms.

The shadows disappeared.

I stood still, staring at nothing, for a long time. I knew that Zane was standing beside me, and I wanted to take his hand. But I didn't. I felt too rotten to deserve it.

"I was wrong," I said finally, still not moving. "I was so wrong."

Zane took my hand anyway. Warm comfort floated up my arm. "You want to go sit down somewhere?" he asked.

I let him lead me back towards the car, where we settled on a bench under a monkey pod tree. I released his hand and pulled my blind back down. I didn't deserve other people's happy feelings, either.

"Albin knew everything," I explained. "He and Kalia might have met at Christmas, but they weren't dating — they were just friends. Albin fell in love with her knowing she was with somebody else. But while she was working at the base, they must have gotten pretty close, because after Emilio died, she told Albin she was pregnant."

"I see," Zane said, brushing back the lock of curls I had allowed to fall in my face.

"She and Emilio were engaged when he left," I continued. "But I guess he couldn't afford a ring, because after he died, his mother refused to acknowledge it ever happened. Apparently she didn't like Kalia, or didn't approve of her, or something. I'm not sure if Kalia ever told her about the baby. But I'm guessing she didn't."

Zane considered a moment. "Hard to see why she would, if she was marrying Albin. Things were different back then. Illegitimacy was a big deal. If Kalia hadn't married, both she and the baby would have been treated like criminals."

I nodded, thinking about the bleakness of Kalia's situation. Supporting a child as a teenaged war widow would have been hard enough, but... as an unmarried mother? Zane was right. In the fifties, she'd have trouble even finding work. And what other options did she have? Illegal abortion? A forever-closed adoption where she would never know what happened to the baby — a living, breathing part of the man she had loved and lost?

It was unimaginable.

Kalia had done the best she could. I couldn't know how she had felt later about her decision, but I did know this. She had made both Albin and her child very, very happy.

"Stop it, Kali," Zane said firmly.

"Stop what?"

"Beating yourself up for having the wrong idea about Kalia."

I didn't bother asking him how he knew what I was thinking. Miserable guilt had to be written all over my face. "I should have given her the benefit of the doubt," I said roughly. "Why didn't I? Why was I so quick to jump to the worst possible explanation?"

He brushed my hair back over my shoulder again.

"Because you knew your grandfather, and you loved him. You never knew Kalia."

"*You* didn't assume the worst of her," I pointed out.

"I never knew either one of them," he replied. "I could be objective. You couldn't. You loved your grandfather very much — it's only natural that your loyal, compassionate heart would leap to what you saw as his defense. Now cut it out."

I looked up at him. "I still feel rotten."

He leaned in a little. "Well, to quote you, I believe the phrase was: *get over it.*"

I smiled at him. In a perfect world, he would kiss me.

Instead, he let out a muffled growl and sprang up from the bench. "We've got to get you back in the water, Kali. *Soon.*"

My smile broadened. He was weakening already. "We can't do a swimming lesson now," I reminded him. "We have to keep watching for more clues from Kalia. I understand how everything came to happen as it did back then, but I still don't understand what kind of danger my dad is in. All we really know is that it has *something* to do with the mystery man at her funeral."

A look of something close to pessimism crossed Zane's eyes, and the sight of it chilled me. He was never pessimistic. "I'll keep my eyes open," he agreed. "But... I'm afraid Kalia may be getting too weak to keep this up. The fact is, I was totally winging those last two turns. She did appear, but she was so faint and blurry I couldn't tell which way she was pointing. When I saw the gardens ahead, I just turned in on a hunch."

"Oh no!" I exclaimed. "But she seemed in such a hurry to have us finish this!"

"She definitely wants us to finish this. Maybe you could call Kylee for advice again? On how to help her get stronger or something? I don't want to scare you, but... You didn't see her face, the look in her eyes... I really think we're running out of time."

I studied him for a second. Then I dug frantically into my bag and pulled out my phone. "I missed a call from Tara!" I cried. "Why didn't I hear it?"

I called her back, and she answered on the first ring.

"Thank goodness," she said without greeting. "Kali, are you sitting down?"

My heart beat faster. "Yes."

"Is Zane there with you?"

"Yeah, I'll put him on speaker." I punched the button, and Zane sat down on the bench beside me.

Tara inhaled, loudly and slowly. "Okay, kids. Brace yourselves. Nobody's driving, right?"

"No!" I replied impatiently. "Tara, just tell us! What is it?"

"I found out quite a bit more than I expected to about Emilio Lam," she began. "The clipping you found was indeed from 1953, from the *Honolulu Star-Bulletin*. I found military records that confirmed everything in it. Except that wasn't the whole story." She cleared her throat. "Are you sure you're sitting down?"

"Tara!" I pleaded.

Zane's arm slipped comfortingly around my shoulders.

"The telegram the army sent to Emilio's mother was in error," Tara continued. "He was reported killed in action, but in fact he was taken prisoner. He was captured in Korea, but unlike most of the other POWs, he wasn't released after the armistice was signed. Somehow, he ended up in China. He was held in a work camp there for over two years."

"Oh my God. How terrible," I whispered.

"I'm sure it was," Tara agreed. "But eventually he did

manage to escape, with some help from the locals. He was part Chinese, on his father's side, and he knew a little of the language. What he didn't know, he must have learned quickly. It took him most of another year, but eventually he made his way to South Korea, and then back to Hawaii."

Zane's eyes met mine. I knew we were thinking the same thing.

"The man at her grave," I said quietly. "It *was* Emilio."

I remembered the feelings surrounding the prostrate shadow, and his grief washed through me all over again. I had been so stupid, assuming both men were at her funeral. How many other times had I seen shadows exist simultaneously when I knew they were separated by time, and in fact, merely overlapped? My grandfather hadn't looked at the other man with indifference — he hadn't looked at him at all! By the time Emilio had made his way back to Hawaii, Albin and my father were already on the mainland, in Minnesota.

"Emilio's return was big news in Hawaii," Tara continued. "But I haven't found any evidence that his story went national. He wasn't the only POW to find his way back as the years went on, and people's sources of news were more limited." She paused a moment. "Kali, I don't know whether your grandfather kept up contact with anyone in Hawaii after he left, or if he even knew who Emilio was, but unless some third party took it upon themselves to alert him, I think it's highly unlikely he ever knew that Emilio came back from Korea alive."

My heart pounded in my chest. "No. I don't think he did." I would like to think that my grandfather wouldn't intentionally keep a man from his biological son, and from now on, I intended to think the best of everyone.

The memory of Emilio's pain at the cemetery gnawed

at my insides, and I was grateful for the warmth of Zane's arm around me. "Emilio would have come home to find out not only that Kalia was dead and gone," I said sadly, "but that right after he was reported killed, she had married another man. And had a child."

Did Emilio know why she had married so soon? That the baby was his?

"Kali," Tara said, anticipating my next question, "I've studied the timeline... when Emilio would have been in basic training and when he shipped out. You do *not* want to know how much time I spent looking into pregnancy diagnosis in 1953 and length of gestation related to infant body weight. But here's my best guess. Kalia might have worried that she was pregnant when she was still in touch with Emilio. But it's highly unlikely she was sure of the fact before his unit hit the ground in Korea. Odds are, even if she did write him with the news, he was captured before it reached him."

"But," Tara continued, "when he got back to Hawaii, there's every chance he would have found out from family or mutual friends that Kalia had married somebody else and had a baby."

Loving wife and mother. "Her gravestone said that much," I replied. "But that doesn't mean he ever knew the whole truth, does it? Even if he had friends who knew exactly when Kalia gave birth, I can't see them falling all over themselves to give him that information three years later when Kalia was dead and the baby was gone. At that point, what chance could he possibly have of ever getting the baby back?"

"Zero," Tara answered. "They didn't have DNA paternity testing back then. If Albin was married to Kalia and his name was on the birth certificate, the baby was legally his son, period. So you're right — it's hard to imagine any of Emilio's family or friends wanting to open that can of worms, particularly when they didn't know for sure. Which no one could have, unless Kalia told them herself. Do you think she told Emilio's mother?"

I remembered the biting hurt in Kalia's eyes as she spoke of Josefa Lam. "I seriously doubt it," I answered.

The more I thought about Emilio's situation, the more it made my heart ache. Either he suspected he had a son but had no hope of ever getting him back, or he believed that the girl he was engaged to had callously replaced him the minute she found out he was dead. Either way, both his grief, and his anger, could only be expected.

I fought back my own sadness. "Tara, whatever happened to Emilio? Did he ever marry?"

"He did," she answered, but with a new and funny note to her voice. "But not until he was twenty-eight. He married a war widow a little older than he was. She had a school-age son, and Emilio adopted him."

At last, I found myself able to smile again. "That's... really good to hear. He deserved to have a happy life."

I felt Zane's arm tighten around my shoulders. I looked at him, wondering why, but Tara's next words stopped me.

"Kali," she said heavily. "You're using the wrong tense. As far as I've been able to tell, Emilio James Lam is still alive. And he's living right there on Oahu."

chapter 21

My body felt stiff with tension as Zane drove us through a seemingly endless stretch of stoplights. The west side of Oahu, I was learning, had a character all its own. While the North Shore was both countrified and touristy, and the "town" of Honolulu was a sprawling jumble of high-rise apartments and multi-million dollar beachside estates, the area where Kalia and Emilio had grown up was clearly "where the regular people lived." It was to here that Emilio had returned after the war and, according to Tara, eventually opened up an auto repair shop. She had given us an address, which appeared to be an apartment building close to his former business on the main highway through Waianae. Every stoplight brought us closer. Every second seemed an hour.

"You haven't seen her again, have you?" I asked Zane.

He shook his head. "Not since before we got to the park. I'm glad Tara's info came in time to spare Kalia any more effort right now. She seemed really weak."

Neither of us understood her urgency. Emilio had lived on the island all this time and was now in his late seventies... it was hard to see how his quiet, law-abiding existence could create any kind of emergency situation for my father. But Kalia had been adamant.

And this time, I intended to trust her.

"I have no idea what I'll even say to him," I worried out loud. "I refuse to believe that *he's* the danger to my dad. You think maybe Kalia is leading us to Emilio because he's the only one who can help?"

"Maybe," Zane said thoughtfully. "Whatever her plan

was, we're on our own now. You're just going to have to trust your instincts and wing it. You can do it." The car turned off the main highway. "Here's the street. We're almost there."

I looked up the block. There was only one apartment building in sight. It was a modest, flat-roofed two-story, with an outdoor walkway along the second floor. As we drew closer, I could read the apartment numbers. "204," I said aloud as Zane pulled into a visitor's spot. "That's his door right up there."

We got out of the car, and Zane took my hand again. With his radiating warmth boosting my confidence, I steeled myself, and we mounted the stairs. I could do this. So what if I had no idea *what* I was going to do?

We reached the door. The paint was peeling here and there, and the iron railing on the veranda was rusty. But overall the building seemed reasonably well kept, and many of the neighbors had cheered up their section of the walkway with potted bushes and hanging baskets of flowers. Zane raised a hand and knocked sharply.

There was no answer.

After another moment, Zane knocked again. I cocked my ear to the door, but heard no movement inside. *Seriously?* I thought in disbelief. *No,* he had to be here. I raised a hand and knocked myself. "Mr. Lam?" I called, my voice distressed. "Emilio? Are you home? Please, if you're here, answer the door. It's important!"

At last, I thought I heard someone stir. But the sound wasn't coming from 204. After a brief moment, the door to the next apartment creaked open, and a tiny Asian woman in her sixties stepped out onto the landing and studied us critically. "What do you want with Emilio?" she asked brusquely.

I thought fast. "We've just come to talk to him about a

family matter. My name is Kali Thompson. I'm... a relative."

The woman's eyes widened. Her face gentled a bit, but she didn't smile. "I'm Tessa," she replied. "Emilio isn't here. He's in the hospital. Did you get a call from a social worker or something?"

Zane and I exchanged a glance. *Or something.*

"No," I answered, as calmly as I could manage. "We didn't know he was in the hospital. What... why is he there?"

Her eyes studied me another moment before she answered. Tessa was clearly a woman who took pride in looking out for her neighbors, and I got the feeling she did not trust easily. But she was perceptive enough to know that my concern was genuine.

"You know about his son?" she asked.

My heart skipped a beat, but I soon remembered what Tara had told us. Tessa wasn't talking about my dad. "The son he adopted?" I asked tentatively.

Her brow furrowed. "I don't know if he was adopted or not. All I know is he meant the world to Emilio. Sammy and him, they built up the garage together. Emilio sold it to him outright a few years ago, but there's no making that man retire. He was up there every day just the same." She sighed heavily. "I guess you haven't heard, then. Sammy's dead. Week ago today he up and died of a heart attack. No warning. Nothing. He was only 61. Seemed fit as anybody."

Zane's hand tightened around mine. *No,* I thought miserably. *Poor Emilio.* After everything he had been through... it was too much.

"It tore Emilio apart," Tessa continued, her eyes hard. "Ripped his heart right out of his body, it did. His wife's been gone for years now, but he never thought he'd lose his child. Who does? And happening when it did... he had a cousin, you know, in Hilo. No surprise about her dying — she was eighty-nine, after all — but still, two deaths so close. She and Sammy were the last family he had."

She looked up at me questioningly. "At least that's what he said. Over and over again, he said it. 'Tessa,' he wailed, 'There's nobody left. They're all dead. Why am I still here? Why me?'" She shook her head. "He's always been such a strong man, but this was such a blow, and such a shock... he was in a horrible state. I've never seen him like that. I've never seen anybody like that. He started talking gibberish — things I didn't understand. About the war, and the work camp — he was a POW, you know. He was on and on about how he had cheated death once, and now it was claiming its revenge by taking Sammy away from him."

She clenched her jaws tightly a moment, then fixed her gaze back on me. "So why is it he never mentioned you?"

"I don't think he knows," I explained. "I only just found out myself."

Her thin eyebrows rose. "You should tell him, then," she ordered. "If he's still alive."

My knees weakened, but Zane's firm grip steadied me. "What happened?" I begged. "Why is he in the hospital?"

Tessa's eyes remained hard, but I could see a glint of moisture beneath them. "Sammy's funeral was three days ago. Emilio broke down in the middle of it. My husband and I brought him home, blubbering like a baby. Couple hours later we heard a thud next door. Like he'd fallen. He wouldn't answer us and wouldn't open up and finally I called the police. He was passed out cold — took a whole bottle of headache medicine. Over the counter, you know, but... It was bad. Ambulance got rerouted, took him to Queens. I keep calling, but they won't tell me a damn thing beyond that. Privacy rules, you know, and I'm not family." She shook her head. "He was still there when I called this morning. But that's all they'll tell me. That's all I know."

"Is Queens the big hospital across from the Punchbowl?" Zane asked, speaking for the first time and startling us both.

Tessa nodded. "That's the one."

"We'll go see him right now then," he announced, squeezing my hand.

Right now.

I got his drift. After giving a heartfelt thanks to Tessa, we got back into Zane's car, drove out of the lot, and immediately began fighting all the same stoplights — this time in the opposite direction. There was no alternative. There was only one main road, and we were on it. And the hospital, unfortunately, was all the way on the other side of Honolulu.

"Three days ago," I echoed dully as we stared at yet another red light. The ocean was off to our right somewhere, but a rise of earth blocked my view. If it weren't for the picturesque volcanic peaks to my left, I could be in downtown Cheyenne fighting the traffic during Frontier Days. My carefree hours with Zane on the beach seemed suddenly far away. "Three days ago was when Kalia first appeared."

"I know," Zane said. "I thought of that, too."

"My dad isn't in danger at all, is he? He never was. All along it's been Emilio. It's his life she's been trying to save."

Zane nodded, his gaze focused on the traffic — and also, I was sure, on the lookout for any more surprise visits from Kalia.

"I wonder if she feels like it's her fault," I said quietly.

"Like what's her fault?"

"That Emilio and my dad are now living within minutes of each other, and neither has any idea that they're father and son. She must feel partly responsible for that, even if she made the best decisions she could at the time. It isn't right that neither of them should know. At least not anymore. It needs to be fixed."

Zane smiled at me. "I think Kalia would agree with you. I think that's why she reached out to you in the first place."

And I almost failed her. I caught myself pushing my feet against the dash. We were moving at a snail's pace. It was crazy-making. "I'm sure she's right that finding out about my dad could help Emilio. But what is finding out about Emilio going to do to my dad?" I tensed even more. "How can I even bring up the subject when he won't talk about *anything* supernatural?"

"You forget," Zane said calmly, "That Kalia has been working on that, too. I don't know how ghosts in dreams work, but whatever you tell him, I don't think it's going to come as a complete shock. He'll believe you, Kali. And he'll come to terms with the truth — however you found out. It will be easier for him now that we understand the circumstances: the fact that there was no deception. It was just three people doing the best they could in a very difficult situation."

I was silent a moment, thinking about how, aside from the forgotten scrap of newsprint, all traces of Emilio Lam were absent from Kalia's memory box. I assumed that she herself had torn out the page in her yearbook — the page her boyfriend had no doubt claimed as his own. I had also assumed that if she were actually in love with someone else, she would have saved letters to remember him by. But I had been thinking about the box all wrong.

The mementos I saw were not what Kalia had collected for herself. She would have kept her yearbook and any letters Emilio had sent, certainly a last love note sent from Korea. She had no reason to hide her past from the man she married, and he had no reason to be threatened by it. But my dad was another matter.

After Kalia died, it would have been my grandfather who took on the painful task of going through her things and deciding what personal mementos should be kept for her son. It wasn't Kalia's box at all — it was baby Mitchell's. And with both Emilio and Kalia gone, my grandfather had every reason to conceal the truth from the boy he was determined to raise as his own. Of course he would not have kept old love letters, and of course he would remove the troublesome page from her yearbook. He would have disposed of the obituary as well if he had noticed it, which I was sure he did not. Albin honestly believed that my father would be happier if the past remained in the past.

And he probably was. Then.

Now, things were different.

"Thank goodness," I gushed as we reached the end of the stoplights and pulled back onto the freeway. I turned to Zane. "What would I do, by the way, without your driving me all over this rock? I owe you at least two tanks of gas. And a bunch of rides back and forth to the North Shore — as soon as my parents get a second car, anyway." I envisioned what he would be doing now if I were still back in Cheyenne, and I felt terrible. He would be out on the water surfing, that's what. Not dodging crazy drivers in rush hour on the H1. "I'm sorry about all this," I apologized, feeling like a drag. "You should be out at Backyards today."

His green eyes twinkled at me. "Nah. The swell

dropped to nothing overnight. Today's worthless. But even if it wasn't, I'd never pass up the chance to help a beautiful damsel in distress — makes for too good an ego boost."

I smiled sadly back at him. "Kalia was beautiful, wasn't she? I almost couldn't believe it when I saw her in the gardens. I'll bet Emilio and Albin weren't the only two men to fall in love with her."

"I wasn't talking about Kalia."

I blinked at him. "Oh."

He chuckled. "You'd better watch that self-confidence thing."

"I am self-confident!" I insisted. "But I'm *not* beautiful. You kept calling me that before, too, and I didn't believe you then, either."

He looked at me sideways. "Are you questioning my taste?"

"Zane!" I protested with a laugh. "I'm not beautiful. I'm flat-chested and I have a big nose. Let's be real, here."

"I am being real. You said Kalia was beautiful."

"She was!"

"Her ears stuck out a bit, and her front teeth were crooked."

I knew he was toying with me, but I took the bait anyway. "She wasn't perfect, but she was still beautiful!"

He smirked in triumph. "And so are you. Now stop arguing and help me look for signs to Queens Hospital."

Despite Zane's efforts to keep my spirits up, the remainder of the journey was as excruciatingly slow as its start, and my anxiety climbed. When at last we reached the hospital and hustled inside, the mere sight of its information desk set my heart to pounding. *Had I gotten here in time? Would he still be alive?* I snatched Zane's hand in a death grip. "Sorry," I squeaked, realizing what I was doing and loosening my hold a bit. "Bad flashback from Nebraska."

He turned to me quizzically, but then his eyes softened with understanding. He reached an arm around my shoulders and hugged me to him, dropping an affectionate, impulsive kiss on the side of my head, through my hair. Though his lips never touched my skin, I could feel a searing heat, and I turned to him with surprise. "You kissed me."

"Oh, crap!" he exclaimed, looking horrified. "I forgot. I mean *no,* I didn't. That wasn't a real kiss!"

I smirked. "If you say so." His resolution was toast.

"Can I help you?" The question from the hospital volunteer brought me quickly back to reality. But I felt stronger, now. Zane was right. I could do this.

I stepped up to the desk. "We're here to see Emilio Lam," I said with authority. "He's my grandfather."

chapter 22

We were standing outside the door to Emilio's room when a nurse stopped us. She was a small, middle-aged woman with an interesting mix of facial features which could have been inherited from any combination of Asian, European, or Polynesian ancestors. Every time I saw a face like hers, I felt a little more at home in the islands. Her flashing dark eyes, however, were less than welcoming. "Are you here to see Mr. Lam?" she asked sharply.

"We are," I answered, bracing myself for battle.

"What's your relationship to him? Are you a relative?" she demanded.

"I am," I said, my tone just as clipped.

To my surprise, the nurse responded with relief. "Well, that's good. Maybe you can get through to him. Our hands are tied, you know. When a patient refuses treatment, there's not a damn thing we can do — not as long as they're of sound mind, which he obviously is. We've had the chaplain and social services both in to see him, but he's having none of it. I'm glad they were able to locate you."

"He's... refusing treatment?" I repeated.

"From the minute he could talk," she said with frustration. "And a fine thanks that is to the people in the ER and the ICU that saved his ungrateful—" She broke off and cleared her throat. "Listen, Miss..."

"Kali Thompson," I supplied. "I'm his granddaughter."

Her lips twisted. "So, he has no family, huh?" She

shook her head. "Look, Miss Thompson, I don't mean to be disrespectful of your grandfather. I'm sure he's a fine man. But I've been through this before, which is why they assigned him to me. He's suffered a huge loss, and he's grieving. He's angry and he doesn't care what happens to him. *Now.* He will, in time... assuming he *gets* that time. But he's not *going* to get it unless he pulls himself together ASAP and consents to dialysis."

"Dialysis?" I croaked. The woman spoke quickly; I was having to work hard to take it in.

"That's right," she confirmed. "He's in acute kidney failure, brought on by an overdose of acetaminophen. Other than that, he's in great shape — better than a lot of men a decade younger, frankly. Odds are, his kidneys could heal just fine, but he's got to have dialysis while they're doing it. If he continues to refuse, he's going to die. Period. Simple as that. You understand?"

I let her words sink in a moment. Then I nodded. "How long..." I began uncertainly, "I mean, how soon would..."

"He could be dead by tomorrow," the nurse said without flinching, her dark eyes boring into mine. Then, without warning, her face softened. "That's why I'm glad you're here." She opened the door for us and stepped back. "Best of luck to you."

I gulped.

No pressure.

We stepped inside the room, and the nurse shut the door behind us. Zane squeezed my hand. "I think you should talk to him alone," he whispered. "But I'll be right here."

I nodded. I let go of his hand reluctantly and moved toward the still figure in the near bed. The figure in the far bed, an obese white man in his thirties, was watching something on a laptop with his earbuds in. Both men seemed oblivious to our presence.

Emilio's head was turned toward us on the pillow. But his eyes hadn't moved when we entered. They were fixed on some random point in space. On nothing. Unlike the patient in the other bed, he was attached to no tubes or wires. He just lay there, staring.

I studied his face. There could be no doubt that this was the same man I had watched in mourning at Kalia's grave. He was much older, of course, but time — if nothing else — had clearly been kind to him. The arm that lay above the blanket was still surprisingly well muscled. His skin might now be lined with age, but the healthy figure of the mature man nevertheless compared well to the gaunt, skeletal frame of the returning POW. Comparing the two, I had the fleeting thought that something about that process wasn't quite right, but I lost it when Emilio's eyes took a sudden dart towards me.

I hesitated only a second. Then I reached out and pulled up a chair, putting our faces level without his having to move. He looked tired. Dehydrated. Nauseous. Indifferent.

Ready to die.

"Mr. Lam," I began, my voice sounding girlish and shaky. I steadied it. He was looking away again. "My name is Kali Thompson. I just moved here a few days ago, from the mainland. I was named for my grandmother, Kalia Haluma. She grew up in Waianae."

His dark eyes shot back to mine. His pupils widened.

I smiled. "I'm afraid I don't look much like her. I take after the Greeks on my mother's side."

His lips moved, but his mouth was obviously bone dry, and no sound came out. He seemed surprised, then irritated at the difficulty. I looked around to see a water pitcher placed close by his head. A full cup of ice water stood ready, straw in place. Had he refused to drink, as well? I grabbed the cup and lowered it down to him, and he sucked greedily at the straw. After a moment he pulled his head back, and I replaced the cup on the stand.

"You have her eyes," he said hoarsely, smiling at me a little.

My heart warmed, and I smiled back. My eyes looked nothing whatsoever like hers, being a light gray to her dark brown, but I chose to accept the compliment anyway. "You were her high school sweetheart," I said softly.

His brown eyes twinkled. His lips formed a small, sad smile. "I was."

"I know the history," I explained, not wanting him to waste any words. "I know that you were reported as killed in action, and that Kalia married someone else. By the time you got back, she had died."

He nodded slightly. The depth of pain in his eyes was haunting.

Enough sadness! "I came to see you today because there's more to that whole story than you know. And I believe that Kalia would want you to know it."

His eyes became more alert. "I've seen her," he murmured.

My pulse quickened. Kalia's spirit had been busy. "Did she say anything to you?" I asked.

He shook his head slowly. "I could see her... but a long way off. She waved for me to go back."

"That's because she wants you to live," I said quickly. "And so do I."

I leaned in closer. "Mr. Lam, what I don't think you realize is that when you left for Korea, Kalia was already pregnant. With your child. When you were reported killed in action, Albin Thompson offered to marry her. He knew the baby was yours, but he agreed to raise it as his own."

Emilio's eyes widened to saucers. His breathing became rapid. I didn't want to stress him, but if I stopped now, I knew he would only stress himself by trying to ask me more questions.

"The baby was a boy," I continued, "and they named him Mitchell. He grew up as Mitchell Thompson, and he never had any idea that Albin wasn't his biological father."

Emilio's head lifted. He shifted his shoulders awkwardly, apparently struggling to make himself more upright. Zane slipped behind me and touched some controls on the bed, and the back of it began to rise slowly, propping Emilio up. I adjusted his pillows and offered him another sip of water, which he took without argument, despite the fact that the movement had made him look even more nauseous. He struggled to speak again.

"She... she told me the baby was Albin's... that it was born a year later..."

"Who told you that?" I asked.

"My..." his jaws clenched. "My mother."

"I'm sorry about that," I said, meaning it. "But I really don't think there's any doubt. My dad was born in February of 1954. And... well, I've had some DNA testing done. It's just general ancestry stuff, not specific to individual people, but Albin was Scandinavian, and I don't have any Scandinavian ancestry, according to the test."

Emilio looked at me for a long time, his eyes drinking me in with awe.

I smiled at him. "I'm your granddaughter."

His still-greenish face beamed. After another long moment, he cast a questioning glance toward Zane, who had moved back to the corner.

"This is my boyfriend, Zane," I introduced, nearly

tripping over the word, which had tumbled out before I could think. *Boyfriend*. I had never called him that out loud before. But he wasn't likely to argue about it now, was he?

"Hello, Mr. Lam," Zane greeted with a smile.

Emilio nodded back. Then he turned to me with a grin. "Well, I didn't think he was your brother."

I laughed. Zane's blond hair and green eyes would indeed be unlikely in my family tree. "No," I agreed. "I'm an only child."

I studied Emilio back, and noticed that his skin, though weathered, was a shade lighter than mine. Still, in the face, he looked Hawaiian. Or maybe I was seeing what I wanted to see. As proud as I had always been of having Hawaiian blood from Kalia, it had seemed more theoretical somehow. Now, looking into the face of a living ancestor who, biology aside, had lived nearly his whole life in Hawaii, I felt something different. I not only felt genetically Hawaiian, I felt... *connected*.

To a military brat who'd been moved around like a chess piece her entire life, that feeling was pretty darn cool.

Emilio's face slowly darkened.

"What is it?" I asked, alarmed.

"What happened to your father?" he asked tonelessly.

My mind raced. Had I said something that made him think — "Nothing happened to my father," I said quickly. "He's perfectly fine. He's a Colonel in the Air Force; he used to be a pilot. He's working at Hickam even as we speak."

Relief spread over Emilio's face, but only gradually, as if he were afraid to believe the best possible news. "He isn't here with you."

I tensed. This is where things got complicated. "No," I began. "But that's not because he doesn't care. It's because he still has no idea that you exist. I only just found out myself, because—" I paused a moment. I was sure that, at some point, I would tell Emilio the whole wildly unbelievable tale of my gift and Zane's and the amazing lengths to which his high school sweetheart had gone to keep him alive. But now was probably not the time. The man had enough to process. And despite his valiant psychological rally, it was obvious that he was still gravely ill.

"It started with a genetics project at school back on the mainland," I explained. "I knew something was wrong when I got the results, but I didn't want to break it to my dad until I figured out what happened. When we got to Oahu, Zane and I... got some extra help and were finally able to put it all together. We went to see you in Waianae and your neighbor sent us here."

"Tessa," he said in a whisper. "God bless her. I was..." He shook his head. "I've been out of my mind."

The door to the room swung open, and the nurse poked her head inside. She took one look at Emilio, and her dark eyes lit up like jack-o-lanterns. "Well, well!" she barked, her lips twitching to resist a smile.

"There you are," Emilio said, his voice as loud and clear as he could make it — which was, unfortunately, not very. "*Finally*. I've been waiting for those damn forms all day!" His eyes twinkled devilishly, and a sudden flash of resemblance to my father made my heart melt in my chest. "A man could *die* in here waiting for you people to get your paperwork straight! You going to get me the damn dialysis or not?"

The nurse's chest swelled and her gaze locked on his, their eyes engaged in a fierce, but clearly not bitter, battle. After a long moment, she let out her breath with a humph. "I'll *think* about it!" she fired back. Then she turned with a flounce and walked out.

Emilio's dry throat let out a sound that was supposed to be a chuckle. "That was fun."

Zane laughed out loud.

"Oh my," I said, offering Emilio another drink of water. "Looks like you and your son are going to get along just fine."

"My son," he repeated, his eyes sparkling. "My son... Mitchell."

chapter 23

I wanted, really badly, to jump back into Zane's car and escape with him to the North Shore, feeling free to do nothing but drink in the soul-restoring sights, sounds, and smells of the wild ocean... to relax and enjoy just being on the islands and being alive... to take a walk with him on the beach at sunset...

But none of *that* was happening. What was happening was that I was about to face the Colonel. And not only him, but his very unhappy soul mate, whom I had hoped to appease with periodic texts throughout the afternoon assuring that my dad was not in any danger. But that hadn't been good enough. My mother's last text had made clear that if I did not return home ASAP and start answering some questions, I was not going to live long enough to vote.

By the time Zane and I pulled up at my house, I was tight as a drum. The hospital had begun treatment on Emilio immediately after he signed the consent, and the smiling, excited man we left looked nothing like the resigned, hopeless one we had first met. But he was not yet out of the woods.

And my father still didn't have the faintest idea about his true paternity.

Nor did he believe in ghosts.

Nor did he like surprises.

"It's going to be fine, Kali," Zane encouraged as I sat unmoving, my hand hovering over my still-fastened seatbelt. "I know it's going to be a lot to take in, but the man flew fighter jets. He's tough."

I nodded mutely. Mitch Thompson was tough, all right. Tough in a lot of ways. Like refusing to believe things he didn't want to believe. Which was pretty much anything that couldn't be proven in a court of law.

What if he rejected Emilio altogether? Could the older man take yet another disappointment?

Had *I* unwittingly set him up for it?

"You want me to go in?"

My head whipped up. "Don't even *think* about leaving me to explain all this alone!"

Zane chuckled. "I wasn't planning on it. Just checking. But you really don't need me, you know. When it comes to handling delicate situations, you're a crack shot."

I had a sudden flashback to a similar statement he'd made as a wraith, after I had helped Matt get out of a potentially nasty scrape with a school rival. He wouldn't remember that. But had it left some impression?

"All I ever do is cut through the nonsense and tell it straight," I insisted.

He unbuckled my seatbelt for me. "Then let's go do that."

Five minutes later, I was facing both my parents across the round metal picnic table on our deck. My mother had grilled burgers, but nobody was eating. The neighbor's children were playing a noisy game in their backyard and ours. Birds chattered in the trees; a fruit fly landed on my dish of banana and pineapple slices. I was trying to decide the best place to begin when my father made his announcement.

"Look here, Kali," he began. "I don't understand a thing your mother's been trying to tell me about where you've been all day, or why it's got her so upset. But I do want you to know that I... uh... I believe that these things you're sensing actually exist. Not your imagination, I mean, but a real physical phenomenon. No reason to think they aren't... just because technology doesn't have the right tools to measure such things yet." He looked at my mother. "You know, two hundred years ago, people would have thought electromagnetic energy sounded pretty fishy, too."

My mouth dropped open. I couldn't believe such words were coming out of his mouth. I also couldn't believe how familiar they sounded. "Wait," I rasped, "What made you... have you been—"

He interrupted me. "Got a call from your friend Tara this afternoon. At my desk on the base, no less. Sharp girl. Always knew she was. Said she had problems with all this business too, at first, but then she started looking at it scientifically, and that made all the difference. Told me to grow a spine and face the facts." He grinned at me lopsidedly. "She's got the cojones, that one. She ever thought about the Academy?"

"Oh for heaven's sake, Mitch!" my mother broke in, exasperated. She turned to me. "Kali, just tell us what's been happening. Please. Your father says he's fine with it, so just go on."

I love you, Tara.

I stopped thinking about where to start, and just started. "Dad, the same day we moved into this house, something else happened here on the island. A man that Kalia was once very close to tried to commit suicide. His only son had just died unexpectedly of a heart attack, he'd recently lost his only other relative, he felt alone and hopeless, and depression hit him like a ton of bricks. They stabilized him in the ER, but as soon as he was able, he refused treatment, because he still had no will to live. They couldn't make him change his mind, and unless he did, he was going to die."

I paused. So far, so good. "Dad, the reason you've been seeing Kalia in your dreams is because her spirit has been making an incredible effort to save this man's life." I explained how difficult it was for her to communicate, but how she had managed to appear to Zane, and to me in a lesser way, and how she had led us to places where I could see particular shadows. Then I got to the hard part.

"She had a tough time figuring out how to get through to us," I continued more slowly. "Because the background to her message was really complicated. And I don't know that she would have succeeded if it hadn't been for that DNA ancestry project I did back in Cheyenne."

My parents' eyes widened.

"You got the results?" my dad asked.

"I got them the last day of school," I admitted. "I didn't tell you because they weren't what we expected."

I glanced toward Zane. His eyes smiled at me encouragingly. *Doing great.*

"That kind of DNA testing is new, and it isn't a sure thing," I plowed on. "But it seemed pretty clear that Albin Thompson couldn't have been my biological grandfather... or your biological father."

My dad's face paled. I charged ahead. "We know now exactly what happened, Dad, because Kalia showed us... I've seen some of it reenacted by the shadows. When Kalia and Albin met, she was in love with a classmate named Emilio. Albin knew that; he and Kalia started out as just friends. Emilio was drafted right after graduation, and before he shipped out, he and Kalia got engaged. But just a few weeks later he was reported killed in action, leaving Kalia pregnant without any family support — her mother was dying and his mother wanted nothing to do with her."

I took a breath. I wished my dad would. He looked like a wax figure.

"Albin was already in love with Kalia, and he begged her to marry him. She was reluctant at first, because she didn't think it would be fair to him, but she did agree."

All at once I saw in my mind the picture of Kalia holding my father as a toddler: the last picture that was ever taken of her. She had been pregnant with her second child. *Albin's* child. The sparkle in her dark eyes had left no room for doubt. She had been happy.

"She came to love grandfather Albin," I finished. "And in what short time they had together I believe they were happy. As far as he was concerned, you were his son. With Emilio gone, he had no reason to ever tell you otherwise."

My father's color was returning. Slowly. He and my mother exchanged dazed glances. I noticed she was holding his hand under the table.

"I don't suppose he would tell me," my dad said finally, his voice sounding surprisingly steady. "Back then, everyone thought it best that way. I wonder if my grandparents knew." He thought a moment. "Probably not. He would have thought it better for my mother if no one did."

We all sat in silence for a moment. Then my father faced me squarely.

"What does all this have to do with the man who tried to kill himself? Is he a relative of Kalia's? Of ours?"

Zane's hand found mine. A wave of soothing warmth moved up my arm.

"Yes, Dad," I answered, meeting his eyes. "He is a relative. Emilio Lam wasn't killed in action. He was captured and held as a POW in China even after the war ended. But no one knew that until he made his way back to Hawaii more than three years later. Kalia never knew, and Albin had left Hawaii and never did find out. Emilio returned home having no idea that Kalia's first child was actually his own son."

I paused. "Until today, that is. He knows because I just told him. Dad... the man we visited in the hospital *is* Emilio Lam. Your biological father."

Silence. For a long moment, my dad's face seemed frozen, unblinking. I really had no idea what kind of reaction to expect from him.

I did not expect anything close to what I got.

He stood up. "Diane, will these burgers keep?"

"Um... well," she sputtered, watching him. "I—"

He grabbed up his and her dishes of fruit and started toward the kitchen. "Which hospital, Kali?" he asked as he moved.

"It's Queens, the one near the Punchbowl, but—"

"But nothing! Time's wasting." He put the fruit in the refrigerator. Or at least, I think that's what he meant to do. He actually put it in the freezer. "You coming, Diane? Just let me find my keys..."

Zane rose. "I can drive, if you want," he offered. "We were just there, and my car's parked right out — "

"Sounds good," my father agreed. He patted his pockets and then drifted off into the living room. "Let me get my..."

"Kali, help me get the rest of this food in the fridge," my mother ordered. "Leave everything else. He won't wait that long."

I blinked at her, still trying to absorb the whirlwind. "I thought he would need some time... that he would ask a million questions... and then maybe tomorrow—"

My mom gave a wry laugh. "Kali, please. When has your father ever wanted to sit around and talk when he could get up and *do* something?"

I thought a moment.

"Good point."

Almost before I was ready, we found ourselves right back at Emilio's door. Only two visitors were allowed in the room at a time, so my dad and I prepared to go in together. He seemed tense, but as I was coming to realize, "tense" situations were the Colonel's forte. Confronting another man, for any reason and under any circumstances, was doable. It was dealing with a teenaged daughter who saw dead people that was a freakin' nightmare.

My dad opened the door and gestured for me to enter first. Emilio, who had been warned of our coming by the nurse, was sitting upright in bed. Despite the fact that he was now attached to any number of tubes and wires, he already looked better than when we left him.

"Hello again," I said softly.

Emilio smiled at me, his dark eyes sparkling. Then he caught sight of my father. For several seconds, he seemed frozen with shock. Then his whole face beamed. "Mitchell," he said, as if making a declaration. He extended his hand. "I'm Emilio."

My dad stepped forward. The two men shook hands. It was a shake like any other handshake. I stayed where I was, watching nervously. Seeing them together, there could be no doubt as to the resemblance. My dad's poise and posture, his entire military attitude, had come directly from Albin Thompson, no genes required. But in both face and form, he was a younger, ever-so-slightly more Hawaiian-looking version of Emilio.

The men studied each other practically without blinking. "I always liked Albin," Emilio said after a moment. "He was a good man — very kind to Kalia. She was a beautiful girl, and when she first started working at the base, some of the airmen gave her a hard time. Albin saw what was happening and put a stop to it. I was grateful for that. Kept me out of jail."

My dad smiled. "Doesn't surprise me a bit. He was a chivalrous soul, my... father." He stumbled a bit over the last word.

"Your *father*," Emilio repeated firmly, nodding. His eyes moistened. "I adopted a son myself. My Sammy's gone now. But I'll always be his father."

For a moment neither man spoke, and I could feel my own eyes moistening. But Emilio's next words were steady and casual. "So, my granddaughter here tells me you were a pilot. What did you fly? Fighters? Cargo?"

My dad pulled up the chair and sat down. "Fighters!" he said with enthusiasm.

Emilio's face lit up. "F16s?"

"F-16A," my dad said proudly. "F-15C too."

"The F15s are double engine, right?"

"Yep. Pratt and Whitney F100s."

Are you kidding me? I thought with amazement. *Is that it?* They were going to cover in less than thirty seconds the emotional aspects of a parent-child reunion nearly sixty years in the making? I waited another moment, then, shaking my head, I tuned out their unaccountably lively discussion of plane guts and sidled toward the door.

Neither of them seemed to notice as I slipped out to join my mother and Zane in the hall. My mom's face was strained, but hopeful. Zane, I noticed, did a sharp double-take in the area just over my shoulder as I was closing the door.

"Well?" my mom asked. "What's happening?"

"They're talking about airplane engines," I said dully.

My mother's face broke into a smile. "Oh, that's wonderful!" she exclaimed.

My eyebrows arched.

"They're going to get along just fine, then," she explained. "Do you think I could go in, now?"

"Be my guest." My mom opened the door and slipped inside. I could hear my dad introducing her as the door swung closed again.

I looked at Zane, all at once feeling totally exhausted. He smiled back at me sympathetically. "Long day?"

I nodded. "The longest. But it doesn't matter. We found Emilio in time." A wave of moisture welled up behind my eyes as I thought of the alternative. For the men to miss each other in time, *again*... It was unthinkable. "I can see now why Kalia was so determined. She really did come back to save a life. I hope she can find some peace now."

"Oh," he said gently, throwing an arm around my shoulders. "I don't think you have to worry about that."

Comfort. Warmth. Safety. Joy. Excitement...

The effect of his touch was as strong as ever, though it was becoming less shocking as I grew used to it. And I could definitely grow used to it.

"You saw her again, didn't you?" I asked. "Inside the room with them?"

He nodded. "Just the briefest of flashes. I don't think she had the strength for anything more. But she wanted me to see her face. She wanted you, and everyone else, to know that she's very, *very* happy."

His arm was still around my shoulders, and unlike the last time he had tried to hold me, he didn't seem quite so tense about keeping it there. Since we were standing in the middle of a busy hospital corridor, I didn't expect the semi-hug to lead to anything more. Still, it was progress.

"She's not the only one," I smiled back.

chapter 24

I was back in the swimsuit. And it was no longer clammy. But I hadn't really thought, when I put it on, that I would actually wind up back at the community pool. I had been sure I could talk Zane into taking me to the beach instead. After all, we were due for a celebration. Emilio had not only started dialysis, but had sworn to become a model patient, and his doctors were optimistic for a full recovery. My dad had stayed with him well into the night and then had sat up chatting excitedly to my mother for most of the rest of it. Or so she had told me at breakfast. Personally, I had slept like a baby.

Now, at last, I was ready for some *fun*.

What I was getting instead was torture.

"Stop looking so glum!" Zane chastised merrily as we approached the gate. "Oh look. There's Lacey."

I lifted my head and saw Lacey, her swim bag thrown over her shoulder, approaching us from the inside. She had obviously just ended her shift, but she did not look like a girl who was happy to be free for the day. Her head hung, her shoulders hunched, and her feet kicked idly at litter along the ground as she moved. I couldn't *feel* Lacey all that well, but even at the distance I stood now, her misery hung about her like a shroud.

"Oh no," I said in a whisper. "It's happened." I stepped forward to meet her. "Hi, Lacey."

She looked up at me, her blue eyes distracted and dim, her lids puffy. Most of her face was puffy. Her lips curved into the briefest of superficial smiles, then pursed again. "Hi, Kali. Zane. How's it going?"

"All right," I answered gently. "Are you okay?"

She tossed her head with a snort. "That obvious, huh? Oh well. Might as well tell you — Ty and I are done. Like, *totally* done."

"I'm sorry," I said genuinely. I hated to see her hurting so much, even if I wasn't sorry she had broken it off with Ty. That jerk didn't come close to deserving her.

"I'll be okay," she said with a shrug, bucking up her voice. "It's all good, right?"

"It's going to get much better," I said firmly. "I'm sure of it." She was probably mad at Matt right now, too. But she would get over it. I gave her a quick hug and smiled encouragingly.

"Thanks, Kali," she said, her voice breaking a little. She turned away from us. "Catch you guys later, okay?"

We agreed, and she passed us and moved toward the exit. But we had only gone a couple steps when she called to us over her shoulder. "Hey, Zane?"

"Yes?" he answered.

"You got a brother?"

He smiled sadly. "Sorry."

Lacey swore out loud and kept walking.

I sighed. "I'll text her later."

"She did look pretty wretched," Zane said with concern.

I smiled at him. "It's going to take a lot of ice cream. But don't worry; I'm an old pro. Tara and I have been through it with Kylee a hundred times."

Zane studied me thoughtfully. "You're going to miss those two, aren't you?"

A wave of sadness washed over me. "A lot. But it won't be forever. I'm already trying to sell them both on the University of Hawaii."

We sat our stuff down near a deck chair, and I looked

out over the crowd with a grimace. The pool wasn't as packed as before, but it was bad enough. Why were there always so many teenaged girls hanging around, laying out? Didn't they have sun in their own backyards?

Zane pulled off his shirt. Female heads turned. Then the random giggling began. As always, he seemed not to notice. Did he act any different when I wasn't around?

I opened my mouth to speak.

"Don't even try it," he interrupted. "Whatever your scheme is to get out of this, it won't work. I'm not that easy."

I grumbled under my breath. "Tell me about it."

His eyes twinkled fiendishly. Aside from the one accidental kiss on the hair (which I had to agree didn't count) my plan was going poorly. Yesterday had been such an emotional minefield, and had ended so wonderfully, I was sure I could break down his defenses the minute we were alone. He must have thought so too, because when he took my mom and me home from the hospital, he had refused to even get out of the car, claiming he was exhausted and had an early surf date with some neighbor guy. Since his hair was still wet with seawater and full of sand when he picked me up today, I figured at least part of the excuse was true. But there was no question what game he was playing.

What was annoying was that he was winning it.

"Do you, or do you not, want to see three generations of Lam-Thompsons out surfing the North Shore someday?" he asked cheerfully, gesturing me towards the pool.

I followed, dragging my feet. "What are you talking about?"

"Emilio, of course!" he answered, surprised. "I bet he was a grom in the glory days of Makaha. Once your dad gets in some practice, I guarantee the two of them will be out there ripping together."

"What makes you think Emilio is a surfer?" I asked.

"Didn't you see his tattoos?"

I had noticed that Emilio's arms were tattooed, but I hadn't looked closely. "What about them?"

Zane chuckled. "Trust me. He's a surfer. It would be a shame for you to break the family tradition, don't you think?" He jumped into the water, turned around, and held out his hands for me.

I hesitated, but only a little. The battle of Zane's arms versus my fear of water was no longer any contest. What was so scary about a little water, anyway? I had been standing in it up to my armpits the other day.

I jumped in. But maddeningly, as soon as I was safely on my feet, he pulled his hands away from me like I was a hot potato.

"You know," I said accusingly. "A girl could get a complex."

His jaw muscles tightened. He moved close enough that he could not be overheard. "Look, Kali. Not that you aren't the bravest girl I've ever met or anything, because you are. But before you write *me* off as a total wimp... I'm not convinced we're feeling the same thing, here."

An intriguing thought. "No?"

"*No.* I touch you, and you seem to feel all fuzzy kittens and apple pie and homemade cocoa and space heaters and God only knows what else."

I grinned. "Sounds about right. Including the something else. But what's so scary about that?"

He groaned. "I'm telling you, it's different for me." He studied my face a moment. "You know, Emilio was right. You do have Kalia's eyes."

I frowned at the change of subject. "Mine look nothing

like hers!"

"They're not the same color," he agreed. "But they have the same intelligent, yet innocent, yet oh-so-enticing lights dancing in them. Your poor grandfathers didn't stand a chance."

I had no response to that. He turned away and led me toward a less crowded area of the pool. "Which reminds me," he added. "Have you thought about the fact that you can see shadows of living people, too?"

I stopped short, irritated at yet another random change of subject. But then I paused to think about it. "You're right. I saw Emilio at the cemetery. I knew there was something odd about that! I always just assumed I was seeing dead people. But I guess the shadows don't all have to be."

I mulled the idea over. Highly charged, emotional moments — burning their energy into space like images on photographic film... Had I left shadows of *myself* around? "I wonder if there's a shadow of us," I mused, looking at him. "When we met again at Ehukai."

He looked thoughtful. "Interesting question. Could you feel the emotions of a shadow me?"

"Ooh," I smiled. "That could be fun."

Zane looked mildly alarmed. He stepped away from me again. "Let's get down to business. First lesson: kicking."

A gaggle of girls sitting on the side of the pool began to giggle.

"He's just her teacher!"

I gritted my teeth. How stupid did bikini #1 have to be to think we couldn't hear her? Most likely she didn't care. Most likely, she was sending a message to Zane that she'd be willing to hook up the second he clocked out.

I sighed.

To my surprise, Zane sighed too. "Self-confidence, Kali," he said quietly. "You can swim whenever you *believe* you can swim. I promise."

I didn't want to talk about swimming. Self-confidence was a different issue. Did I have reason to *be* self-confident?

The girls were still tittering and squealing. He was ignoring them. I was trying to. "Be straight with me," I begged. "Do I have anything to worry about with girls like that?"

He smiled at me, his eyes holding mine. "Absolutely nothing," he assured, quoting me. Then, although he didn't know it, he quoted himself. "Don't ever doubt it, Kali."

And I didn't.

I grinned at him through moistening eyes. "Then will you take me to the beach now and forget this learning-to-swim crap?"

He drew himself up with a frown. "Not a chance. I'm a man of my word, and if I have to go another day without kissing you, I'm going to lose my mind. You are *going* to swim, dammit. Right now."

He leaned away from me and backstroked to a position about ten feet away. "Don't make me call you a wuss," he taunted.

He was being so uncharacteristically demanding, I had to laugh. So, he *wanted* to kiss me, did he? Whatever he felt from our supercharged interactions was powerful enough to totally freak him out, but like any surfer, he must consider the thrill worth the risk.

"Swim over here, Kali," he ordered. "Just do it."

"She can't!" bikini #2 declared with a laugh.

"How old is she, anyway?" bikini #3 chided.

"I'll just wait," bikini #1 reported. "It's probably only a

half hour lesson."

Zane didn't look at them. His gaze was fixed on me. *Come on, Kali,* his eyes begged.

My heart pounded in my chest. How hard could it be? Kick and stroke at the same time. Why couldn't I do that? I'd learned more complicated dance choreography when I was five. I had only been afraid of the water — but I wasn't anymore. Not really. Zane was standing no deeper than I had stood with him the other day.

"You don't think they're dating, do you?"

"No way! He could do better than *her.*"

EAT MY BUBBLES, WENCH!!! I jumped up into the water. I kicked. I windmilled my arms. I didn't sink. And I still didn't sink. And then I was *moving!*

I was moving, and I kept on moving, and I could see Zane ahead of me in the water. I was almost there, and then he was gone.... I couldn't believe my eyes... he was moving *away* from me!

Furious, I redoubled my efforts. No way was he getting out of this. No way could he walk backwards in shoulder-high water faster than I could swim!

He kept on moving, blast him, but I plowed through the water like a steam engine until at last my hand connected to his retreating shoulder. I grabbed hold of him and wrapped my arm around his neck. I stopped kicking and let my legs drift to the bottom.

He swept an arm around my waist and pulled me close, laughing. "You did it, Kali!" he shouted, his face glowing. "You did it!"

"I did it," I gulped, my breath coming in ragged pants, my chest heaving. "Thanks to you."

The bikinis weren't taunting anymore. But I wouldn't have cared if they did. Those girls had nothing on Kali Thompson. Kali Thompson was beautiful like her grandmother. And Kali Thompson could *swim*.

He was holding me as close as he ever had. He wasn't tense, exactly, but I wasn't the only one breathing heavy, either.

He leaned his head down toward mine, our noses nearly touching. The euphoria I felt was so intense it couldn't possibly get any better. Or could it?

"I believe..." I breathed, "that we had a deal."

He smiled lazily, revealing the irresistible dimples.

"Now," I ordered. "Kiss me."

His green eyes twinkled.

And he did.

epilogue

At exactly 1:34pm on that very afternoon, the Pacific Tsunami Warning Center documented an underwater earthquake measuring 4.5 on the Richter Scale centered about thirty miles off the southwestern coast of Oahu. The quake occurred near an underwater volcano and caused a minor tsunami of eight inches at Waianae and two inches at Honolulu. The tidal wave did not cause any damage and no tsunami warning was issued.

It *could* have been a coincidence.

But we didn't think so.

about the author

USA-Today bestselling novelist and playwright Edie Claire was first published in mystery in 1999 by the New American Library division of Penguin Putnam. In 2002 she began publishing award-winning contemporary romances with Warner Books, and in 2008 two of her comedies for the stage were published by Baker's Plays (now Samuel French). In 2009 she began publishing independently, continuing her original Leigh Koslow Mystery series and adding new works of romantic women's fiction, young adult fiction, and humor.

Under the banner of Stackhouse Press, Edie has now published over 25 titles including digital, print, audio, and foreign translations. Her works are distributed worldwide, with her first contemporary romance, *Long Time Coming*, exceeding two million downloads. She has received multiple "Top Pick" designations from *Romantic Times Magazine* and received both the "Reader's Choice Award" from *Road To Romance* and the "Perfect 10 Award" from *Romance Reviews Today*.

A former veterinarian and childbirth educator, Edie is a happily married mother of three who currently resides in Pennsylvania. She enjoys gardening and wildlife-watching and dreams of becoming a snowbird.

Books & Plays by Edie Claire

Romantic Fiction

Pacific Horizons

Alaskan Dawn
Leaving Lana'i
Maui Winds
Glacier Blooming
Tofino Storm (2020)

Fated Loves

Long Time Coming
Meant To Be
Borrowed Time

Hawaiian Shadows

Wraith
Empath
Lokahi
The Warning

Leigh Koslow Mysteries

Never Buried
Never Sorry
Never Preach Past Noon
Never Kissed Goodnight
Never Tease a Siamese
Never Con a Corgi

Never Haunt a Historian
Never Thwart a Thespian
Never Steal a Cockatiel
Never Mess With Mistletoe
Never Murder a Birder
Never Nag Your Neighbor

Women's Fiction

The Mud Sisters

Humor

Work, Blondes. Work!

Comedic Stage Plays

Scary Drama I
See You in Bells

Printed in Great Britain
by Amazon